PROSPECT>EARTH

by

Craig Jenkins

First published in Great Britain in 2015
by LionheART Publishing House

Copyright © Craig Jenkins 2015
ISBN: 978-1-910115-38-1

Science Fiction, Fantasy, Futuristic, Sci Fi, Aliens, Thriller,
Mystery, Apocalyptic, Suspense Colonization, Dystopian, First
Contact, Space Exploration, Adventure

Cover Design by Gareth Hughes
Edited by John Goodfellow
Edited and Prepared for Publication by
LionheART Publishing House

PROSPECT < EARTH

PROLOGUE

MONSTER

2424 November 15th
Avatar Operations Control: Algeria.
Avatar Deployment Combat Model: G47.3 12th Generation
Nigeria.
Combat Operation: Rashad.
Parameters of Mission:
1) Destroy terrorist group known as the E.O.T.
2) Infiltrate to Retrieve and Confiscate Important Technology.

'Okay people, we're approaching Combat Zone Alpha. Suits on and deploy your avatar.'

The hangar bay was one of many housing simulator units used by soldiers to control the combat drones. In other hangars across the field were similar operations using other types of drone. Combat models of aircraft, and dog and ram drones had already been deployed and were heading south with the convoy. There had been a time when fewer people were needed for the armed forces, as a quantum computer could manage thousands of drones at a time. What had happened in recent times was perhaps more of a choice than a necessity as AI, limited as it had remained for hundreds of years, had been replaced by the best and most instinctive intelligence of all.

Men and women, specifically trained combatants, were now seated in their pods and connected to the various types of drone. They could see, hear and act via the use of the machines and in this hangar – housing five hundred pods – were the best regarded drones

1

of all: the human drones. Two hangars were dedicated to a thousand machines designed to manoeuvre as instinctively and fluently as possible for their operators. No one went into combat for real any more, except for those on the African continent who would stand against this flash invasion. They had no such technology, meaning this operation should be swift and encounter no serious opposition.

Colonel Phillips watched as the specialist ensemble of soldiers finished the process of uploading to their machines from within the pod units. He then walked to his own pod, lifted the lid, and sat down within the small chamber. The inside of the metal case was virtually empty apart from a reclining seat with several injection syringes surrounding the headrest. The seat fell back a little and he waited and braced himself for the inevitable first stab of a needle into the top of his neck.

Transfer pads had once been used to interface with the machine. Now, due to some bright spark advising that deep penetration contact with the spinal cord was better, the pads had been replaced with monstrously thick needles. The interface had not improved and the only real benefit was that if a person's body flinched or jolted during combat, the pads would no longer fall off or come away from that essential point of contact.

Colonel Phillips felt the back of his neck as a ten-second countdown began. The scars from previous injections were now thick and bulbous, yet the ferocity of the needles would be accurate and puncture the very same locations without any trouble. Phillips inhaled from a small canister to allow a chemical agent to make its way through his body and prevent any bleeding from the injection sites. The first injection was administered: a tiny prick that would numb the rest. A second, third and fourth followed in quick succession.

'Neural-synaptic synchronisation complete.'

A fuzzy feeling filled the colonel's head. He opened his eyes, yet they were not his own. He stood up, looked to his left and then his right. A vast proportion of the machines was located on the war path many miles south at the border with Nigeria. His machine, the one he had now become for the operation, stood next to many others on the

2

airfield outside the hangar bay where his actual body was located, within the pod. Over a hundred machines began to run at speed towards the jets, and Phillips moved towards his own F250 fighter plane.

'Colonel Phillips, this is Command, patching through Captain Jarvis of Air Drone 2032.'

'Understood,' Phillips said in a hollow, mechanised voice. His machine spoke his thoughts even though the thought projected a response automatically through to the command centre.

'Captain Jarvis, I need a sit rep.'

'Free as a bird and soaring like an eagle, Colonel. Full complement moving on schedule. No sign of hostile forces. One moment – bogey spotted at seven hundred feet, eight klicks south of our location.'

Phillips commanded his machine – seated in the cockpit of the fighter jet – to receive visuals from various drones now surveying the area. Simultaneously he launched the jet vertically into the air. He set the craft for stratospheric altitude so he could be on site in less than ten minutes. Within seconds the world below became a map and the jet headed south. Phillips watched as the live feed showed him the unknown craft hovering above the vast jungle canopy. The view projected into his left eye was quite clear and, on zooming in to gain an even clearer image, Phillips became very concerned.

'Jarvis, what the hell is that? I seem to be having trouble identifying bogey at your location.'

'This is Flag General Dean. Be advised that this is the craft logged from the Earth intrusion on September 18th. Craft is conjectured to be possibly alien in origin. Approach with extreme caution.'

'General Dean, this is Colonel Phillips. Why have we not received information on said craft prior to this?'

'All information is classified, you have permission to engage only if fired upon, Colonel. Is that understood?'

'Copy that, General.' Colonel Phillips noted the formation of over eight hundred jets surrounding his own while he thought about this new report of intelligence from General Dean. *Arseholes*! The operation should have been child's play, yet even this assumption depended on whether there would be repercussions from other states that had opposed this operation, that some had deemed to be an act of war; Phillips, along with the rest of his contemporaries had been led to believe that a substantial opposition was unlikely.

Phillips noted that the Germans had arrived with another squadron of jets equal to his own.

'Colonel Phillips, this is Colonel Weber approaching with Beta Squadron on flank position, please acknowledge.'

'Received and acknowledged. Have you received update on foreign craft?'

'Affirmative. Approaching with caution.'

'Ground Team One, Captain Jones, please give the order to halt all vehicles on encroach path east to west, we have a situation due south of your location,' Phillips said.

'Roger that, Colonel. Bogey has been spotted, convoy will be held until further orders.'

Phillips looked around and saw the mighty force of sixteen hundred jets swarming around him. His own jet passed over the mass of vehicles below. Enormous jungle crunchers at the front of the convoy had stopped creating a path for all combat vehicles, which had also come to a halt. Ahead and hovering above the jungle canopy, thousands of small fighter drones waited. They were small jets which had no human drones on board but combat avatars directly linked as their pilots.

Further ahead of these, motionless and without making any sound, the alien craft hovered and waited. It was jet black with smooth surfaces reflecting the sun as though covered with mirrors. It was strange and yet familiar in a way for it had eight wings like a butterfly, except they were sharp and rhomboid in shape and they moved at two main points attached to a narrow mid-section. It had a bulbous back end while the top half of what could only be described as its body was narrower with a large, sharp harpoon for its head, or possibly a cockpit. It could be thought of as a spider with wings and no legs, or some insect perhaps, except this thing was enormous with a wing span of a hundred metres. On the underneath of its body, blue pulsating light emanated through what appeared to be thinner transparent plating that shimmered and rotated. This could be assumed to be its engines or even lungs.

'This is Captain Vale of the gunship *Shadow Light*. Please acknowledge our location at three thousand feet above set jet height of combat zone.'

Three thousand and thirty eight lights winked on the cockpit display of Phillips' jet. Jets and drones alike, all linked to human pilots, confirmed they knew the combat zone parameters beneath the colossal airship that had arrived to offer support.

'Colonel Phillips, this is Captain Jones. Do we have permission to set blanket defence?'

'Position tanks and silos but do not activate unless air support is compromised. I do not want cross-fire zones, no matter how accurate these machines are.'

Phillips sat within his avatar – he had become his machine, seated within a jet hovering and waiting as the unusual craft did the very same thing only a few miles away. Thousands of hovering air drones and jets created a deep hum, sounding like a great swarm of bees. On the ground, thousands of combat vehicles, tanks, trucks, dog and ram drones, along with human drones also waited. Above his position the airship floated as perhaps the most deadly killing machine of all, and further above this there orbited a weapon satellite. A laser cannon held its position as further backup.

There was enough firepower at this location to obliterate a country the size of Nigeria within a few hours and render it a grave of ash. This was not the objective. This operation was meant to be swift and accurate, and cause a minimum of collateral damage. Now Phillips wondered at the thing that had stopped this mighty war machine in its path. The unknown caused fear, and taking a risk might prove essential to the timetable of this operation which was slipping away fast. Silence engulfed the world as Colonel Phillips considered that this thing might be destroyed with ease, and it could not cover the whole width of the battlefield that stretched across three hundred miles of convoys heading south.

'Captain Jarvis, come in.'

'Received.'

'Order one of your team to send in a drone. Full identification notice protocols need to be followed.'

'Understood.'

An air drone flew ahead over the canopy, its gunmetal jade hull almost disappearing as it shot over the sea of green beneath. Anyone below this machine would also struggle to see it as its hull projected the same colour as the sky through adaptive light emitters. The drone slowed and hovered twenty metres from the alien craft. The alien machine appeared to watch and tilted its attitude towards the human machine.

'This is a message from all allied forces of the United States of America and the United States of Europe. Please identify yourself.'

The alien craft did nothing.

'You are in the direct path . . .'

The alien craft fired a bolt of energy at the drone. It melted and dropped from the sky, hurtling in a molten blob into the forest canopy below.

Phillips gave the order to engage as the craft opened fire on multiple targets as it moved. Faster and faster, more projectiles of energy found targets in all directions. Drones and jets fell from the sky en masse as the hostile craft moved up, down, left and right with impossible and mechanised accuracy as if a dragonfly above a pond.

The swarm of drones and jets fired missiles and fifty calibre rounds from stampede cannons. The airship fired one-tonne bolts that managed to hit the target repeatedly. The alien craft jerked with each impact yet it deflected the rounds and missiles with some sort of shield that could only be seen as forked lightning flashing upside down and away from the alien craft's hull.

The human aircraft continued to fall like molten rain from the sky. Human drone pilots ejected from the jets and parachuted to the ground; there was no sense in wasting the machines by allowing them to crash. Some of the drones were half melted and on fire as they fell to earth, and by now the ground battalions were running around as though an ant's nest had been disturbed.

Tanks, trucks and drones alike were pelted by the debris of their own destroyed air support; the world below was on fire as the jungle burned. Colonel Phillips took his jet to high altitude and neared the airship for cover. In the medium distance he could see the alien creature hover and fire relentlessly at the allied aircraft. Energy bolt after energy bolt snaked their way with staggering accuracy.

From above, an energy beam shot down and hit the black beast dead on. Its shields shimmered and took the heat blast of over one million degrees. The craft tilted upwards and fired its own narrow blast of high-yield energy into the sky. In orbit above the combat zone, the military satellite melted and fell into Earth's atmosphere. It lit up like a flare falling in the night sky.

The craft took more hits from the one-tonne rounds and turned its attention to the airship. As it rose, the Zeppelin-styled military vessel fired a staggering display of missiles and stampede turrets. All found their mark and yet the alien craft appeared completely unscathed.

'We're losing this battle,' Phillips voiced over the comms. 'We need to retreat now.'

The alien craft bombarded the airship from fore to aft down its port flank. The thick metal plating surrounding the ship's inflated innards melted, allowing helium to burst out along the two thousand metres of hull. The ship listed then toppled over. It sank through the air until it eventually hit the ground, crushing hundreds of drone assets. Something within the ship exploded, releasing a blast that snuffed out a vast portion of the raging inferno taking hold of the jungle in one massive gust.

One of the thousands of bolts fired by the craft headed directly towards Phillips' jet. He manoeuvred but the bolt of light seemed to know where he was headed before he arrived. He hit the ejector seat.

The canopy blew away and he shot out as the jet turned to vapour. Phillips then watched the full horror of the drone massacre from this new and open perspective. He may have been in a drone, had become the very robust drone and was out of danger, yet with such an immersion into technology he felt that he was really there, naked and floating in Hell. As Phillips parachuted to earth, he saw the alien craft move towards him. An eternity crept in as though the world had paused. The craft leapt on him, was right next to him. It seemed to look at him and tilt itself as though analysing him.

Phillips woke within the metal pod. He was drenched in sweat and his head spun wildly. He vomited violently and sat for a moment to find his bearings. The pod opened to reveal chaos had erupted at the base. People were running around shouting this and that; Phillips was not sure what. He climbed out and grabbed the nearest person he could find.

'What the hell happened?' Phillips screamed.

'World War Four just happened!' the man shouted back.

Three Months Earlier

THE TURN BACK

Location: Carina Quadrant – uncharted system
Date: Earth reference 2424 August 8th
Mission: Retrieval of Medical System One. Return unit to
original designation.

A memory could deceive and even a photographic memory could be manipulated by time and emotion. The alarm on the bedside cabinet was a quirky tone chosen in another time and place which now seemed less fitting. The woman lying in bed next to him seemed just the same so that inadvertently the mornings came earlier and the nights later. The life in her womb was the only anchor to any focus and any kind of future.

The kitchen was clinical and removed the taste from breakfast; it had become habitual and was now only thought of as fuel. The memory of the journey to work was peripheral as cars were followed and passed by while so-called experts on the news channel argued about the climate. Some company – yes, the one that paid the bills, paid the mortgage – was a powerful conglomerate which was changing the face of the planet. The House of Ecology was still building rainforests and with that came rain. No one seemed to like rain even though they liked the break from the heat and sun.

The office came into view within a large, tall, elongated rectangular building of reflective black glass and, as he approached the security gatehouse and the flags on the main building fluttered, a thought of surreptitious fascism crossed his mind.

The reception of the building was cool inside and the people seemed fresh and full of verve in suits and ties with shiny shoes. Women were conservatively dressed with blazers and neatly tied hair. Some of their counterparts elsewhere in this very land were covered from head to toe and it was a crime to show their faces outdoors.

The cruising along to the lift and up to the second floor was thoughtless and the final part of the journey down the corridor to the office a mundane chore. The office was too cool because the cleaning staff were too hot during the evenings when they performed their duties and they forgot to return the air conditioners back to seventeen degrees. By morning it was always a chilly five or six. The desk was a flat piece of glass-woven fabric which tilted as a fully voice-activated monitor and keypad. The chair was a comfortably padded synthetic; no one ate meat any more unless someone broke the law, and leather was off the furnishing menu for the foreseeable future.

A few tasks came to mind and he remembered that the fat Turkish man needed to be called soon, but he liked to barter and more time had been scheduled for some official wasting.

'Hey, you're getting earlier and earlier, you know that?'

Can I ignore this man?

'Ologun? Snap out of it, you know you don't look tired but you seem totally fu . . .'

'I'm thinking. I have things to do.'

'Okay, okay, stay cool, my American friend.'

Ologun activated the desk and dialled the fat Turk. The screen made fractal patterns as the server connected. 'Hello.'

'It's me, Mr M, Ologun.'

'Ah yes, you were meant to call me yesterday, Mr Jowett. I must let you know that unfortunately for you I have decided on fusion.'

'Fair enough,' Ologun replied. 'May I ask why? Look, I understand the lenses take up too much space, yet if you integrate them into the building design you save space and as I said before, much less maintenance and a lifetime guarantee, not to mention the cost of manpower. Fusion costs what? At least five hundred man hours per week and raw materials per year in the form of ballast for the lasers and gravity nullifiers for the sphere to form perfectly in its initial and continuing existence.'

'Maybe so, Mr Jowett, but the price is too high for the lenses and you know with this dip in spacecraft production I'm getting a good deal on the initial installation so I think I'm okay with the yearly maintenance. Also, people are cheap and I can pay little enough for labour and still it wouldn't come anywhere near the cost of the lenses in the first six years.'

Ologun sat back in his chair and swivelled round to look out the window. Quartz had become so expensive over the last few years that his job here was becoming very difficult. 'Look, Mr M, I can't come down on price any further so I'm sorry for inconveniencing you today. If you change your mind . . .'

'Goodbye, Mr Jowett. I trust you will have a good day.'

*

Lunch was unappetising: a paste smeared on crusty bread washed down with kiwi fruit-flavoured water. It was all just ritual, and conversations with colleagues seemed tired and pretentious, with talk of investments and tomorrow's stock and gadget items bought and analysed for their product life cycle. The late finish at work was also pointless with little achieved and a stern pep talk from the manager led nowhere.

The clockwork storm at 6 p.m. had started on the drive home, and yet today and out of all that had happened as usual lately, the storm seemed especially rough. The open window let in static which was building throughout the air, and the night sky was black with clouds which seemed filled with more intent than usual.

A drink at some unknown bar was an unusual set of colours among the dark clouds overhead where people were perpetually fascinated by the weather and talked of nothing else. The fancily named gin with a super-bitter twist took some of the edge off; perhaps a little too much as the first stages of the wind-driven downpour began. Everyone was cautious on the highway as the endless flats were blotted from view by weather. He thought about the woman he had left at home that morning. *She hates everything,* Ologun thought.

The couples at the bar served to remind of what life used to be like. Now it all seemed claustrophobic and thick with anxiety. Every gesture and attempt to renew the hope of it and the effort to find change in it was shot down with contempt and disgust. Her attitude was of indifference and agitation yet the ambition of obvious solutions at this stage were confused, for in three months the new addition would be here. The value of a wedding band diminished by the day and yet the feeling of the expected child allowed for something, but his daughter could not be allowed to come into this world in such an atmosphere. Something had to change, the feelings buried for the sake of dignity and false portrayal. Tops were about to blow.

The comms blinking on the dash came on several times and finally deserved a look. Another falsehood: a picture of a man in a comedy pose hiding the reality of who he was and what his past represented.

'Ologun, are you there?'

'Dad, I'm driving, what is it?'

The old man's voice seemed different; concerned, no, frightened.

'Ologun, I need you to come to the Memorial Hospital right away.'

'What? What happened, are you okay?'

The comms suffered interference and the rest of the conversation was lost in the digital abyss.

Ologun snapped out of his day-long trance of introspection and put his foot down on the accelerator. He switched to inter-spectral camera mode and turned on the dash's monitor.

He finally reached the hospital after much frustration and traffic. Further east out of town there had been a substantial car accident with a number of deaths already reported. Ologun fought the storm as he headed for the hospital reception. The car park's surface danced with rain and temperamental wind as it changed direction every few seconds. Cars rocked violently as they sat in rows and an IMC flag swooped by, then disappeared as though the great empire had come under attack and lost the battle. Forked lightning filled the sky, an orange bolt followed by a deafening clap of thunder. The storm had now engulfed the city.

Ologun glanced in reflex towards the panoramic view of buildings as the lights went out. He entered the hospital reception as emergency lighting took over. The reception lobby was painted a menthol white, lit by chemical burners of a similar colour. At the desk, Ologun queued for what seemed an eternity. Once there he provided his name and query along with a quick DNA sample to be analysed there and then. Identity check complete, the receptionist seemed busy and told him his wife was on the third floor of intensive care room 6A.

'I don't understand. I'm here for my father.'

'Oh, let me see, your father is in life-span maintenance, three buildings down. I'm sorry Mr Jowett, but your wife arrived two hours ago along with a Mr Hashem.'

Ologun felt sick with confusion. One of his good friends and his wife were here in this hospital. 'What's going on, why are they here?' Ologun demanded hysterically.

'Mr Jowett, please be calm, they were admitted into the critical care unit . . .'

'Please, sir, come this way.' A nurse placed a hand on Ologun's shoulder. He explained about a car accident on the highway heading east away from the city. Ologun followed the man, feeling ghost-like as he reeled at the situation. Finally they arrived at his wife's room. *But why?* Ologun asked himself. *Where were they going?*

He entered the room quietly and stood near the door as it closed. The nurse disappeared without a word and Ologun was left in a room lit only by the faint glow of the storm outside and the sounds of the rain on the window pane. As he paused in the dimness, a beeping noise from some apparatus became louder until he realised the machine was keeping his wife breathing. He approached a bed situated against the wall, where a small figure lay unconscious under a thin sheet. Special chemical wraps covered her arms and legs, and a device hanging above the bed pulsated a beam of the sort that rebuilds broken bones as it holds them in place. Ologun moved closer and finally recognised his wife.

Something clicked in his mind and his sense of unease increased. Kneeling down, he saw that her stomach was too flat. Blundering to the door, Ologun slammed hard against its wood surface. He then exited into the corridor, looked both ways, and saw that to his left and through a window in another set of doors, a woman was seated at a desk. He sprinted to her, smashing his way through the doors as he went. 'My wife was pregnant,' he blasted at her.

'I'm sorry,' the woman replied, utterly startled.

'My wife, Hiba Jowett, was pregnant, where is my daughter?'

The woman checked something on her desk's surface which held a large inbuilt computer pad. 'Please place your thumb on the DNA scanner, Mr Jowett.'

Ologun placed his shaking hand on to the device and waited, wild eyes twitching here and there without patience.

The woman read more information from the surface of her desk. She seemed uncomfortable and Ologun noticed a small red light flashing on the surface of her desk's computer screen. 'Please take a seat, Mr Jowett.'

Ologun went numb as the pressure in his head increased. 'What's going on, is my daughter alive? Where is she?'

A man accompanied by two armed security guards entered the corridor. 'Mr Jowett, I'm Doctor Mubarak. I need you to come with me please.'

'No,' Ologun replied. 'I need to know what's happening, my wife was pregnant, where's my daughter?'

The security men tensed and the doctor raised a hand in order to stand them down. 'Very well,' Mubarak said. 'We performed an emergency C-section operation on Mrs Jowett an hour ago and I'm pleased to say that a baby girl survived the operation and is now in specialist care. Mr Jowett, can I ask you what arrangements you had with Mrs Jowett for this pregnancy?'

Ologun felt his heart beating faster even through his relief at the news. 'I don't understand – arrangements?'

'Mr Jowett,' Doctor Mubarak continued, 'the DNA results show that the child is not yours and under state laws we are unable to provide you with any more information and certainly no access at this juncture.'

Ologun almost lost his temper when he noticed his father standing further down the corridor. He took a moment to think about this statement in silence, and finally realised the truth of the situation. Utterly devastated and feeling completely removed from himself, the voices of the nearby people echoed around his head. Ologun turned around and quickly moved away from them, feeling exposed like a raw nerve. Through corridors he marched until outside amidst the raging storm. Somewhere on the outskirts of the car park he collapsed to his knees, vomiting violently.

Someone placed a hand on his shoulder and he shrugged it away with force. 'I'm sorry, son.'

Ologun recognised his father trying to speak above the din of wind and rain. His father knelt with him, shivering and wet through. He wore a large overcoat, and underneath he had on a hospital gown.

'How did you know before me?' Ologun asked.

'I didn't.'

Ologun looked at his father and saw his face was pallid and almost drained of colour.

Gavin Jowett looked at his son in empathy for a moment, then his face suddenly changed to an expression of intense pain. Gavin exhaled loudly and slumped over on the soaked ground. Ologun jumped to his feet and knelt over him in further panic. 'What's wrong, what is it?'

He tried to manoeuvre and pick his father up off the floor, but his father placed a hand on his shoulder. 'Intersections come in all shapes and sizes, son.'

Ologun dismissed this famous philosophy of his father's and tried to lift him again. Hospital staff were now running in their direction, shouting his father's name.

'Time's up, my son, I am sorry, you know that, right?'

Gavin Jowett closed his eyes and Ologun felt the life leave his father's body.

*

Ologun watched as though an invisible entity while the hospital staff dragged Gavin on to a stretcher. They shouted this and that as they frantically worked their way back to the safety of the building. Ologun turned his head and stared out over the city.

Sometimes a thing could change a person's mind. They said there was a part of the brain that received chemicals which in turn were emotions. They said that too much of one emotion eroded a person's capacity to enjoy the full range of said feelings. It was also said that a person could never change and yet some things change a person forever. An utter transformation, as though a different version of one's former self might emerge through a complete overload, whether it was through the pressure of time and consistency or an instantaneous assault on one's senses.

A moment, almost tranquil in many respects, fell across Ologun as though from some great defeat. The clouds parted and he looked at the sky as great apparitions floated around and danced like phantoms weaving across the open expanse.

A terrible thought took hold in his mind as though a splinter-inducing guilt which could never be banished. He had lost a daughter who was not his real daughter. He had lost a father who was not his real father. And, as terrible as these deceptions had been, Ologun felt freedom wash over him so that much of his grief was nullified or cast aside never to resurface. In the way that even a photographic memory could not illuminate, he realised that maybe this was the point in his life where feelings would never be felt the same again. No anchor to stop what was to come and no restraints to stop him from taking a path which would only lead towards alienation and isolation. The ones who came for him would classify him as crazy; they wanted crazy. He was no sociopath, yet for all intents and purposes he might be even better.

*

Ologun had visited these memories of loss and change from time to time depending on mood or perhaps from some unknown trigger that tormented him. The alien craft he had entered, the ones who had attacked the basin upon the shard. The ones he had killed and destroyed without mercy had, it seemed from spite, crashed into the ocean upon this world where he resided. Ologun could not help but feel bitterness toward those whom he thought had shaped his life until it had come to this. He blamed himself, he blamed his father, the alien organism that had made him. What if his wife had never cheated on him or left him? What if? That is what Ologun found himself pondering more and more as time went on.

*

Being here, exiled on this planet had almost driven him insane and for a long while he had become a thing, an empty and unreal object. Physics and chemistry created biology which consumed and multiplied and mutated and adapted and evolved. The ocean had changed from red stagnation to that of a dark, cool machine lubricating the planet and allowing an explosion of life. How long had it been? In the beginning he had been adrift in the ever-changing, noxious waters. So much energy and so many storms had felt like both entertainment and punishment from the heavens. Lightning attacked the seas and much of it had struck him over and over again. That was the worst part in the beginning, for every time he lost consciousness, or more specifically his life, he would wake deep down near an ocean floor of endless thick red cloud. Swimming up, before long it made no sense as to which direction he had come from and to where he was headed. No need to breathe or sleep or eat or drink or be anything that he used to be.

So much energy attacking this world and its incessant ocean had now subsided. And the nightmare, his worst nightmare of deep, vast seas where there was no escape was just a memory. It was, however, far from being anything that would lead to relief or catharsis.

*

The ocean crashed heavily against the shore as the sun set on another day. The light turned the ocean water into a black and violent surface, a moving landscape of tall pyramids chopping and swaying which seemed to be far worse way in the distance. Two and a half moons orbited close to this world, and would not let the oceans lie in peace, never giving them rest. By now it had become an existence of routine made of and filled with the utter chaos of base reality; and yet still it was a far more simple life compared with that of before, so he was now without the contrived and complex notions of morality or paradoxical dualities that were the concerns of man. There were no sentient beings around to perceive or pervert and to do things or make statements which swayed the mind into the realm of dilemma. Ologun missed people, yet at the same time he was not sure if he could cope with ever seeing them again.

*

In a small valley leading to a cove by the sea existed what Ologun thought of as his responsibilities. Each day was different with some spent in despair, others in satisfaction, or wonder and entertainment, but through some absurdity he had found a sense of duty in this place. As he sat high up near the cliff tops on a small ledge gazing out over the ocean, he waited and felt the change that always came. They knew it and they somehow set their tiny minds and tiny lives by it, for it was now time and it was all he could offer; and what a gift to them it was.

He did not like to think of it as being consumed, for even now as they made their way, there was that realisation that life was increasing in this place and far more rapidly with him being there than without. For the moment there were only insects and plant life to make this world a living place. He did not count the ocean, for the creatures there may have been more evolved and more complex, yet they were out of sight and out of mind and none of his responsibility.

The insects gathered next to him in vast numbers, creating a deafening roar of buzzing and clicking noises. They waited and felt just as he did: *enjoy!* As the blackness engulfed him the various insects took what they could: burrowing, scraping, chewing and sucking. They ate him, they ate each other and the frenzy continued so that he had a thought, the same thought every time this offering happened, as he chose to perceive it. What if these creatures could think and what would they think of him, this thing that was always there for the taking? He felt a wasp-like creature enter one of his nostrils and knew he had little time left before he was done. In moments he would be temporarily deceased for what he thought was a few hours, before he was made new again. In the time shortly after regeneration and when he was temporarily immune from attack, he would make his way to his other responsibilities.

*

It was daytime when he regained consciousness. The binary white suns bleached the landscape and the seas were a different realm. He usually had two modes of existence, either dead or alive via the nature of the way things were. For him this meant that when he was alive there were two primary responsibilities and that now, as always, it had to be the other's turn.

He headed away from the coast and deeper into the valley through the grass and under trees of varying types, heights and colours. Many were typical and leafy with a whole range of flowers to attract the insects of lesser size that lived without the necessity for flesh and blood. These things were nice but none of his concern, for his garden lay in open grasslands deep in the valley and within the darkness of shade. Photosynthesis was not their main source of sustenance as they were there for him – or was it that he was there for them?

He approached the shadows lying out of the suns' reach and just beyond the last stretch of purple sward. They were tall with thick necks and with one peculiar trait. If he had remembered what he himself looked like, he would have realised that the pods at the top of each plant were shaped like heads and that the face on each one was meant to be his. Thick black wool sprouted on top of each pod and strange marble-like balls could be taken for eyes on the features of each face. There were even strange flaps of red resembling mouths, yet when close up it was easy to recognise what they were: coconut pods on stalks, a mimicry of true horror, or was it just some parody? He sometimes got the two mixed up.

He came on a flat stone overlooking a thousand faces in the short distance where they looked more like men; exactly like men. This served to remind him of another, more sinister time as they were more akin to skulls placed on spikes and each skull was his own. Perhaps it was a coincidence and just a random act of nature. Either way he had been here long enough to forget and would not worry about it any more.

These plants were less needy than the insects and could wait for weeks at a time before he returned, except that there were always more of them which had caused him to spend every other day covering sections of this vast expanse of man-eating pods. Some were withered and dead while others had branched out and had grown two or three pods to make them look far more monstrous. On the ground, their barbed vines stretched out in a crowded and confusing entanglement containing insect traps at varying points; perhaps another adaptation as he was becoming less reliable. Time and motion. He could not be everywhere often enough to nourish them all, and how such a failure pained him. This plant, however, had adapted towards him and had flourished because of him and because of what he truly was. Each drop of blood or pound of flesh was worth a thousand times more than if it were from any other. He had something which allowed for life to rush forth and for mutation to take place at a staggering, even supernatural, pace.

He waited patiently and for a long time, watching the plants sway in the breeze until he felt the cycle complete within his body. That was the way it was, this switch where he felt his flesh return to its state of vulnerability. He quickly made his way down the slope towards the section of plants he had scheduled in his mind. Standing a few feet away from them and taking a deep breath, he stepped forward on a vine and was snared. Now each of the pods swayed back and forth, hissing and releasing long tongue-like feelers from beneath their black woollen mimicry of hair. The tongues pierced him and drank, and the vines released longer needles which twisted and ground his skin so that, as with the insects, all these things left of him were his bones.

*

His life had been like this for much longer than that of his other original existence, and to him it was neither better nor worse. He never ventured from the valley as there was too much going on outside, and he never found the courage to exceed this peculiar comfort zone. Perhaps it was primitive and vicious, but then certain values just did not apply to him here. Somehow he could condescend to these creatures which never really took anything that could not easily be replaced. Sometimes he grew tired of it and dreaded it and was at times concerned, being very aware that this course of fast-track evolution could have profound consequences which he had no way to predict. From witnessing the thick viscous pools of broth mutate and divide, to the white lice and basic forms of algae, to the first moss and plant to the more complex progression of those insects, life was getting bigger and, if it could be perceived as such, better, and he was sure had already vastly superseded the natural order of time needed for a more natural course of evolution.

Another waking moment, to be reborn within the forest of pods, came as the suns set for yet another day and he wished to know how long the days and nights actually were and why there seemed to be no difference in season. It was always hot and humid and the rain came in a firm rhythm as with everything else. Or was it the lack of apparatus to measure anything that led to the perception of such cadence? Either way, without seasons as such, it was hard to gauge time and he experienced existence as only night and day, rain or sunshine, with a smattering of the odd typhoon every so often; always extreme, particularly violent, and unfailingly devastating. That was all there was to this place, if it could ever be thought of as usual.

*

Ologun made his way back to the coast, and on to the sandy cove and watched as the ocean breeze created a flurry across the surface. Tonight he gazed across the horizon and on the calmer seas. With acute eyesight adapting perfectly to the dark, he spotted something unusual and made his way towards it. On the beach he found a pale mound, small and curved. He picked it up, a light object which, when brushed of its quartz and lesser shell debris, shot an electrifying realisation.

Alien skull in hand, with a thumb in an empty eye socket, he sat down to reflect and to remember. Every language he had learned of his kind had to be exercised and kept as things might change. He knew this because of the whispers; the noises carried on the ocean breeze and which sounded like an omen, like that of a hollow rasp between two close objects holding the code.

Remember who you are!

*

The echoes in his mind came and went. They were not always there and, as much as he could not remember when exactly it had started, it had definitely been recently.

For the first time ever, he saw something leap from the surface far out to sea; a big fish maybe . . . or something else. It disappeared as if a trick of the weaker moonlight, and so he returned to his thoughts and tried to grasp more whispers as they passed.

It's stupid, he thought. *How can someone exist in two places at once or even . . .* The notion was confusing and what confused him even more was the notion of being lost. This planet could be within the outskirts of the Milky Way, another galaxy even, or it could be—

It made no difference for he was lost and refused to entertain it. He had, however, discovered something unique about himself, to which he had become so accustomed that it was now inconsequential with no one to tell and no audience to watch him showing off. Then again, how could he be surprised considering everything else he had done?

He took the skull and threw it towards the breaking tide, then smacked it with his mind. The skull banked left with force, went further out over the water, plopped down, and rapidly sank out of sight. *What's it all about?* As clumsy as it had been (he had aimed to hit the object upwards), it was still some form of telekinesis. *Is that really what it is?*

He remembered finding land, finding solidity, yet he was so angry, frightened and frustrated, abandoned and stupefied. He had found a huge rectangular rock and hugged it for so long and in such despair. Eventually he had lost his mind and had beaten the damned pillar with his fists until his hands were mush and his empty; stifled screams had nearly caused his lungs to collapse.

In one final blast of emotion at his beloved monolith, this inanimate thing he had clung to for refuge for what seemed like decades, was suddenly gone. It had stopped him in his mega-tantrum like a slap to the face. He peered out over the valley towards the bay, frantically searching for his pillar of strength and safety, panicking with thoughts of loneliness without his silent friend.

A faint thud in the distance drew his gaze and he zoomed in with a focus akin to a bird of prey. *What?* Had he hit it so hard as to launch something else that weighed a few tonnes, causing it in turn to land half a mile away? He had killed the pillar, his only companion for so long, but he did not care. Something had happened.

When he had found the answer through mind-numbing and exhausting concentration, long before life had spread to land and had launched into a frenzy of mutation courtesy of his blood, he had found a new skill.

It was not the truest sense of the word skill. Skill meant he had expertise or competence. Hitting a boulder in one direction, for it to flip up and land in another, which had consequently crushed and temporarily killed said skilled person, did not justify the terms skill, talent or competence. He never got any better, however much he practised.

Then, when time had passed and his responsibilities came along, he rarely hit anything with that invisible mind trick, for it was a pointless trait which made no difference in this place and, even after all this time, he was as inept as when he had first discovered the ability.

His thoughts dissipated as the broken moon sank into the horizon. This was the only true calm time of each of the three cycles this place had and when he felt most relaxed. Then, as though something hard had hit him, he jolted and stood up like a shot on the beach glaring out to sea and beyond. He felt it, knew it was there without a doubt.

*

Far away and approaching rapidly like a bolt of energy across the system, it passed the planets and the moons and through the rest of the vacuum, outrunning the light. His heart raced as it hit the stratosphere and swung round. Across the sea and moving towards him he saw it, a speck of black which had connected with him the moment it came within range.

Juxtaposed with him it beat his senses, and hovered – a mighty craft of war and prey. A wing span blotted out the fading moonlight with lungs of pulsating energy kicking up a storm of debris across the beach.

Say my name!

It hovered in circles and pointed itself at him.

Say my name and I will believe it is you!

The noise it released took his breath away; a boom of other worldly bass. '*Ologun,*' it said.

Through time unused and in this strange world's atmosphere which he had adapted to breathe, he attempted to speak. A peculiar name for the thing he was a part of and which was also a part of him. 'Creed.'

Regardless of cryptic whispers gathered on the wind, and the illusion of having responsibilities, he thought his goodbyes and subdued the emotion of having to leave them behind. *How would they . . .? No.* He had to think more realistically and stop being pathetic.

He wanted to leave and was so relieved to be found, yet he did not want to go and wished he had not been found at all. Collapsing to his knees on the shore, the tide washed him slightly deeper into the sand. They would be fine without him, for he had to face up to the reality that he would have to leave this place, be snatched away.

Looking at Creed as it waited patiently, excited in some way due to this unannounced and sudden reunion, he said, 'You're humongous.' He smiled a little at the comic factor of the first sentence he had uttered in a lifetime, his voice sounding alien and croaked to his own ears. His gaze dropped to the floor, hoping Creed would make this easier and simply abduct him before he ran away.

The craft made a deafening sound, its own language of crude noises letting slip that which had not been possible to know. Ologun was dumbfounded, for it had been much longer than he had expected and much less time than it had felt. It had been eighty six years, three months, eleven hours and twenty seven minutes since he had entered that enemy ship and been stolen away.

The craft was anxious to go. It opened a slit along the underside of its bulbous undercarriage and released a long tentacle. The appendage reached down and hoisted Ologun towards the opening as though it would consume and digest him. Ologun gave it little thought and was happy to be handled, a feasible excuse for leaving his responsibilities behind. His mind went over many things and to him all this meant one thing in particular.

The turn back had finally arrived.

PROSPECT

Location: Prospect/Lambda Quadrant/Scutum-Centaurus Arm.
Year: Earth Reference 2424. July 8th
Prospect Reference 2404 November 12th/Space time variation
adjustment.
Mission: Not applicable.

The copter jet shuddered then corrected itself automatically as the pilot sat back from the controls and turned to her passenger. 'Final approach on auto, Emissary Gibson.'

The craft hovered more slowly over the city and lowered itself gently towards the government's capital building; a mighty structure, a fortress constructed using the asaronite shell of a decommissioned flag ship cruiser once called the *Given Alignment*. Far below on the streets and among the many other dwarfed skyscrapers, the protests raged on. Not that any normal person could see from such a distance, but then her eyesight was special and she could read the picket signs and even the emotions on the faces within the crowds.

'Judith.'

'Sorry?' the pilot asked, not quite understanding her.

'Call me Judith, I mean seriously, when I said call me Judith about umpteen times I meant it.'

'Affirmative, ma'am.'

Judith rolled her eyes and leaned over the open hatchway of the copter jet to gain a better view. How had it come to this? She had spent yet more weeks in the wilderness, hundreds of miles south of civilisation, providing more resilience against alien diseases, parasites, viruses and any organism that needed to be fixed for the prospectors living on the frontier. This she knew to be laziness on the government's part, for they had the capacity to make medicines for anything needed. Yet her intervention was far more sophisticated in that the indigenous life on this world was also protected against everything humanity had brought with them.

*

The people who lived and survived outside the safety zone of the six cities of the empire, and had done so in very tough conditions, were the real prospectors as far as she was concerned. It was a different story for the rest of the people on this planet who were far from content under this new iteration of government. People were pointless and expendable and a nuisance for the empire. They had enticed billions from Earth and other colonies, told them they would find a new world of untold wealth and prosperity. Now, almost a century later and with the empire deploying their new toys, things were looking even tougher for those wanting to remain within the confines of the six sectors, all of which seemed pointlessly unfair.

The craft touched down on the building's landing pad and Judith exited quickly without a mask and made her way to the uppermost access hatch. The pilot nearly took off her breathing apparatus, almost forgetting that this was still high altitude and that the person she was with was beyond such restriction.

Down the corridors and inside the warmth and protection of the building, Judith marched towards the director's conference room or, as those in power had called it for the past fifty years: Base Chamber. The 'democratic' government, as they saw themselves, used this place to gather both for extraordinary levels of security and out of the need to establish some tradition.

Her mind worked over everything that was happening, that had happened over the past ten years. The people were less important, and exploration and many other forms of progression had been reined in and restricted.

Minus the politeness Judith had learned over the years, she barged in mid-conference, stopped just inside the doorway, and absorbed the entire scene within a split second. At the centre of the enormous room was a huge conference table that seemed to be tiny and isolated within its clinical surroundings. Three walls of charged transparent lenses were the partition to the outside world; they lit the room a dull grey amidst the haze of cloud, and reflected a stark sheen on the black marble floor. Apart from the table and chairs there was no furniture or technology within this place in any form for the sake of security, and if need be they could enforce a further lockdown of asaronite-plated walls with an added force field to surround them. All thirty members of state, including the chairman, looked across at Judith, following her as she approached the conference table; the power base of this world.

'Back so soon, Judith,' the chairman enquired politely, yet with a hint of malice and agitation in his voice. The other directors – governors as such within the only officially occupied country of the planet – held silent, many of them hoping Chairman Huzima would not agitate the situation any further. Whatever the chairman, this president, thought of Judith, all within the room remembered that Judith was something else. No matter how she had worked with any of the many politicians throughout the three generations that had helped govern and develop the Prospectus Colony, this creature was very powerful and possibly very dangerous.

'When are you going to make up your mind?' Judith demanded.

'I'm sure I don't know to what you're referring,' Huzima said.

'The more of those machines you deploy, the less work there is for the people. The less work there is, the less currency they have on which to survive, Simple, obvious stuff,' Judith pointed out with both scorn and sarcasm at the chairman's insolence.

Huzima smiled. 'Don't you have another jungle or swamp, some other mining town or farmland to aid with that precious gift of yours?' He rolled his eyes, searching for the answer on the network implant embedded deep within his brain. 'Grid seventeen south-east, lovely area with something new for you. A hundred cases so far and a very ferocious type it is too.'

In her youth Judith would have struck Huzima, regardless of the fact he was the most powerful man on the planet. She looked exactly the same as when she had first arrived: young and with the same fierce eyes that gave the impression to others of ruthlessness and ambition; yet on the inside, she had become complacent in many ways and even exhausted by it all.

'The people are moving too fast because you are . . . look,' she said, moving towards the wall past the conference table to take a look at the city and its streets below. 'People are moving into the frontier lands in uncontrolled numbers and becoming exposed to too many alien flora and fauna. It's not just the organisms, it's the wildlife too. Choose to drop the Version service project or make it all free, abandon Limit-ism – it's just aggressive capitalism dressed in left-wing clothing. This is all ridiculous, I hope you've all gathered in order to see sense.'

'Preposterous!' one of the board members blasted from way down the table.

'Now that's a word I haven't heard in a while, especially from a fat idiot like you, Bowens,' Judith taunted.

What could they say? Judith had been there from the start and had known everyone who was anyone, including the parents and grandparents of Chairman Huzima. To dismiss this creature that had not aged one iota in eighty six years had to be considered the most preposterous aspect of it all. The real issue that anyone in government had with this thing, this being named Judith Gibson, was that because she had made no true attempt towards the realm of political power, had not indicated that she had any tangible desires and in particular appeared to have needed nothing whatsoever to survive, her values were always being questioned. What exactly did an unkillable being want? How could her judgement in terms of dealing with the natural order of things be trusted? Could she relate to what people really wanted or needed?

'Fine.' Judith finally surrendered, sick of it all. 'Let the masses find their own way, replace them with those things, and have this grand old shipyard to yourselves.'

Judith peered out through the transparent wall again and over the city, still wondering after many years how exactly she was able to see through such thick mist with exceptional clarity when many other aspects of life were in such a haze.

She had been there when they chose the ships that would land to form the initial base points of the city. Other metals, apparently from another universe, had been used for their hulls and this ensured no corrosion and no fatigue, so that even now and across this immense city they were just as they were when they touched down; or so she assumed. Some of them were now government buildings or factories and some were accommodation blocks or technology research centres. They were relics of the war between the new world independence seekers and those from the old world that had not been spoken to in over sixty years. Now the city was complete and had been erected amongst the old war ships so that they faded away from the days of victory and out of this generation's mind which knew nothing of sacrifice and had never tasted glory. Judith remembered and she yearned for those progressive times of prospect and exploration, long before this clapped out era of political and social dysfunction, and the inevitable backwardness of greed, selfishness and corruption. *Your fathers knew better!*

'Okay,' Judith finally voiced, her blue eyes flashing a deep purple in the fading light. 'Do what you want. Build those things and displace an entire workforce with those slaves, but I quit. You all think this makes you powerful, but do you know what happened to every civilisation whose hegemony became engulfed with greed? Of course not, you're all just children, babies.'

The members of the board seemed to glaze over at this statement, seemingly without a clue as to what Judith was referring.

'There's a plaque downstairs in the lobby containing all IMC and Prospect Division values and core objectives. Much of it is jargon, but I suggest you read the parts on progression and sacrifice and that you all stop lining your own pockets at the cost of what others before you managed to achieve.'

No one said a word to her as she left. In fact they had not seen her leave at all, despite the ten metres distance between the table, the empty floor space and the door.

*

Judith made her way through the crowds until she hit the central canal. It ran through the city's oldest district dedicated to the Prospect Foundation government and military headquarters. She climbed the steps to one of the cable sway bridges to gain a better vantage point among a group of people wishing to keep a safe distance should anything go wrong. Thousands had gathered on this autumn night, angered by the government's callous approach to supplanting an entire workforce with the newest models of the Version.

Equal amounts of drones – advanced bio-mechanical anthropoids – now did most of the labouring within the mines, building infrastructure, farming, and aiding the military. Anywhere with labour intensive jobs would now utilise these bipedal machines that were stronger, faster and far more reliable; that were simply indefatigable. They would serve humans and make life easier for people, it had been said.

That would have been an excellent idea were it not for the fact that this country had yet to change its economical and ideological infrastructure from that of flat-base capitalism to something else, something that did not rely on people earning money in order for them to live. What else there could be in terms of such an infrastructure was difficult to fathom, yet whatever the answer, the heads of business within this state had fallen too quickly in love with the idea of free labour without considering peoples' lives.

Judith could not believe the level of idiocy of those now in power. No society could survive without being held together by people that worked and functioned, and, it had to be said with some regret, the competition of commerce that involved people. Human beings were like that, they needed a certain fairness on the playing field. Replacing tens of thousands of them with creatures grown for war against a virtually unknown alien species, that potentially deadliest of enemies, was against all fairness; it just made everything pointless. *Isn't that why robotics on Earth have been kept at that crude and archaic level for hundreds of years? Shouldn't values be based around human interaction and production? Isn't that the whole point of existing?*

The masses were being fired up by various ringleaders who stood on stools and other makeshift pedestals at specific junctions amidst the chaotic scene. The roar was deafening, making Judith feel hemmed in underneath the autumn mist now blotting out the view of surrounding buildings only ten to fifteen feet above the streets. Cafés, bars, restaurants and most other businesses were closed; their shutter doors pulled down and locked. Something was brewing.

There was no point in loitering to see what would happen, so Judith continued until the crowds thinned and the noise became a low din behind her. She wrapped her heavy coat around her and wandered the east side of the city and towards the new military and technology foundation that was now located on the outskirts. Her mind went through everything in logical fashion for there had to be a constructive, even a peaceful way, to get past what may end in riots and bloodshed.

Her main concerns were about the Version drones which led her to walk towards the train station. Once there she would take the shuttle train and get to the military complex faster, for she wanted Version's mk36 creator Doctor Glynn Sharplin to pull the plug on the drones if things got out of hand. Judith then decided that such a visit should wait until the morning, and continued past the station. Deep in thought, she mulled over the disturbing fact that there were now at least two thousand Version patrolling the city, up high on the roof tops out of sight, ready to deploy if so much as a loaf of bread was thrown out of malcontent. *Would the Prospect government, the police or army really do it?* Judith wondered. She turned to face the city, pushed her eyesight to its very limit, and could see the armed response teams along with the Version in the distance scanning the streets below, where only the machines and Judith could truly pierce the shroud of mist now descending further on the streets.

For too long she had ignored this problem, which had started as a weapons-defence project and had slipped over into the domestic lives of the masses. Turned a blind eye and ignored it. Got on with the mundane job as main competitor to this world's natural order and became its replacement Mother Nature. Stopped the ecosystems and all they churned out from harming people and vice versa.

In the end it had been the brave men and women who had finally stood up for their rights on this matter. Yet at this stage there were only a few options: move to the frontier land and carve a living from the landscape and survive, maybe prosper; or put up with what the powers that be dictated.

Prospect had always been more of a totalitarian empire regardless of its proclamation as a democracy. Those directors of the company, its stakeholders back when it was seen as a company, had claimed ownership of this planet and set up as a government with no intention of allowing a voting system that involved the people. Through hereditary and other biased forms of promotion, each generation of directorship came and went with little say from any of the masses. Maybe the forms of democracy within all countries on Earth were flawed, even an illusion when it came to electing those the voter wished to be in power, yet even so, at least there was an attempt at empowering people into becoming content with the idea of options, with choice.

Judith wished she was wearing a second skin for many reasons. It was her battle suit as such, and even though technically she had never gone to war she knew that her first reaction to any of her people coming to any harm would be to fight for them. The protesters were brave indeed for the Version drones, even though deployed as slaves for hazardous mining operations and all menial tasks across many industries, were tough battle machines and it would take only two or three to kill thousands of people.

A strange breed created from silicone-based biotechnology, progressed from the old Keeper range of fleet pilots that had been designed to position process ships to circumvent vast distances of space through portals of some kind. The Keepers were as old as Judith and still in service, and were now being used to control and manoeuvre this vast army, which to her seemed strange and very dangerous.

Judith had by now gone way past the train station and was within the city's external park of grasslands, golf courses and various club houses for the Prospect military houses. Next to the main path and away from the park stood a tall mesh fence and, on the other side, numerous training academies for the Prospect war machine. Building after building shrouded in the mist worked their way into the distance. These were mostly two-storey structures of a white chalk-brick exterior holding the flags aloft out front to signify each division: Air combat, Fleet, Army, Navy and so on. *Perhaps they'll be replaced,* Judith thought.

Her relationship with the armed forces had been eroded over the years and, as she watched the young cadets loiter outside the buildings through the fence as she walked by, it became apparent that none of them would know who she was or what she had done for this world. Time had sent her on another journey and, whilst the military council of the Prospect division long ago thought her a weapon or something else of importance, the newer generation thought little of her at all. Alienated or forgotten to the greater extent, she still had access to the technology foundation where all the might of war was created, including the factory where the Version were produced; an indication of how important her counsel used to be.

If the Prospect Empire wanted to reclaim the land after people had worked so hard to forge a living then they would, regardless of humanity. At least in comparison to those who lived in the city, she found the frontier folk in general to be happier and more accommodating with a better sense of unification; the present circumstances of the city dwellers excepted. Her mind pressed on and she began to relax. She told herself that things changed and this was a young state of independence with only one mega-city divided into six sectors and only a few billion people. Things would work out.

Perhaps it was better that people went to the frontier to build towns and villages and have their own piece of Prospect; the downside was that the government had not once acknowledged anyone's claim for anything.

The mist was thicker outside the city where the leafless trees in the park made for creepy figures as the mixture of vapour and back-lighting threw their shadows with outstretched arms and fingers. A commotion ahead distracted her and, regardless of her abilities, what lay ahead still made her anxious for it was the new recruit section of the barracks where all the cadets who had recently passed entry congregated after hours.

In line with the times, the younger generations appeared to be more arrogant, vicious and cruel. It was even more apparent that this newest generation of the military were no exception and that no matter how many times she walked through this part of the park she always had to endure the gangs of men and women, or rather boys and girls, who should stay on their side of the fence. They had pestered her, thrown bottles, balls and rubbish, and shouted obscenities; yet with the grace of age she had ignored them. Tonight, however, was different, for apart from Judith being more highly strung than usual it was nearing Prospect Independence Day when the war with Earth had been declared over. If they were drunk and disorderly on top of being their usual selves there would be trouble. Judith had never said a word to them, never revealed who she was or what she was capable of. Things were about to change.

A scream, then more commotion pierced the fog. Judith quickened her pace out of concern and curiosity for it came from a woman, perhaps a young girl. Her eyes adjusted to see through the thick vapour. Horrified, Judith sprinted towards the unthinkable. A group of recruits had surrounded someone on the ground and were taking it in turns to kick and stomp on them.

Reaching the commotion, she immediately threw one of the gang to the floor, and took in the scene in a heartbeat. A young man and his girlfriend were slumped on the damp grass and had been beaten badly. Judith rushed to their side and tried to call for assistance using her neural implant. *Signal jammed.* 'You bastards!' Judith shouted at them. 'Where's the jammer?'

One of the gang rushed in to kick Judith in the face.

'Wrong answer,' Judith said, grabbing the boy's foot, breaking his leg at the knee, then flipping him aside. Another came at her with a knife, but it was too late. Judith had broken and twisted each individual before they even realised she had moved.

All eight of the Prospect basic army recruits were laid out cold with various injuries and broken bones, and were no longer Judith's concern. She knelt down to aid the young couple and to her horror found the young man was already dead. The girl, however, was alive but in a critical condition. Judith investigated her from head to foot quickly, then did something she had learned to do with great expertise and efficiency. Taking the knife, she cut the girl's clothes from her arm and cut into the skin on her bicep. Judith then cut her own wrist and fell into a slight trance of concentration. From inside the cut a thread, a capillary, worked its way out like a long, thin worm that slithered and wriggled its way towards the cut on the girl's bicep. Within moments Judith linked her nervous system to the girl's as the thread burrowed deeper. This was the true magic of her ability:

that she could inject her own capacity to regenerate into the girl so that in only a matter of minutes she would be as new, physically at least. Judith found this one difficult for the girl had a partially crushed skull and internal bleeding. The hideous operation to rectify bone and manipulate tissue on this invasive but necessary scale continued until Judith knew she had won. The girl's eyes flickered open and she immediately began to scream hysterically, then broke down crying.

'It's okay,' Judith said, grabbing her and pulling her close. She wrapped her coat around the girl, holding her firmly. 'What's your name?' she asked the girl in order to fend off shock. There was no answer. The girl just sobbed, almost unable to breathe as she was so upset.

'Calm down, it'll be okay, I've got you,' Judith said in her most comforting tone. The girl was only sixteen years old, a baby in Judith's eyes, and so she searched the gang of unconscious animals, wondering which one of them had stamped so hard on this girl's head that they had crushed her skull and which at any other time would have killed her. 'It'll be okay,' Judith whispered again, now rocking while cradling the girl in her arms.

Judith felt deeply emotional about it all as though a decade's worth of ignorance and acceptance had suddenly engulfed her. Things were not okay and she had had enough. She had managed to send for help over the network, listening as the sirens drew closer in the distance, and now kept watch as most of the cadets poured out of their compound to see what was going on. None of it concerned her and she was happy enough to stay there a while with the child, feeling something she had always longed for and that had always failed to happen.

FLOWER

Location: Spectra Vessel/Unknown.
Time: Earth Reference 2424 July 3rd/ Comparable reference unknown.
Mission: Unknown/Withheld.

Ray . . . Ray. Oh, come in Ray, I have something for you.

The whining of his second skin went away at last and he returned to watching the breed fly overhead below the liquid lens sky. Ray was in no hurry and observed just how much this place had expanded over the decades.

The old accommodation cabins that he was sitting amongst occupied a large network of scaffolding, which was now a naked and exposed structure of pipes and boxes that had once hugged the inside of the basin's shell. The north wall it had been called, but it had long receded into the distance so that this curved structure of scaffolding was nothing more than an elaborate trellis for thick vines amidst a seemingly endless forest.

The old mining city and farmlands had been engulfed long ago, yet from this position he could still see the lake that glowed a stark orange with the presence of the Spectra. He summoned one of the larger craft, one of the newer and younger castes to take him to the old fortress; another human-built structure that stood like a volcano split in two now that the south wall had receded. The thing swooped down, grabbed him under the arms and darted off over the canopy below, over the lake and further still until it dropped him off outside the entrance to the old fort. *Ten minutes!* Ray thought of the three-hundred-mile journey. This new type of craft was ultra-quick, but could they fight and protect the rhombus into which the broken shard had morphed?

Nature, or rather the super-nature present within this pocket world, had moved on regardless of man-made things. A dull metal object high up amongst the trees – apparently caught and pinned among the branches over the years – could, on closer inspection, be identified as one of humankind's war machines: a tank.

Ray, hurry along, I have things to be doing.

Within the courtyard of the fort a number of very young craft scurried around on another vehicle that had been buried deep within the foliage. Why had the infant war machines insisted on digging up destroyed relics left by humanity? Ray had no idea. He at least remembered what had happened here at this place all that time ago, and smiled to himself at the pathetic behaviour he had witnessed.

Ray, how long? I have no time for your dilly-dallying, so hit the flow.

Ray made his way to the rear end of the fortress and to a burrow that had once existed within the basin's wall. As the wall receded to make way for the garden, the tunnel ended up on the ground. Ray exited the rear half of the fortress where all rooms and compartments were exposed, having lost their rear wall of protection. It all looked like a giant mound of shrubbery where hardly any of the grey concrete showed through the thick foliage that had latched on from the bottom all the way to the top. He then looked at the burrow on the floor and shrugged, then jumped in, fully aware that by now there should have been better ways to get down below. Two thousand feet of sheer drop later, he hit the flow of Spectra, or should it be said the plasma within which they survived; they may not have been present in this blood of energy, but then who could ever tell?

*

One gut-wrenching ride later, Ray hit the final pool to be greeted by Hina.

'This better be important,' Ray said exiting the pool. He then sat down and waited for his right collar bone, which had snapped on impact, to straighten out and re-set itself.

'Hurry,' Hina insisted. 'You have been bestowed a great task this day.' He then cackled loudly and ran off into one of the many tubeways leading away from the pool.

Ray followed the curvature and deep slope of the tunnel that became more illuminated as he descended. Soon he was walking deep underneath the ocean of light, deep within the rhombus. This was an unusual place to be, a place he had never been in fact. This tunnel – normally created of a black marble shell – was instead composed of a transparent gelatinous substance that dipped in small circles under the weight of each footstep.

It was also extremely bright from being surrounded by the sea of Spectra so that Ray had to wait for his eyes to adjust until he finally saw Hina at the far end of a section of tunnel within an enormous bubble. As he approached Hina, he noticed varying mutations of what could have only been described as eels or marine snakes. They were everywhere: underneath, above and to either side. More complex than ever they floated in various shapes and sizes, yet their main feature or texture was still that of a luminous ghost-like energy. Ray watched as these phantoms of the Spectra swam or floated by and watched him. This had all served to distract him from what lay within the bubble at the end of the tunnel, the thing sitting next to Hina, who had been patiently waiting.

Ray entered the orb and was transfixed on the thing on the floor and at its centre. 'What is it?' he asked Hina.

'This is your mission,' Hina replied.

Outside the confines of the orb within which the two stood, and directly underneath the thing that had Hina so excited and Ray mesmerised was one of the ghostly creatures. It was enormous and had no definable shape or features and appeared to be attached to the outside of the orb, which it may have actually created.

'Are we . . . ?'

'Inside it? Yes. Say hello to your surrogate mother, Ray,' Hina jested.

Ray brushed the comment aside for he knew how it all worked. What lay directly in front of the two men, however, was even more peculiar and of great interest to Ray. The object could have been likened to a large plant made of dark-blue flesh, and its flower, held aloft on a thick trunk only a foot above the floor, was large enough to engulf an adult human.

'That thing grew this?' Ray asked, although he was really seeking a full explanation beyond this obvious question.

'You know,' Hina said, moving to stand next to Ray and admire the flower of flesh, 'we are actually standing within its womb. Oh but don't worry it's quite all right, I just needed to get you here on time to see this.'

Ray had witnessed a variation of this with the thousands of craft developed and born in hordes hatched from great pods that hung from fauna and looked akin to flora. These were all grown and incubated from select types of creature that aided the Spectra, the ones from another realm. They had been utilised and developed but never offered progression or sentience. Ray had thought about this both philosophically and logically. He and the others shared something that had belonged to these creatures. Did that make them related or, even more disturbingly, did it make this creature in whose womb he now stood, however enigmatic it may seem, into his mother as Hina suggested? *Too many parents,* Ray mused, believing full well that such a level of splicing made notions of belonging pointless.

'Wait for it,' Hina said excitedly, and grabbed Ray by the arm as though he were trying to escape.

Ray watched as the flower opened; its flat, meaty petals spreading out to reveal a thick white mucus bowl at its face. Ray crouched down as the flower flexed like a muscular animal to disperse the liquid. What he saw made his eyes widen and he was unable to break his stare.

'Well?' Hina asked. 'What do you think?'

Ray remained deep in concentration in a world of his own until Hina's question sank in. 'Beautiful,' he whispered softly.

UNINVITED

Location: Earth/Quadrant: Closest Reference Identifier Orion Spur.
Time: 2424 September 10th/Origin Reference.
Mission: Surveillance of Surrounding Cosmos/last hostile contact/time lapse 86 years 3 months 5 days.

There was a terrible intangible pressure with having such a short life span. There had been a time long ago when such a thing was restricted; when people lived too long; and, above all, when there were too many people.

'Natasha Forbes to the observation lounge immediately please.'

'On my way.'

A faction of humanity with a terrible and selfish agenda, had found a way to beat the speed of light many times over and, on August fifteenth 2338, eight hundred ships appeared above Earth's stratosphere and the world changed. Every country and especially those considered to be superpowers was brought to its knees in a matter of hours.

Decimation of cities and a way of life was not enough, however, and the death toll from such a devastating bombardment was just the beginning. Much of Earth's scientific resources were now being directed towards the protection of Earth and, more importantly, vengeance.

The observation platform Dakota 2 hovered one hundred and thirty thousand feet above the Nevada desert and was ideal both for such research and for keeping surveillance of the surrounding universe. Of course there were satellites and various telescopes that could observe just as adequately, the Dakota had access to all of these, but more importantly the platform was a symbol of security and a place to centralise key protocols in how to keep an eye on Earth's solar system.

Natasha walked the complex corridors and through the final lounge area, avoiding the great window and its view of the world below from such a height. She only had two weeks left in this place before she would return to C.E.R.N to continue research on how to create an energy cascade; the world was still a long way off from creating one.

'Natasha, you need to see this right away.'

Bryan Bates ushered her on to the observation deck and the two of them walked past people working on consoles within the coliseum-shaped room. The transparent roof to the whole complex was dimmed down to a dull grey and Natasha suspected something was happening here. 'What is it, Bryan?'

Bryan pointed to a large holographic representation of Earth's solar system and drew her attention to a region of the Kuiper Belt. 'If your theory on light consumption as pre-emptive to a cascade is correct, we're about to have company,' Bates said.

Natasha studied the hologram and then began keying in information on a screen on the console below. An etched representation of the space-fabric phenomena illustrated a convex shape as though a bubble ready to burst. 'It isn't large enough to be a battleship, it's approximately one hundred and ten metres in diameter,' Natasha stated.

'It's large enough that everyone's seen it. Chatter's been intercepted from China, Europe, the Middle East, Russia and the African Allied Council.'

Colonel Young had entered the room. 'How long before a confirmed contact?' he demanded.

'Could be as little as a few minutes,' Bates offered, to the annoyance of Natasha who wondered what Bates knew of such things. In fact she had often wondered why a civilian scientist would suck up to the military on such a continual basis.

'Anything up to twenty minutes,' Natasha intervened, and the colonel nodded as he was aware this was her domain of research and expertise.

Natasha sat on a chair in order to monitor this event, the likes of which had not been recorded in over sixty years. 'What do you estimate it could be?' she asked.

'Could be a natural event with an asteroid or small debris,' Bates speculated, which annoyed Natasha even more. As she reeled at Bates' stupidity, the console's display changed and the convex shape on the screen opened up. The whole room exploded with activity as the colonel barked questions. Natasha shut everyone out and began to read the information as it scrolled along the screen.

'I need to know what just exited the aether, now!' Young shouted above the commotion.

Natasha felt a little bewildered and lost some objectivity as she began compiling the information. 'It's a small, something. Fifty feet is the length of the main body with a wing span of one hundred metres.'

'A craft of some kind?' Young asked.

'I'm not sure, it's just changed shape. Oh . . .' Natasha was stunned by what she was witnessing.

'We have a reverse-mass wake . . . it's headed for Earth,' Bates told Young.

'Earth atmosphere incursion in eight minutes. Mark,' someone shouted from behind Young, causing him to hurry out of the operations centre and into the adjoining room. Once there, he removed a flat hologram-projector tablet from his uniform jacket pocket. He placed it on a desk and typed in a code on the screen. The screen blinked and then projected a 3D picture of a man from the waist up.

'Colonel Young, I need a sit rep now,' the man in the holographic image ordered.

'Admiral Wass, sir, we have a breach.'

'I know, Young, it's not exactly a subtle entrance. What is it, do we know?'

Colonel Young moved to switch on another display and fiddled with the machine's interface. He then grew impatient and ran to the doorway of the room and shouted for one of the scientists to assist him. 'You! Make this screen show what's on that screen in there!'

The scientist entered and quickly configured it so that the observation lounge's main monitor and the side room monitor were both the same. Young watched as the intruding vessel passed the moon and entered Earth's atmosphere at colossal speed. It then looped around the planet over and over again; each orbit slightly smaller than the one before.

'We just shut down all air space within our jurisdiction, Young, but this thing is travelling in excess of two hundred thousand miles per hour. Where's Forbes? I need to talk to her now!' the Admiral blasted, causing the tablet's speakers to distort at the bellow.

Colonel Young walked to the doorway and shouted for Natasha Forbes. Natasha in turn left her console at the centre of the observation room and followed Young into the side room. 'Forbes!' the Admiral boomed at seeing her. 'What's going on here? We haven't had time to react to this. You said you could design a system that would give us plenty of forewarning. Now there's something scanning us.'

'It's a little more complicated than that, Admiral. This thing is not like any ship we have on record,' Natasha argued. 'It's more fluent, fluid in its use of reverse-mass ability. Its speed alone should cause a massive tidal-wake in Earth's atmosphere, and yet it's as though it isn't there. It gives off no adverse effect which may also be why it can move so fast.'

'Any ideas where it's going?' Young asked.

There was no need to answer as the vessel began to slow. It had seemingly finished its full inspection of Earth and was now headed north towards the African Continent. It then disappeared as it flew low over the Cape of Good Hope.

Colonel Young and Natasha listened in to Admiral Wass who had left the visual domain of the tablet. 'Get me the President now.'

*

The Version stretched back in rows of a hundred wide and a hundred in depth. They remained dormant and as still as any inanimate object. Dark crimson skin made them seem as though a human being had been flayed and the exposed muscular structure beneath had dried. The differences from the older types of Version were that these newer models had arms, legs, hands and feet. They had eyes with which to see and they had small slits for ears with which to hear, though no nose with which to smell nor mouth to speak or consume nutrients. As bio-mechanical beings they would obtain these through an umbilical on their abdomen; they had a navel through which a large hose would inject specialist food. This seemed to be a major chink in such a tough armour, and yet creating a machine that could self-repair and actually become fitter and stronger with use was in fact a smart move.

Judith Gibson stared at them for some time with concern. The Version were of three distinct shapes and sizes: the ectomorphic for speed and agility, and the mesomorphic that were powerful entry units developed to take incredible punishment and the top category, which troubled Judith as they were designed purely as wrecking balls. The standard ectomorphic Version were eight feet tall and not to be dismissed as feeble by any means, yet the mesomorphic TL37 Version was, as it said on the tin, a Titan, a tank that stood at fourteen feet in height and weighed in as a useful tonne of enhanced carbon alloy-laced bone and toughened alligator-type silicone flesh. All were initially designed to counter the alien threat that had entered the basin over eighty six years ago, although the menace had not shown itself in all this time and had seemingly disappeared.

'You're in a trance again, Judith,' Doctor Sharplin called from above. He sat in a control room adjusting the code to the original pilot Version units so that he could patch various issues for when they controlled the soldier Version.

'Bet you never saw these things taking over the labour market,' Judith quipped with malice.

'I know, they'll have them as butlers and maybe even use them as prostitutes, the limits are endless.'

Judith grinned at Sharplin. He had once been called Glynn Langmead and had changed his last name to his mother's maiden name due to having a closer relationship with his grandfather than his parents.

'I'm amending the fail-safe code on these thinkers, I mean they're becoming archaic and these new budget restraints are causing problems. We should have new thinkers developed really. Hell, this one here, number 6, is over a hundred years old.'

'Built to last and not to mention the fact that the Spectra helped develop them. Can you honestly say you could make better?'

'Do you miss it?' Sharplin asked.

'Miss what?'

'The shard, the basin, the alien entity . . . the combat with the others?'

'It was more than a lifetime ago. I miss your grandfather, I miss . . . I do not miss your grandmother,' Judith mused.

'There, if these things get out of hand I have my own personal deactivation programme.'

Judith climbed the steps from the hangar bay and into the open office dais. Glynn swivelled on his chair seemingly satisfied. 'Are you allowed to do that?' Judith asked.

'Do you trust General Feng?'

'He's an arsehole like any other these days. You need to watch your posture, you're beginning to get kyphosis,' Judith offered and massaged his shoulders.

'All right,' Glynn argued, shrugging her off.

'Speak of the devil and he shall arrive,' Judith said, seeing that the general and twelve soldiers were outside the vault security door. The general and his men entered and walked across the factory floor amongst the machinery that helped grow and assemble the combat drones. Eventually the group climbed the stairs to the control room on the opposite stairs to the hangar bay that housed the completed Version units.

As the general entered he ignored Judith completely. 'How is the interface programme coming, Sharplin?' Feng asked.

'That's Doctor to you, Wei,' Judith interrupted.

General Feng ignored her again. 'I need the human interface upgrade completed by the end of the week, Sharplin.'

'Well, you asked for a complete upload . . .'

'Get her out of here now,' Feng ordered. 'This is classified, not for her.'

The soldiers moved to place hands on Judith then paused, knowing who and what she was.

'I think I'll stay.'

45

'I'm afraid that your security clearance has been revoked due to recent criminal activities,' Feng said with glee. 'You see, the police are looking for you due to causing grievous bodily harm to six cadets the other night.'

'Oh you mean the six that murdered a man and nearly killed a young girl? I'll go right away then shall I?'

'They were in a Prospect military zone and so they were justified in their actions,' Feng said.

Judith remained calm at this even though she knew the information to be untrue. The couple were in the park outside the fence perimeter, but the so-called facts in such a fascist state meant little.

Judith received a message from the space port informing her of Hershal's arrival. 'Saved by the bell, Feng, I'll see you later.' She gestured to Sharplin.

The soldiers seemed relieved as Judith made her way from the factory and into a lift which took her to the surface. She exited through a secure airlock chamber and out into the crisp autumn evening. Walking quickly through the compound and past various buildings, Judith noticed that everything was very quiet with no one around at all. She took her truck from the compound, signed out at the gatehouse, possibly for the last time, and drove towards the space port, ignoring speed limits.

Twenty minutes later she found herself denied access to the docking area, yet waited patiently for Hershal to meet her outside the port main gates. Things were getting out of control, she reasoned, and simply figured that she had had her day; it was most likely over.

Judith watched Hershal as he walked across the car park, talked to the guards at the gatehouse, then exited from the main gates.

'Long time no see,' Judith offered, smiling.

'Yes,' Hershal said with a smirk. 'The day is here at last, although I think we need to talk.'

'There's a nice restaurant around the corner,' Judith suggested.

They were soon sitting in a rather swanky facility overlooking the city from a thousand floors up in one of the ex-ship buildings.

'So,' Hershal said after some time, 'you're in a spot of trouble at last. I thought this sort of thing would have happened many years ago.'

'It's not what it seems.'

'No, I believe that utterly. I'm suddenly having problems. The treaty to establish contact and hopefully peace with Earth is being revoked.'

'Can they do that?' Judith said, astonished.

'No. And they will not, either. I have just spent fifty years preparing their new fleet and I'll be damned if they get any of those ships back if they continue down this avenue.'

'The shell work as expected?'

Hershal thought about the most reasonably short answer as he absorbed the scenery of smartly dressed waiting staff and a hideous waterfall feature at the centre of the restaurant. The fifty years of difficulty, trying to coat the enormous warships with the virtually indestructible marble, secreted almost as though excrement by the Spectra, had been pretty farcical and utterly tedious. 'Heat is our problem. I mean the shell can take anything thrown at it, but you have shockwaves that could rip the crew apart and energy transfer of any so-called energy weapons that would simply boil, even vaporize anyone inside, except the Version units that can withstand much more.'

'Better with than without,' Judith stated. A young girl came over and they both placed orders for drinks.

'I need to leave this place now,' Judith continued. 'I have as you say . . . come to the end of my time here. Either that or something will happen.'

Hershal sat eerily still, displaying no body language as usual, as Judith tried to gauge what he might be thinking. His bright blond hair and pale blue eyes drew looks from a table nearby, where slightly overweight businessmen in suits began a typical mockery with the words 'albino' and 'freak' finding their way across the otherwise pleasant atmosphere.

'I understand,' Hershal said. 'Could you hold off a while? Find somewhere remote and give it a year, just one year until this last endeavour is achieved and then we can abandon this place, maybe concentrate our efforts on Earth, if that is we can be forgiven.'

'Well, be sure to break me out of prison, I'm wanted right now.'

'This is a tricky situation. The problem is that the new generations have forgotten what we are,' Hershal said with a certain malicious intent. 'I've been dealing with the new administration and met with the lead of the council, President Tsar Huzima.'

'Oh yes,' Judith said.

'Luckily Hina doesn't wish to leave the ship.'

'If only Ologun were here. I think the whole cabinet would be buried by now, revolutions are right up his street.'

'You still think about him?'

'I think about a lot of people,' Judith said and Hershal noted the glum look on her face.

Hershal nodded to the waitress as she placed the drinks on the table. The years had rolled by and he found it puzzling to have attended all Judith's social gatherings. The odd Christmas at Frank Sharplin's house or the summer holidays at some resort that Judith insisted were important. Then there were the funerals of Doctor Siren and Frank Sharplin; funny how a married couple could pass away within months of each other, so it seemed more than just coincidence. Then there were the boyfriends and the endless love affairs and also the one time that stood out where Judith had spent a decade with a woman. Judith had not seemed that invested in the sexual aspect of the relationship; that being said, these things were private. Yet it was apparent to Hershal that the physical part was indeed a worthwhile price to pay for something quite deep and spiritual. Juan was her name and when she left Judith for whatever domestic issues that had occurred, it became evident that Judith had been crushed beyond any foreseeable expectation. He thought carefully about his next words and was very aware that being hurt and lonely were sometimes symptoms only evident because of one's exposure to love and all the emotions found within this most tedious of paradoxes; something in which he had never been remotely interested.

'Ologun is back on Earth,' Hershal finally said, unable to find tact.

Judith sat bewildered at the news, and then shot up to leave.

'Judith, hold on a moment.'

'I'm going to Earth with you and Laughing Boy.'

'I gave you this information and hoped we could discuss a few things.'

'There is nothing to discuss.'

'Something else is happening and I don't know the details. Look, he wasn't just found after all this time. Hina says that Creed left three months ago after some instruction from the Spectra and now all of a sudden Ologun has been taken to Earth.'

Judith paused as she thought about this and then sat down. 'They knew where he was all along,' she seethed. 'Eighty years go by and they knew all along. Well, where has he been, is he okay?'

'I know little at this point. All I know is that Ray is also there on some mission that Hina refuses to divulge, and it's all in the run up to the Prospect Fleet peace envoy which, might I add, is now in jeopardy due to this new administration's disinterest in affairs planned long before they were ever born.'

'I can't stay now,' Judith reasoned.

'You are one of the predominant reasons this world has worked, you need to keep an eye on this army of machines. I don't know, I feel a disaster approaching somewhere. Earth, Prospect, I feel it in my bones, Judith. I see the wealth being drawn from the bottom and kept at the top, I see the fascism creeping in towards something inhumane as at times it does. I expect you to put your foot down at some point. I expect that if you see things getting out of hand here that you will become an agent that acts with extreme prejudice. I expect you to destroy this administration and take over if justified.'

Judith was horrified and became more anxious as what he had said sank in. She gulped on her coffee as though the mug would hide her reaction for a few seconds. 'What you're saying is unrealistic,' she said, placing the mug on the table.

'What I am saying is that your personal craft is en route as of today and will arrive in under a week's time.'

'You want me to get involved here on a level that was never intended,' Judith said, lowering her voice.

'I want insurance from someone I trust!' Hershal said.

Judith sat back, looking out of the window as the sun broke

49

through clouds and hung low between two of the flagship skyscrapers. The crimson ball cast a sheen on the metal hulls that lit up the whole boulevard into the distance. Protesters had already begun their daily activities and were gathering en masse. 'You think such action hadn't crossed my mind? Hershal, I can't even begin to understand the ramifications if in fact I agreed with you.'

'I'm talking about a precision-based course of action if required.'

'You are talking about an abuse of my abilities and playing a game of power that can never end well.'

Hershal smiled and moved to sit back, perhaps in wonder. 'The fact that you have considered all of this means that you are capable and will do so sensibly if necessary.'

'If anything happens and they use the Version then I'll react. The machines were never created for domestic use and God help us if they're used against the population.'

Hershal considered this statement from Judith and nodded in agreement. An army of machines designed and created in order to help fight the alien force that had attacked Vanguard and some years later the basin, was now being applied in unexpected ways.

Hershal inspected the space above and around the city rooftops and saw at least twenty units scanning the crowds now gathered on the streets. To him it was the least ethical way in which to deploy such lethal apparatus. Regardless of using these things for cheap and effective labour, which to him was no great surprise, utilising them as a force to intimidate or even supply an active level of force was unacceptable. Hershal understood Judith's caution over the issue and he admitted to himself that the crux of the conversation was orientated around the machines and how far the Prospect government was willing to go regarding their use.

'I'm already in trouble,' Judith said in frustration.

'With who? Not the people – I am quite sure if something happens here, they will support you.' Hershal stood and surveyed the city through the panoramic window lens as the sun finally disappeared, leaving a red hue over the atmosphere. 'Kill anyone and everyone who supports what I believe to be an unacceptable oppressive environment. Judith, when this next year is over I will help you achieve what you have wanted for quite some time. I-I think that when the then Prospect Division of IMC attacked Earth for independence . . . I think it was wrong and unforgivable. If I had been a different person all those years ago and had any real foresight, empathy, I would not have agreed.'

'You couldn't have stopped it, we were never meant for any of this,' Judith reassured him and watched as he began to walk away. 'You didn't say what you thought I wanted.'

Hershal turned and smiled before saying, 'You were thinking that what any of the men you have been with over the years could have given you, was what you wanted. It's surprising really, as you are so biologically hostile that I would imagine you wouldn't need any of us, but even I would offer this to you.'

'Offer me what?'

'A family.'

*

'How the hell could this happen?'

'Madam President, we are compiling as much information as is reasonably possible at this time.'

Aarti Kawle had only been President of the United States of America for a few months and had inherited what she considered the mother of all shit-storms that would likely start World War Four. She took a moment to consider the news and if her instincts were correct, it gave her the optimum opportunity to turn congress against Operation Rashad. The politics of this operation had been what she considered both insane and exhausting, and above all had reinforced the fallacy of her being called Commander-in-Chief. Rashad was the last administration's legacy and, as ill-timing and democracy would dictate, that administration had failed to see it through. Business pays for a presidency and as Congress continued to support the operation, it had proved almost impossible to retract or even delay what was to come. President Kawle would tread carefully as she had done for some time. She had never said that she opposed the operation and had always danced around the subject using carefully chosen phrases such as "re-assessment before execution". Corporations had their old, withered hands in all the right places and had all the will, might and connections to remove a Commander-in-Chief. With a world war, or rather a defeat instigated by one of the biggest corporations the world had ever known just shy of a century ago, it appeared some lessons had not been learned.

Colonel Young stepped forward to be the next in line to talk with the President. She had not hooked up to the war bunker via holographic imagery, she had come in person and was with much of the military top hierarchy hundreds of metres under the southern outskirts of Washington in one of the most sophisticated blast-bunkers ever built. Now every head of every division was scurrying around the war room making calls to find out information or organise spec op missions and, as far as Young was concerned, was liable to blow the whole operation wide open. Young waited for President Kawle to leave the confines of the dead room. She would come out for a while, get a call, then disappear back inside. It was no secret that the first few hours of the day had been spent in meetings with various figureheads from around the world. The Italian prime minister, the German chancellor, the Chinese president, the Russian tsar, Europe, the Middle East, in fact everyone except the alliance of Africa had voiced their concerns and were now preparing for what they thought was a second impending contact from Prospect.

The President exited the dead room and sat at the conference table. 'I can't read this report. I mean, what exactly does this chart represent?'

'It's an inter-dimensional representation of the craft using reverse-mass-inside-planet gravitational and atmospheric conditions,' Colonel Young answered.

'In English, not Scots, Colonel please.'

'The craft was only partially in existence within our reality and was quite able to move at record-breaking speed while causing only a minimal slipstream as it went. This craft was not attempting to hide and, simply put, it was showing us just what it was capable of. Madam President, this thing scanned every last inch of this planet in under seven minutes and it made sure we knew that.'

'He's right,' Admiral Wass interrupted, 'this thing just screwed us royally.'

President Kawle rubbed her temples and thought hard about this. 'How do we stand in regards to the mission?'

'We have brought the timetable forward by three weeks and we will be ready for launch within the next two.'

'This thing disappeared for an hour somewhere over Africa. It then left very quickly and is now oscillating around the Kuiper Belt as though searching for something. So I'll ask this again. What did the invading craft do when it flew over Great Karoo and then vanish for that hour? I'm calling for a congressional meeting tomorrow at 9 a.m. and I cannot continue to endorse the operation without further discussion.'

The room continued with the din of voices and a multitude of suggestions until the President had heard enough. She had a monumental headache and felt hemmed in. There was no easy solution to what seemed to be a situation spiralling out of control and doomed to failure. President Kawle could only predict that her first term in office was likely to be far shorter than anticipated.

ACCLIMATIZATION

The sun had risen and set twice and another morning had begun. Ologun assumed that the dirt track road would have had some traffic by now. He knelt there as though perhaps meditating and taking time to accustom himself to less gravity and to thinner air, adjust to the different rain, flora and fauna, the sounds and the smells. The sun in the sky was how he remembered it yet it looked so different from the binary suns and the moons that protected the world he had just left. This world felt simple now with its one and far less precarious orbit around a single star and a perfectly stable rhythm.

It had not taken long to catch his breath and to grow more capillaries. It had not taken long to adapt at all. But what of meeting people and learning to cope with more sentient contact?

There was not much time left now to contemplate his social abilities for in the distance a truck pulled nearer. On a dirt track surrounded by jungle, the wait seemed both long and short and the weather quite changeable with fleeting clouds of rain followed by breeze-broken patches of heat. The truck finally pulled up directly ahead. Almost immediately three men jumped out and shouted at him. He recognised the language; he had spent the first ten years of his life speaking it.

'Who are you, white man? What are you doing in our road, white mongrel?'

A nice warm welcome with unsheathed machetes and a pointed gun. Nice to be back and have the same old feeling of a rifle butt to the face; nothing new at all.

The men dragged their newfound prisoner into the back of the truck and tied a zip cord around his wrists and ankles. They punched and kicked a few more times and were convinced they had found an American or German. The men did not seem to like Americans or Germans at all, yet it could be that they were just being racist towards any white man. Some people liked their prejudices.

Memories of fighting in the school yard and exclusion from social activities at the office sprang to mind; home sweet home. The truck had not gone far when it pulled into a large military complex. It appeared they took the back entrance as it turned out the rest of the roads were nicely made and led off to a far more swanky and official-looking entrance further north.

As it stopped, another man in camouflage gear yanked the truck's rear door open. 'Who are you?' he demanded using English.

'Ologun.'

The soldiers laughed hysterically at this and it was remembered that such a name could be mocked in this part of the world.

'Okay, okay, where are you from?'

'Nigeria.'

The man leapt on to the truck and held a razor to Ologun's throat. 'We shall see, white boy, eh?' Ologun heard the man saying in Nigerian to the others, 'Why is this American wearing a wetsuit in the middle of the jungle, and why is he so disgusting? He smells like pig shit!'

Large grey buildings and endless hangar bays housing fighter jets and jumbo tankers suggested that Creed had been a bit of a bastard for dropping Ologun directly behind a very active and very large military installation. Of course Creed came into the solar system with a fanfare akin to a loud brass band. No stealth was ever initiated until trying to fool the countries throughout Africa into believing it was a normal aircraft. There was something else odd about the craft's choice of drop-off point. This military installation was less than twenty miles from the devastated city of Sokoto, the place where the IMC once had a major military and construction complex and where all experiments on the very young Ologun had taken place.

Two soldiers smelling strongly of dried fruit and old, spicy sweat dragged Ologun across three roads, one field, and then into a wooded area near livestock and many wooden cages, where pigs, chickens and even a chained elephant resided. Still, the main point of interest was the prisoners lined up in the small wooden cages across the way. They were all white, with perhaps the general look of the Anglo. Five of them were alive and in very poor health, and separate cages housed two dead women of the same ethnicity.

Ologun was swiftly tied to a nearby tree and smacked around the face a few times when one of the prisoners began taunting the soldiers. 'Hey monkey, that's right, ape.' He then made monkey noises in animated fashion.

'Give me the blade,' Ologun insisted. 'I'll cut the racist shit.'

'Are you making fun of my accent?' the soldier screamed at Ologun. 'Are you making fun of the way I talk American?'

'No this is the way I speak, this is my accent,' Ologun insisted, feeling bad that he had offended his brutal captor.

'You make fun of me,' the soldier snapped, and stabbed Ologun in the stomach with a short knife.

'No, wait, we need to question him, Ghalib,' the other soldier shouted and grabbed his colleague to drag him away. Soon it was just the prisoners, with a few chickens, pigs and an elephant to keep them company and Ologun wondered how his insects and plants were doing on that other world.

'What are you doing here, man? Are you from Recon Team B? I see your seal suit is still on, I think, is that a Dutch slender? They must have grabbed you pretty quick!'

Ologun tilted his head and looked the man up and down as he sat decrepit in his wooden cage. 'I just came home after a long break . . . but the neighbourhood has changed a little. Actually, scrap that, it's always been like this.' Ologun thought for a moment. 'Why are you people here and why do these soldiers hate Germans and Americans? Actually don't answer that as I don't really care.'

'Are you on drugs, did they drug you?'

Ologun ignored the question and began to think about this situation. The man he had ignored was German and, along with the Americans, seemed to be wearing military attire. Ologun guessed that they had all been caught doing something they should not.

The place fell quieter at last and Ologun remained where he was for the night. He watched the three men and remaining two women as they slumbered or were unconscious through dehydration and malnutrition, or perhaps they had all been tortured quite badly. *Should one get involved?*

Ologun enjoyed the wisp of the breeze through the trees and all the noises that nature brought to the vast rain forest surrounding them. As morning came he heard the voices of the soldiers as they traipsed nearer. Five men eventually arrived along with the same man who had held a razor blade to Ologun's neck the previous day, and Ologun surmised he was in charge. The men sat on thick logs placed in a large triangle and lit a fire. They had coffee and some sweet pastries and then fruit. 'Please,' a prisoner voiced to the captors, 'we need water, food and medical assistance.'

One of the soldiers moved across and poked the prisoner hard with a stick. 'Shut up!' he sneered, and the soldiers laughed at this cruelty and continued eating.

The one in charge had a device attached to his belt in which Ologun took great interest. It was a small remote computer, and might be the key to gathering information whereby Ologun reasoned he might be able to use his second skin to start doing some research. His second skin could gather information as complex as that needed to store the genome of entire species; the question was whether it could be used to hack and store other information.

'What rank do you hold, I see no epaulettes?' Ologun asked.

'Our new American friend is keen to begin.' The man gestured to the others in his native tongue and then laughed loudly, waking a few more of the other prisoners. 'I ask the questions,' he said in English, with a more serious tone.

'Be careful about the day ahead,' Ologun said in Nigerian.

'What did you say to me, American?'

The man seemed unnerved by this and went over to the prisoners. He chose and unlocked a cage occupied by one of the female soldiers. He dragged her out by the hair and threw her to her knees. Grabbing her arm he held it out and then lifted his machete. 'You let your women fight and spy for you, you cowards!'

Ologun had already released a strand of second skin and destroyed the rope binding him to the tree. He then did the same to twist and break the fabric zip cord around his ankles. He moved before anyone had taken another breath and snapped the blade-wielding man's arm with a simple move, then smacked another soldier in the face and chest with two polite jabs that broke his jaw and a few ribs. A few moments later the other soldiers were given similar treatment and soon lay unconscious on the thin sward. Ologun knelt down next to the woman. 'I think we should move on quickly.'

The woman looked up at him and appeared to be quite ill. Ologun moved her on to her side as she vomited and shook with fever. Leaving her side, he moved quickly and smashed open each of the cages then dragged each and every living prisoner out into the clearing among the trees. Chickens roamed around at random and the elephant trumpeted as though it agreed with the proceedings. Ologun set about each of the prisoners and began healing any ailments. Wounds that had turned into gaping ulcers, parasites and other infections were quickly remedied. One of the soldiers had two broken legs and a broken back and seemed to be slipping away. The others looked on in bewildered fashion. 'What are you doing, who are you?'

'Shh,' Ologun insisted and leant over the particularly injured man. 'What is your name?'

'His name is Corporal Faith, I mean Carl,' one of the women answered.

'Okay Carl, this is going to hurt like hell, but don't worry, I'll keep your heart beating for you.' Ologun released a strand of second skin, then several more and stabbed the man along his body so that the silky threads were inserted deeply within him. 'Oh by the way,' Ologun said to the platoon of prisoners, 'this is going to be hectic.'

Carl screamed in agony as both his femur bones moved and cracked into position. They began to set correctly as planned, but Ologun found the man's spinal cord was severed, making things more difficult. 'This is going to take a while.'

'We should leave him,' one of the German soldiers suggested.

'No one gets left behind, not even the dead!' another soldier argued.

'Shit, that was complicated,' Ologun remarked.

Carl sat up and then slowly climbed to his feet, and stood as though testing a new body. 'Who are you?'

'Come on,' Ologun said, ignoring them and walking over to the elephant. 'Are you coming with us out there? There are nuts and berries and bananas.'

The soldiers had begun planning their route of escape by now and had no idea Ologun had suppressed their curiosity as to who he was or how he had healed them. Slight re-programming of each individual's mind when healing them would allow things to move more smoothly. Ologun just was not sure if nullifying their interest in him would be permanent. Tensions ran high among them and Ologun decided to remain silent as he took the unconscious soldier's computer pad.

'We need that, pass it to me,' Carl said.

'Give me five minutes with it,' Ologun replied and untied the elephant while watching as the dead were dragged over to the trio of thick logs.

'We cannot bring them,' the German argued and then cursed.

'How about Pebbles here takes them?' Ologun said, stroking the elephant's large ear. 'You'll do that for me, won't you, Pebbles?'

'Is this all a joke to you?' an American soldier shouted.

'Okay, Abe, keep it down,' Carl ordered. 'We take the elephant like he suggested.'

'Ologun,' Ologun offered.

'Ologun, as in Logan right?'

'Absolutely,' Ologun said with a hint of sarcasm and impatience, wondering when they would get going. He suddenly felt as though he had things to do.

The bodies were strapped on to the elephant without commotion using the twine from the wooden cages.

'So we head south through this bush land and to the fence. The fence has no doubt been rigged with alarms so we . . . shit!' Carl threw up his hands. 'Everyone feeling okay? I'm not right yet.'

'Look,' Ologun interrupted the increasing chatter, 'you people head south to the fence and cut it open. This blade is asaronite and will slice it open quickly. Take the elephant and keep heading north-west until it's safe. It's a long journey so pace yourself. Now, I just took this thing off the grid,' Ologun said, gesturing to the pad.

'Grid?' Carl asked.

'Network, whatever, so they can't trace it. Use it with the real-time map application.'

'I know how to navigate,' Carl said, taking the device. 'You seem in better shape than the rest of us, I think you should take point.'

'I'm staying here,' Ologun stated, only half-listening. He was already intent on finding out if his skin could use the data band frequency of the computer pad in order to hack other systems. Within moments he had pretty much imagined stealing a large amount of virtual cash from a bank. Moments later he had achieved it.

'Oh really, and what do you intend on doing?' Abe asked, taking the machete as Ologun passed it to him.

'I'm going to hang around for a while for when you set that alarm off on the fence.'

'And get yourself killed?'

'I might die for a minute or two, but then I'll just come back and mess some shit up.'

Jake, Abe and the others all thought the same thing. The man in the strange wetsuit looked utterly wild and insane with a raggedy long beard and matted, bouffant hair, not to mention a pair of electric blue eyes that twitched as though he were on amphetamines. If they were going to get a head start with the use of a decoy willing to stay behind, this might be the man to use.

*

'I thought I'd find you here.' Judith turned at a voice, to see Glynn Sharplin had made his way to her.

'It's funny how things move too fast,' Judith offered. She gazed out over the mist-strewn lake and watched her breath condense and dissipate. She glanced at Frank's grave once more and began walking across the grass and down towards the water's edge.

'It's freezing out here,' Sharplin complained.

'You should get out more. Don't worry, spring is on the way.' Judith looked at him and shook her head. 'You need a skin shot.'

That was the thing with evolution. You could traverse thirty thousand light years to a planet twice the size and mass of the one your species had evolved on and you had all these little problems. In the beginning there had been mechanical suits to help people move around with the increase in their own weight. Oxygen-thinner tanks and masks had been provided until the generations passed and people could breathe unaided. Muscle, organs and bone adapted to be stronger, yet skin seemed to lag behind and literally sag with that extra pull. Judith was obviously different and was up and away within hours of her arrival. Unfortunately the saying 'as long as you have your health' seemed to be wasted on her now as she felt the weight of the universe pressing down hard on her.

'We should head for the boathouse,' Judith told Sharplin. They headed around the lake in silence among the naked trees and through the mist. Judith could see Prospect agents loitering in the distance. 'You should keep your distance from me right now, G.'

Doctor Sharplin scampered after Judith as best he could and found he was beginning to lose his breath. 'They can't touch you, I mean they still haven't figured out how you work, right?'

'I was talking about you being safe, G. Look, I might not be staying much longer.'

They approached the boathouse, a small cabin attached to a pier that seemed a little old and run down compared to what Judith remembered. 'We had some great summers here, G,' Judith said, continuing to use Glynn's pet name. 'You were young back then and your grandfather was such a fusspot over you.' She smiled.

Sharplin used his handprint on the security access lock and they entered the boathouse. As the two of them made themselves comfortable, Judith took a look around. It had been unused for a long time with tired cobwebs along the ceiling and beams as well as the grubby window panes, and all the surfaces were covered with thick dust. Sharplin sat down as Judith rummaged around for an old kettle. She noticed a picture on the wall, a motion active yet particularly old type Flickr file. It showed Rita Siren, Frank Sharplin and many friends gathered for a summertime pose on the lake shore. Judith saw herself and, apart from not ageing one iota, saw that she was nevertheless somehow different: she was happy. It was peculiar how people worked. Frank and Rita had an unusual permit for limitless lifespan replenishment due to Siren's position within the division.

Judith could not believe it when they had both died but had later found that for some time they had both purposely stopped receiving the span treatments. It had been the beginning of the end of any anchor Judith had had with Prospect, and even with Glynn partially in her life, Judith still felt that a real change in her circumstances was imminent.

'How is your mother?'

'She's looking to retire from the fleet soon.' Glynn had lit a fire within the old cast iron furnace by this time, and sat back to watch the flames. 'I've been thinking about the peace envoy to Earth. You lived there once, do you think there's any point? I mean they're backward barbarians and I can't imagine there would be any real point.'

Judith stood in silence as Glynn went on and she became upset at Glynn's perspective. 'You might be right, but let me tell you this to clear up a few of your assumptions because you know jack shit of what you're talking about.'

Glynn watched and was startled as Judith began slamming cupboards and throwing this and that around the kitchen. 'The first ten days of that war three billion died. The next ten after that another billion. Then there were twenty years of totalitarian rule by the Division as they chose and took people from Earth and brought them here. Each of Earth's governments were allowed to be maintained in order to, well, keep order and control. Then the empire left for good and with that they left a sophisticated virus in order to complete the Integer project and thin the numbers down to the desired parameters. The people on Earth are not . . . there will be no peace, and you should think before you open your mouth.'

'All right, dry your eyes, Judith.'

'Really?' Judith said. 'You want me to come over there? Because I will!'

'Listen, I wanted to ask you for a favour,' Glynn offered, trying to rapidly change the subject.

Judith filled a kettle and washed two old camping mugs in the sink. 'It's about Feng, isn't it?' she asked, wiping the cups dry with her long jacket. She found some fruit-flavoured tea in a sealed capsule, sniffed the tea bags and was satisfied.

'No,' Sharplin said. 'Why would you say that?'

Judith sat down and gave Sharplin one of the drinks. He took a sip and continued. 'I fancy someone at work.'

'That's fantastic and about time too,' Judith said. 'What's his name?'

'No, that's not it, I mean it's a she, why would you . . . ? Anyway, she's nice but a bit strong-willed you know, I need some advice.'

'Just ask her out, I mean come on, G, you're thirty two years old. I've been wondering whether you were ever going to ask some boy or girl out for, well, decades.'

'The thing is,' Sharplin said, 'she's on the probation programme. She just spent eight years in prison.'

'So what?'

'She tried to kill her husband.'

Judith grinned at this and then laughed. She threw some logs on the fire as she searched the domain for personnel files until in her right eye a picture of a sweet-looking blond woman was held. 'May Jarman, as in the wife of General James Jarman of the Frontier Rangers?'

'Yes, Judith,' Glynn said, exasperated. 'I talk to her every day and I, I just need some advice from a woman and you're almost like a woman.'

'Thanks G, I'm flattered. Look maybe I can put in a good word or suss whether she's even up for any sort of relations.'

'Dear God no, I just wanted your opinion, Judith, not for you to ruin any chance I have.'

A bleeping sound in Judith's pocket drew her attention. 'I have to go, I'm being robbed.'

Doctor Sharplin felt Judith kiss his cheek followed by a gust of air. He blinked and realised that she had already gone.

He ran out the door after her. 'Judith, don't you ruin this for me, please!'

*

Hershal had spent the day taking the sky train around the six cities and contemplated upon the fact that it was both enormous and tiny depending on one's point of view. As a hub of civilization it was both pragmatic and well-designed. He had finished his tour and now stood at a lake which was located at the centre of the surrounding six circular districts. People were huddled on the beach in the cold air with fires lit at intervals along the way. The lake was over a hundred miles in diameter and stretched far into the distance with various boats and yachts sailing near to the shore. Further out there were larger ships, and on occasions Hershal caught a glimpse of submarines; it seemed to be the fashion to have personalized one-man vessels to ride about in and there seemed to be more of these in use than any other craft.

It was the same as it always was, Hershal felt. One great city for leisure and art, restaurants and clubs. Another two districts for business and training, schools, colleges and universities. A further city for the political farce that would be a military state disguised as a democracy and two more loosely designed city districts for accommodation. It was these two cities that always confused Hershal for even when those taken from Earth had arrived and were allocated houses and apartments, it had not been long before certain groups had begun to move and segregate into communities. It was perhaps down to religion or ethnicity, or maybe it was due to culture: he just could not quite grasp the nature of human movements. The white and the black people seemed to exist together as though there were few cultural differences. Those from the Asian continent of Earth and those from the Middle Eastern countries, however, had created their own vast and seemingly impenetrable cliques en masse. It did not appear that there was hostility or racism and it was not as though all the groups combined refused to go to work together or allow their children to go to school together. It just became an oddity to Hershal that some natural occurrences happened no matter how new and different the environment. Some things never changed and some differences between people, whatever they were, never went away.

Hershal waited for a ferry to dock and paid the fare to travel to the militarized district, or what everyone had come to accept as the political district. He wanted more time to venture through the forests and farmlands that filled the immediate circumference that surrounded the six cities. It would have been nice to see nature in the autumn as it began its journey into hibernation for he had only ever seen the tropical side to the wild back on the rhomboid. Hershal watched the clear night sky and the water as he leaned over the railing at the aft of the ferry. His eyesight took in the stars, the distant galaxies and nebulae and then watched the starkness of white foam escape into the distance as the ferry's jets disturbed the water. The air was thin and crisp and the wind took away any warmth left over from the day. Hershal enjoyed the new sensation of cold and pulled his thick coat tighter even though he was warm enough.

The ferry docked and Hershal made his way across the wooden harbour and towards a car parked beyond a set of buildings near the lake's edge. A man in Prospect military uniform was waiting next to the rear door of the vehicle and nodded as he opened it for Hershal. The car journey was less interesting than any other part of the evening as it drove through the grounds of a campus and through various other military compounds. The car stopped near to a wire mesh fence that was very high with barbed wire coiled across its top. Hershal made his way to a security booth and signed in via a palm scan device handed to him through the booth's window. The guard inside seemed tired and indifferent as security officers sometimes did. A large set of gates opened and Hershal entered on foot on to a large area covered in grass. The whole area was lit up via a massive digital lens roof whereby the air was warm with a cold breeze sapping the temperature from time to time. Hershal stopped to look out and over the proofing grounds, a large rectangular-shaped field of various assault courses and mock towns used in urban combat testing. The whole area covered ten square miles; the brain child of a nation that wanted to put its armed forces through its paces. Hershal could hear the sound of various types of gunfire coming from one of several skyscrapers in the distance and noticed three solders abseiling from a building that was over a thousand feet in height. He saw a party of people already gathered outside the training ground's entrance gate, recognising a few people from previous visits over the years. Admiral Langmead and General Feng were chatting away and next to them was a young man that Hershal remembered, who should not be so young at all.

'Good evening, Hershal,' Admiral Langmead said, offering her hand.

Hershal accepted the offer and saw that Feng was less enthused to see him.

'Glynn Langmead,' said the young man.

'Hershal,' he offered and shook the man's hand. Hershal scanned Glynn and considered it very strange that the man was officially called Sharplin but had given him another name, his mother's name in fact. *People were so peculiar and petty!*

'How was your journey?' Admiral Langmead asked. She had her hands planted deeply in the pockets of her coat and appeared to be cold.

'Fine.'

'The Version are down on the field now. We just have to wait for a thinking unit to become available,' Glynn said.

'Thinking unit?' Hershal said, contemplating the pilot Version's designated name.

'I hope that if and when required, you won't have to wait for a pilot to become available; emergencies are very scarcely planned in advance.'

'We need to get to the point where they can think for themselves, or so that they have enough of a subconscious to navigate and have their own instincts,' Feng said, defensively.

'And why would you want to achieve that?' Hershal asked. 'I'm sure such an achievement will make these things better bartenders or gardeners.'

Feng, Langmead and Glynn looked at each other in a mixture of embarrassment and discomfort.

'Obviously none of us makes policy when it comes to the allocation of the machines,' Admiral Langmead replied.

'I have to admit to you all that none of this interests me,' Hershal said in a frank tone of voice. 'I know little about artificial intelligence, although I do know that the Spectra helped make the Version pilots in order to, how shall we say, dream their way into other dimensional spaces; a conventional computer that humanity would create cannot achieve an energy cascade. So I ask myself now, having given these new drones little to no thought whatsoever, what is the point?'

Silence engulfed the proceedings as soldiers moved around them in their various duties. One of the soldiers said something quietly to Feng and Langmead. He was dismissed and walked away, glancing at Hershal as though intimidated.

'I'm not sure what you mean,' Glynn said.

Feng folded his arms and seemed agitated. 'I'm sure that being what you are, many things escape your understanding.'

Hershal looked at Feng as though a machine himself, with no facial expression. 'It was said that the military would work on ships of varying types. It was stated that, due to the main danger coming from above, it warranted huge investments in planetary shielding and an armada that had a better chance against the enemy,' Hershal stated.

'What enemy? There's been no sign of anything, ever,' Feng scoffed.

'We have three hundred ships dedicated to the Version with new hull specifications . . .' Glynn intervened.

'And yet when your people attacked Earth to find independence you had over eight hundred vessels,' Hershal interrupted. 'It was planned that three more planets would be colonised, that several more cities would be created on this world alone.'

'I hardly think this is the time or place, and we are hardly the ones to discuss this with,' Admiral Langmead said.

'I see. Well, let us watch this spectacle of drones and see if they are worth the fuss,' Hershal said.

'I'm afraid the demonstration has been cancelled,' Langmead stated. 'There are no pilots available.'

'Well then.' Hershal smiled. 'I think you have demonstrated quite enough, don't you?'

'My apologies,' Langmead said. 'We can still give you a tour of the new ships. They are quite something.'

'How many ships have you dedicated to the drones?' Hershal asked.

'Fifty,' Feng answered.

'Good. I'll be leaving now. I see no reason to look at more ships, and to be honest I have better things to do.' Hershal nodded and began to walk back the way he had entered.

Startled, Admiral Langmead looked at her son Glynn, and then Feng.

'I apologise once again,' Admiral Langmead offered.

'Never mind. I just hope that if anything does happen those pilots are not too busy. I know how important their duties are as bell-boys and chauffeurs, fruit-pickers and doormen,' Hershal said with a hint of sarcasm.

Feng and Langmead began to talk and things became heated. Glynn chased after Hershal and found himself having to half-run at an awkward pace as Hershal sped on.

'It would be good if you took a look at the ships,' Glynn said.

Hershal continued walking until outside of the lens and exposed to the full cold of the night sky. He stopped and turned to Sharplin, who in turn became hopeful that he might return to look at what they had achieved with the Version ships. 'Why aren't you older?'

'Excuse me?' Glynn asked.

'You were born sixty years ago and yet you appear to be no older than your mid-thirties, you certainly don't look like a sixty-year-old on span treatments . . . so what then?'

Glynn thought about this and decided not to answer the question. Hershal stood there watching his own breath dissipate with some fascination.

'None of us make policy here, I'm sorry,' Glyn offered. 'Those ships are the main achievement of this whole project, won't you come and see what we made for the Version?'

'This was just a visit out of pure courtesy, and all I can say is that it doesn't matter.'

'I don't understand,' Glynn said.

Hershal continued to walk through wide streets among the very measured and precise buildings on either side that were all exactly the same: tall, white stone blocks that were all about efficiency rather than style. 'My opinion does not matter, just as Judith's opinion does not matter.'

'It matters to me,' Glynn said.

'You never knew Earth, you never lived through the cost of this world. You don't know your own kind there or have a sense of all the hard lessons that world had to endure. You think I'm a part of this, or that the Spectra has some hand in protecting this world. That somehow Prospect is their favourite and that I'm part of some form of plan to help protect you?'

'No one knows what you are for. No one trusts what you or the creature are for,' Glynn said.

Hershal considered the use of the word 'creature' when referring to the Spectra. 'The organism, the Rhomboid, has been roaming the outskirts of the Milky Way for the past fifty years. It began a specific change of course and turned back just three months ago. It concerns me, and all I wish is that the hostile species that we encountered would also be of concern to those who are in charge of this world.'

'Are you saying we should be afraid of the Spectra?' Glynn asked.

'Good luck,' Hershal said, walking on.

'You're wrong about Earth. Some of us try to understand.'

Hershal stopped yet again and turned to face Sharplin.

'In answer to your question, I am young. I was in stasis for the first thirty years of my life because of my grandmother.'

'Who?' Hershal asked, with interest.

'Rita Siren.'

'She wasn't your grandmother!'

'My granddad's wife, then. When I was five she had to look after me one afternoon. It's a long story but I was always too smart . . . I ended up sneaking into her laboratory at her house and became exposed to one of her, how can I put it, developments. It was a modified flesh-eating virus and she could not synthesise a cure. By the time they put me under I needed a synthetic liver, kidneys and heart and they couldn't clone new ones until I was cured. The chances were that I would die during any transplant anyway.'

'Why didn't she use Judith?' Hershal asked.

'My grandfather and mother . . . it's complicated . . . it's the reason my parents got divorced, it's the reason for a lot of things.'

'I see,' Hershal said. 'I'm beginning to realise that things are not complicated at all, the exact opposite in fact.'

'It's the legacy I'm a part of. It was my grandmother's curse, her obsession, just as these Version machines are mine. I want you to know I'm trying to do the right thing.'

'Yes,' Hershal said, 'aren't we all?'

*

Judith walked into the lobby of the high-rise apartment block. She had seen the police cars out front and was now doing a head count of armoured police present in the vicinity. It was evident by the way they watched Judith that they were more than likely here for her. The building assistant at reception seemed nervous at the intrusion. There were armed police in the lobby and more of them stood to her left in the bar and restaurant. Judith stopped walking as she saw the two Version drones standing directly outside the lifts. They were indeed formidable creatures, especially when seen in such a domestic setting. The things towered above everyone as though hideous demons sent from hell, with their heads being only two inches from the ceiling. Judith broke off from staring, and recognised that a Captain Zhokov was approaching her. 'Captain.'

'Judith Gibson, I am arresting you . . .'

'No you're not!' Judith exclaimed and walked past him, heading straight for the lift where the Version remained. The police raised their rifles, which Judith found odd considering that they must know who she was and of what she might be capable.

'Fine!' Zhokov shouted, and nodded to the armoured police to move in.

As one of the police tried to manhandle Judith she smacked him in the face through pure reflex. 'Oh I'm sorry,' she said, holding her hands up as the man held his mouth and nose.

Zhokov nodded to his men to back away. The staff on reception had by now moved into a back office behind the front desk and the policemen cleared the area. 'You wanted this the hard way,' Zhokov said and walked out the front door and into the street. At this the two Version units that had been stationed at the lift leapt at Judith, grabbing her by the neck and legs. They dragged her from the lobby, out on to the street and threw her into the back of a truck. Zhokov and a few other men moved in quickly as the Version held her down.

A worried look then fell across his face as he realised that Judith was not moving. A crowd had gathered to watch the show, and a news camera crew team that had turned up for the protests had found something of more interest. The Version towered above everyone as hulking creatures scanning the gathering masses. One of the machines released its grip from Judith's legs and distanced itself from the other Version in order to keep a more tactical position.

'Shit, shit!' Zhokov shouted after checking Judith over. 'You killed her, you idiotic machines. Brent, we need to back off now.'

Detective Brent looked over at Judith, who was lying quite still in the back of the police truck, and could see that her head had been twisted backwards and her neck had been completely broken.

'We need the A box now!' Zhokov shouted into the air. He was relaying an order through his server chip to a truck hidden down the street, yet some thoughts could not help being voiced.

The Version held on tightly and Brent saw movement as Judith's head began to twist. 'Get the box up here now!' Brent shouted. 'It's happening.'

The clumsy operation had by now been observed by hundreds gathered on either side of the street. An explosion of movement jerked the truck and threw the Version backwards. A blur of movement and the crowd gasped as something was attached to the machine's upper body. Back and forth the Version moved, trying to prise the thing off itself. The second Version unit leapt in and began trying to grapple the creature that had begun to crush the other one's head.

'Move, move, move . . . move!' Zhokov screamed as the other truck pulled up. The police opened the back of the truck and removed a thick canvas sheet from on top of a large, empty box. It was of a thick metal which seemed very heavy as it was lowered and crunched into the metal lace tar of the street surface. The box was opened as Zhokov continued to scream his thoughts at the Version that were struggling to respond to his demands. Eight more Version had by now climbed down from the surrounding buildings and another six left their varying positions as security guards to banks, museums and art galleries. A severed head belonging to one of the machines flew across the street and in turn was stolen by a member of the crowd. As its body hit the floor it appeared that the other machine that had attacked Judith crumpled at its extremities as though by an invisible force. Its legs snapped and its arms twisted and broke so that it, too, fell into a contorted heap of mess.

Judith was now standing still and calm and was surrounded by the fourteen machines. 'What's it to be, Zhokov? You know how this works, you know how this will escalate beyond anything you could possibly imagine.' She walked towards him and he froze, realising that there could be thousands of Version there and even with his unit now pointing their rifles directly at her, she would eventually win and possibly kill him.

'This is not over,' Zhokov said.

Judith moved close to his face and could see that he was shaking with fear. 'You don't know what the hell you're talking about.'

Judith then turned to the crowd as though a gladiatrix that had won a match. 'Anyone fancy a drink? All drinks are on me.'

The street erupted in cheers that shook the building's digital lenses. Zhokov ran to one of the trucks and got in. The truck lumbered slowly through the crowds that were now pelting and rocking the vehicle. 'This is Zhokov to General Feng. You were wrong, sir, they were useless against her . . . I mean it.'

MEMORY LANE

No one had been killed so far, which was a bonus. The stolen helicopter shuddered as it gave up under the final missile attack; the ground was better for him anyway. One military installation destroyed and plenty wounded, although the relief of not killing for a change felt good. Ologun was not sure of anything at this point and knew nothing of the place where he had returned. He felt the guilt of vandalism regarding the military base. He appreciated the good old-fashioned fact that being so utterly destructive was unjustifiable; he had got carried away in the moment.

As the aircraft hit the jungle canopy he was thrown through the cockpit window and flew through branches and foliage with force. Two hundred feet later his body twisted and broke as he hit the floor. Tranquillity followed as he lay there wondering which way was north. Ologun stood up and made his way underneath where he thought the helicopter might be stuck in the trees. Using the ability to manipulate atoms in that vague, unskilled fashion, Ologun shook the trees this way and that. He could hear the aircraft fall a bit at a time until finally the branches released their grip only for the thing to fall directly on top of him. *Clever boy!*

Ologun pushed the wreckage off himself and searched the remains of the cockpit. He used a small knife retrieved earlier in the day's events and dug out a navigation device from within the control board. He looked it over in its dead state and then inserted a strand of second skin. The machine was powered up and a marker was set for Laghouat. If Ologun was to find his bearings he would need to start where the third part of his life began. He looked around and took a deep breath. There was a lot of jungle between where he was and where he wanted to be; the border into Niger was his next objective and would hopefully be reached without incident.

*

'Colonel Young, sir, you need to be briefed.'

Young sat up in his bunk. His head hurt and his eyes burned with only three hours of sleep. Young took a teeth-cleansing capsule and glanced in the mirror. As he dressed, the thought of retirement in the next few years crossed his mind. At thirty two years old he had been lucky so far in that The Virus, the universal virus that the world suffered from, had yet to take its full toll on him, although when it did there would not be much time before he was incapacitated. The thought was depressing him and knowing there might be only two to three years of life left was a burden he refused to face.

The bunker was still a hive of activity with officers working at their consoles. There were only six weeks to go until Operation Rashad commenced. One of the officers informed the colonel of the meeting within the dead room. Once there he acknowledged Admiral Jones and Admiral Wass, then sat down among other members of the presidential cabinet. Vice President Eric Blane was sitting, typing busily on a built-in console screen on the conference table. Young said nothing for several minutes and decided to pour himself a cup of coffee from the facilities provided at the end of the room. As he poured the cream the dead room door opened and he immediately recognised the voice of the General of the Army, General Annette Dean.

'At ease, please be seated,' Dean offered.

As the conference began, Young could see Vice President Blane seemed particularly stressed. Whatever the briefing here was about, it did not look to be positive news.

'Three hours ago the German government launched a mission into enemy territory in order to rescue soldiers registered as M.I.A.,' Dean began. She sat down next to Blane at the head of the table. 'Three American Delta Force operatives and two Spezialkrafte soldiers were lifted from the jungles of South Niger at 06:00 hours this morning. I don't need to stress the dire implications for the forthcoming operation. However, the intelligence we have gathered has been . . .' General Dean stopped talking for a moment as though considering what information to impart. 'The rescued operatives were captured six weeks ago and held at one of three military installations located twenty six miles north of the city of Sokoto. Fifty two hours ago we monitored this satellite feed.'

At the centre of the conference table and running the full length, a screen rose up, and an iris-locating, two-way holographic emitter projected imagery taken by a high orbiting satellite.

'This is the military base from which the captives escaped. According to statements taken, a man calling himself Logun helped the operatives escape. This individual was described as Caucasian, particularly short at around six feet in height and wearing what was described as an ocean wetsuit of a strange material.' The holographic projection, a top-down view of the base, seemed to show nothing of concern until a large explosion was followed by a mass of gunfire. The holograph file was paused.

General Dean continued, 'This happened within moments of the captives escaping through the southern security fence to the compound. This is the best image we can retrieve of the man we believe to be the individual described.' The holograph image zoomed in and on a man who, as described, seemed petite in stature. 'This footage was reduced a hundred times in speed in order for us to track this individual,' Dean added.

'I don't understand what you mean,' Admiral Wass said.

'Without slowing this recorded information down we simply could not track his movements.'

'You mean he's that fast? What are you saying here exactly?'

'What we have here, people,' Blane voiced, 'is a catastrophe of epic proportions. Young, you were resting at the time, but a vote was held in congress this morning regarding the viability of Operation Rashad. The operation has been approved to be brought forward a whole month. This incident has put Nigeria, Niger, Kenya . . . let's face it, all of the African states on high alert. Our job just became almost impossible. Now General Dean, please continue.'

The general sifted through notes on the console embedded in the conference table surface. 'Admiral Wass, you need to report to the fleet immediately. A stratospheric flight to Miami is waiting for you. Admiral Jones, you are to remain here as scheduled and greet President Kawle when she returns at fifteen hundred hours. That is all, you are both dismissed.' The two men left the room promptly as Young prepared himself for whatever came next.

'Colonel Young,' Dean continued, 'you are to be reassigned to New York base Charlie Six. The civilian contractor Natasha Forbes is en route and will meet with you there. You are to set up a task force in order to locate this individual and if possible, work out what the hell his or its intentions are.'

'It?' Young asked.

'Colonel Young, I have taken the liberty of speaking with Ms Forbes and in her opinion we are dealing with something unprecedented here. I have uploaded all of the information regarding her theories on to your secure domain. Colonel, this man destroyed a class three military base in under an hour. Also, there are reports that there were no fatalities whatsoever, which we find to be of interest to us, so consider this to be an assignment of the utmost importance. That is all, dismissed.'

'Excuse me if I seem out of touch here but Nigeria is harbouring terrorists,' Colonel Young said, 'and this individual rescued our people, and then attacked a Nigerian military base, so wouldn't that put him, or it, on our side?'

'We know little at this point and we do not like to assume anything,' Blane replied.

Colonel Young nodded, stood up then made his way to exit the room.

'Oh, and Colonel,' Dean said, 'next time I expect you to be on the ball. You can sleep when you're dead.'

*

'I want you to travel on the *Full Result*,' Hershal said.

Hina gazed at Prospect and her red moon in thought. 'Are you sure Judith is up to the task?'

Hershal stopped contemplating and looked at Hina curiously. 'Why, what do you mean?'

'I mean she isn't that proactive, and being reactive in light of things is risky.'

'I still have no idea what you mean,' Hershal replied and started typing something into one of the console units.

'Oh come on, Hershal, ten thousand machines made for one purpose. They should be tried, tested and then left in storage. It's as though every cliché to do with AI is on our doorstep. One minute you're hanging your washing on the line and then suddenly the hordes of Jericho come crashing down and you wonder why you washed your dirty knickers in the first place.'

Hershal stopped typing and raised his head to look at Prospect once again on the main screen. It was a colossal-sized planet with vast oceans and varying terrain and landscapes. He saw the six cities of the Integer project; the Prospect Empire had been built and designed as it had been in the basin with a large lake at the centre and all the cities surrounding this liquid epicentre. For all its efficiency of design and all the hopes of its founders, the city from this distance looked akin to a large target. Things had changed over the years and Hershal worried about the fact that Hina had thought the very same thing.

'You know there are limitations to our role. I told Judith to react accordingly, yet I am aware that any proactive action may lead to what you might call a self-fulfilling prophecy.'

'Damned if you do and damned if you don't,' Hina said and cackled to himself.

The bridge to the flagship *Ryu Yo* was quite dated now that thirty years had passed, although the ultra-manoeuvre class of ship was one of only six to be coated by Spectra shell. The weapons of such a ship were also unconventional compared to the rest of the Prospect fleet. There were no stampede turrets, no missile silos and no rail cannons. Much of the old ship had been gutted and now held vast quantities of active Spectra blood. This in itself was a loose term used to describe the incredibly viscous gas of energy that in turn would normally house the mass of unified consciousness, the micro-organisms that had been named Spectra. The importance of these new ships was that if the alien race that attacked the basin ever came back, these ships would hopefully match their fire-power.

Hina nodded and made his way to the transfer. Hershal began monitoring the rest of the Prospect fleet of sixty ships of varying types. He was tired. Deflated, as though the levels of work undertaken over the past eighty years had left him an empty vessel. The Spectra had done much of the work even though it did not understand engineering on such an archaic level. Try telling an ocean of high-functioning consciousness that people needed to access and egress the ships. Try telling it that the ships needed to move around in this reality, the vacuum of space in this dimension and not just be able to access portals as the Rhomboid did. The Spectra secreted and applied the transparent gel that solidified into a dull black shell of that godlike 'other' toughness; the entity had literally defecated all over the chosen six Prospect ships. An adequate allowance for thrusters was made, yet remained the main point of weakness throughout the ships' impregnable shell.

Hershal closed down the feed to the remote drone orbiting the ship and waited for the crew to board. A small crew was all that was required for each ship. Three hundred and sixty naval personnel divided over six warships. Three bombardment class and three ultras were now a short time away from launch status; their objective, Earth.

*

Captain Perry entered the bridge followed by five other officers. They took their posts within the rectangular room, hooking neural threads into consoles.

'Emissary Hershal.' Perry nodded.

'Captain,' Hershal greeted the man.

'You moved Emissary Hina to the *Result*?'

'Please dispense with calling me Emissary, Captain, I assure you I am far from requiring an absurd rank. Hina is quite capable of taking command of the *Result*.'

Perry seemed uncomfortable at this for reasons Hershal could not gauge.

Commands were given for a position access. Hershal remained silent and very still as each ship created an energy cascade portal into the aether that buffered between this universe and another. This was the place of echoes and the indescribable, where all sensory feeds to the outside of the ship were best cut off or else madness would grip anyone exposed. The Version pilot on board was put to work and began its constant process of working out the reality of obscene variables. It could be six weeks or several months before Earth was reached, but this was to consider the contrived nature of time as perceived by humankind. Here in the place between realities, time as it had been rationalised had been made a mockery.

*

The world was an empty place it seemed. There was the fact that nature had taken over in all its glory and yet without the constant occupancy of human interference, it all seemed to be derelict. City after city, villages and towns that were once heaving seemed to be abandoned and left to decay. The several-day journey via a bullet train starting at the city of Lagos had finally ended at Nouakchott. The journey west had been against all original plans, if indeed there had been one in the first place. The journey had also been a lot quicker and a lot more peaceful than anticipated. The world above tree tops had whizzed by as distant sky-scrapers and city-scape stood as half-abandoned relics to a time when the world was overcrowded and bursting with activity.

Heading north had been a bit of an issue from the start. There seemed to be activity in Niger, Libya and Algeria of the magnitude that was best avoided; something big was happening. A more indirect route had been required and it turned out that heading west was a sound solution. Once over the border of Benin, the reality became more of a standard affair. People here and there were aware of the colour of his skin, treating him as a hobo, and yet they minded their own business. The train journey was long and enchanting. The super-speed mag rail had woven through dam structures and man-made mountains and their tunnels, and across the tops of jungles, through more old cities and across expansive lakes. No one wanted to sit next to the smelly man with matted hair and beard and so it was peace and quiet all the way. Many hours were whiled away learning how to hack this system and that; the ticket for the train journey was just the beginning for everything that was to be had and falsified in the whole of cyberspace. There were many programmes to be uploaded, although most were pointless. Most that were tried had distorted reality and made the brain think and see peculiar things. That was the rage nowadays. Making the colours of the world alter, making the detail and texture of the world change: day for night, winter for summer; childish gimmicks that were deleted from the second skin after only ten minutes of play.

A man with black, almost purple, skin and blond dreadlocks would be the first person he had talked to in many days. He was sitting on a wooden pier on an old deck chair drinking alcohol from a large bottle.

'I need to hire your boat if possible, please.'

The man took his time and winced at seeing a small, grubby white man standing next to him.

'Jason, is it?'

The man nodded and glanced at the small sign where he sat: JASON BOUNTY BOAT RIDES.

'So,' Jason said, 'where ya wanna go?'

'My name is Ologun . . .'

'Not what I ask you.'

Ologun sighed deeply as there never seemed to be the patience to have these conversations.

'I'm going to Morocco.'

Jason laughed his way through the next several seconds and then wiped the smile from his face as though it had all been fake. 'You need speed for that kind of trip!'

'You have a six-thousand break horsepower triple injection minx drive with a reinforced power chasse made by Provost,' Ologun reeled off, courtesy of the information highway zooming through his head. Jason seemed unimpressed, which made sense due to the fact that everyone could access any information they wanted on demand and have it on hand to see within moments of it being required; learning anything had become pointless.

'She can go all right, but ya see, due to a card game I no longer hold the necessary balancing conduit for the engine to exceed fifty knots.'

'Right,' Ologun said and sat down with his legs hanging over the pier edge. He stood back up on seeing the water below. 'How much do you need for a new one?'

'It take two day to have a delivery round here, eternity ya know.'

Ologun knew about eternity and had a better understanding of it than this man. Ologun had grown up around hybrid accents all his life and was puzzled by the half-Gambian, half-whatever-it-was accent. He took a voice sample using his second skin which then came back with the answer of Jamaican. Ologun shook his head at the pointless curiosity that had led to this last use of the information highway; he was becoming addicted.

A car pulled up at the seafront which seemed to make Jason flinch then stand up in a hurry. 'What ya gonna do for me?' he said.

Five men of well-built stature exited the vehicle and began to make their way down the pier towards them. They appeared to be relatively well-dressed, although the heat of the day had driven them to discard their jackets to reveal sweat-soaked shirts with recently removed ties.

'Do for you?' Ologun replied. 'Let's skip eight sentences here. You owe them money, they took a piece of your boat, I need to go somewhere, so I'll pay them what you owe them seeing as you're a crap card player. Agreed?'

Ologun walked straight towards the men as Jason looked on, seemingly nervous and bemused. The men spread out across the pier as though they knew what to expect; they had no idea. Ologun sped up drastically and smashed one man around the head so hard that he flew into the man next to him, knocking them both unconscious. He then rendered another two unconscious while they tried to reach their weapons. Ologun carried on without a pause in his deliberate set of movements and grabbed hold of the man he assumed was in charge. He smacked the man hard across the back of the knee while grabbing the man's neck tightly.

'How much does he owe you?' Ologun demanded to know. The man was choking and could not speak and Ologun released his grip slightly. 'How much?'

'Three!' the man screeched.

'Three what?' Ologun asked Jason, who by now had begun to pace the pier with anxiety. 'Ya gonna get me killed, white man, killed!'

'Jason, Jason look at me,' Ologun pleaded.

'He's a dead man, you're a dead man, English fool.'

'I'm not British,' Ologun replied and smacked the thug across the top of the skull.

'Three million,' Jason said.

'What currency?' Ologun blasted in frustration. He decided to work it out for himself and accessed the appropriate information via the Net. Ologun then inserted a strand of second skin into the man's server port behind the left ear and hacked his personal account. Ologun transferred the money which was automatically exchanged into dirham through the man's account settings. He then dragged the man to his feet and pulled him close, causing him to cough as he caught a whiff of something putrid.

'You stink,' the man observed.

'What's your name?' Ologun asked him.

'Dubai,' the man replied, rapidly going into shock.

'I need the component for that boat.'

'The car, the trunk of the car.'

Ologun had already placed strands of second skin into each of his victims and checked their vitals; they would be fine apart from something else that had been bothering him. Ologun gestured for Dubai to walk towards the car as he followed. All he could think about was the fact that he disliked piers. Nothing good had ever happened to him on a pier.

Dubai retrieved a small cylindrical object from his car and handed it over. Ologun in return took Dubai's pistol and threw it into the sea. Ologun apparently vanished before Dubai's eyes until he realised he was now handing the piece of engine over to Jason. Dubai looked over at his unconscious colleagues and then at the man who had done all this with little effort. Dubai rushed to the driver's seat of the vehicle, started the engine and drove away as fast as he could.

PERSEVERANCE

Midway between Edison and South Plainfield, west of New York City, somewhere hidden beneath the ruse of an old school building, a new assignment had begun.

Another lift to another war bunker, except this one was sparse and derelict, dusty and archaic. Technicians were at work upgrading the neural lace ports that had been outmoded many years previously as other labour mopped and cleaned to make the place more presentable.

'Colonel.' A female soldier saluted.

Young saluted back. 'Is the control centre operational?'

'It's partially online, but we have managed to complete a dead room within one of the old conference rooms.'

'Good work, Corporal; that will be all, thank you.'

The colonel arrived at the operations room and surveyed the area. The chemical lighting seemed a little dim and old, casting shadows across the main desk at the rooms centre. Old-fashioned consoles filled the room's exterior walls, which had a dull plasma-concrete finish. The digital displays that worked were tired and had finger-mark indentations from overuse; this just would not do. 'Excuse me,' Young said to one of the workers, 'when will we have hologram emitters?'

'Give it a few hours, we're expecting a delivery. The power here is good old-fashioned eight phase mark three. It's about the only thing here that is good news and ironically, once the sockets have been gutted and replaced, we have a better compatibility than most other places.'

'Good,' Young answered even though he had switched off at the word 'power'. He went over to one of the old internal communication pads that seemed operational. 'This is Colonel Young, any news on Natasha Forbes and the rest of the team yet?'

A garbled mess of noise came back over the receiver. Young then became more optimistic as he watched a remote HT station being wheeled into the room. He waited for the delivery men to leave, walked over to the small table and activated an encrypted file on his server domain. The holograph projectors on the table's surface fired up and he watched as particles of dust danced within the light.

The colonel loaded all the files compiled for the mission thus far and set the holographic emitter so that only his eyes could receive the information emitted. Two files were loaded and Young began watching the footage of the craft that had entered Earth's solar system, or rather what could be seen of it that had been captured. He then moved on to the incident at the military base. In his left eye he typed notes as he thought them and saved these thoughts at intervals. From his right eye Young watched the holo-file in mesmerised fashion. Even in slow motion the events seemed difficult to fathom, and what seemed to be even stranger was that within the first few minutes of the main event, this person referred to as Logan had purposefully destroyed three trucks as they headed south towards the escaping American and German soldiers, the strangest part being that the trucks had hit thin air and their engine units crumpled up on said impact. The man, this Logan, had looked at the trucks as they smashed into nothing as though he had expected or instructed this action to happen.

Colonel Young rewound and watched the satellite recording over and over, and specifically from the point just before the trucks crashed one by one. He then paused the footage and looked over at the rest of the table and was satisfied that each place had a carbon block placed for each of the expected arrivals to have their own private briefing.

This whole affair was an incredible addition to something that was all very strange. Young mulled over what he knew about Operation Rashad. Over the past five years a terrorist group calling itself The Eyes of Truth had attacked locations across America and Europe. The group had recently struck at locations in Central Africa, which all seemed puzzling. They claimed that the weaponized and very complex virus sweeping the globe was not of Prospect design. What The Eyes of Truth claimed was that certain governments, a web of hegemony, had taken over old IMC military facilities around the world and released The Virus in order to wipe out the world's population to prepare for the Prospect Empire's return.

America and certain European countries, most notably Germany and Italy, had declared war on the group. The terrorists were, however, far from being the rag tag militia the media portrayed. They did not just plant explosives that had taken out power stations or key buildings within the affected countries. They had raided military installations and used tech that had sunk one US aircraft carrier and one European alliance airship; to describe such a thing as both stunning and impressive was an understatement. Either way it was all tragic, but none of it made sense to Colonel Young.

Now this terrorist group were in Central Africa and had threatened to destroy one of the countries from the inside out. Most agreed that Nigeria was most likely the target which is where things became very complicated. America and Europe had called for a resurrection of the United Nations. When Russia and China and the Middle-Eastern countries declined, the United States and the European alliance told the Nigerian government and made a statement to everyone that they were going into Nigeria in order to hunt for the EOT; thus Operation Rashad was conceived. The entire situation was precarious. The United Alliance of Africa was behind Nigeria in its response to this operation and had declared it an act of war if any American or European military entered any air space south of Algeria. The rest of the world meanwhile looked on in quiet disagreement but not much else.

Young sat back. Several things seemed to be happening. There were whispers that the terrorist group were so well-equipped that they would create a catastrophe in Africa and that the only country able to match their military technology was South Africa. Still none of it made any sense. Young was a patriot but was no fool. His country and Germany would not be doing anything unless they were after something and so far there seemed to be nothing of political or physical importance on the continent. There were either a number of lies or one colossal lie here which had yet to reveal itself.

'Evening, Colonel.'

Young turned to see Natasha had finally arrived. She pulled a large suitcase behind her in one hand and walked across the room to place a flat computer on the HT table that in turn blocked part of the holographic image as it remained on pause.

'I trust you checked my latest report?' Natasha asked.

'I read the file,' Young replied. 'I don't think I fully understand.'

Natasha left her suitcase upright and switched the computer on. 'Well, I'll explain it to you in more detail as we go, I'll put it into some context for you, Colonel. If I'm right in what I have discovered in the past thirty six hours, there might be serious trouble ahead.'

*

There came a point when certain places were or should be out of bounds. The music was not as good as it used to be, the men and women or so-called youth were always seen as the most lame generation, and, all in all, things had been better back in the day.

'Give me another, make it a double,' Judith ordered the barman. She was now on the precipice of being tipsy and would soon be far less cogent. The club was unspectacular and Judith had forgotten its name on entry. She sat on a stool and watched a transparent soundproof booth from an elevated position from the other side of a dance floor. She necked the double tequila she had ordered and realised something had been deposited in her mouth. She moved it with her tongue and retrieved it with her thumb and index finger. Judith saw that it was a grub and swallowed it before setting off away from the bar and across the dance floor.

She made her way through the crowds and as she walked received a message on her social domain. 'Hi there gilf, fancy a drink?'

Judith scanned the room and saw that a man was thrusting his hips and winking at her. 'I'm no one's girlfriend, chum,' she sent back.

'Grandmother, not girlfriend, babe,' the message came back. Judith carried on through the crowd even though she wanted to grab the man by the testicles and push his head through a speaker. She arrived at the small dome, looked inside, and found the person she was looking for. The door to the pod opened automatically and Judith sat down inside the transparent soundproof capsule. The music being played in the rest of the club was cut off with only the bass remaining as a low thump in the background.

The five occupants of the capsule sitting around a large round table seemed to be upset about the intrusion. 'This is a private capsule, now piss off,' one woman hissed cattily.

'There's an open tab at the bar, I suggest you use it unless you want me to rearrange that hideous thing you call a face,' Judith said, nodding to the capsule door.

One of the girls whispered something and the colour drained from the face of the woman that had been rude to Judith. Four of them left with haste as Judith grabbed the fifth by the arm and pulled her back into her seat. 'Not you, honey. I'm Judith, by the way,' Judith said, offering her hand.

'I know who you are, you're all over the news, right,' the woman said, declining Judith's hand.

'Oh, well that was just a slight misunderstanding.' Judith flashed a wicked smile and placed her hand on the table. 'I know you too, May, and I have to say you should be ashamed of yourself.'

'Really, I . . .'

'Attempted murder is still a fail. You should have cut off his nuts and shoved them down his throat.'

'That's great,' May said in agitation. 'I need to leave now if that's okay.'

'Listen, May. How's the new job?' Judith said, ignoring her protest.

'I clean toilets at the R&D block on military campus, you know the same job those little robot arms do,' May said, becoming angrier.

'Good,' Judith said, 'this is great.'

May stood up to leave.

'Wait,' Judith insisted.

'Why, are you going to kill me?' May said, with sarcasm.

'I'm here for a friend who has a crush on you. I said I'd put in a good word.'

'Well your friend chose well by picking you then, didn't they?'

Judith laughed, sat back and began to see something she liked in this girl. 'I should have waited until I'd calmed down, I'm sorry. All this fighting with machines and being wanted for . . . things.'

'You're crazy,' May said, in disbelief.

'Look, my friend is really shy and . . .'

The door to the capsule opened, causing May to flinch as the music blasted in. Judith turned to see that General Jarman had entered.

'Well, this is inappropriate. Here, pull up a seat, General, the drinks are on me tonight. What can I get you, a pint of wife-beater perhaps?' Judith said.

'May, I've come to take you home, I forgive you,' the general said, ignoring Judith.

'I'm not going anywhere with you, why can't you leave me alone? Please.'

'You are still my wife and you will obey me,' Jarman hissed, clenching his fists.

Judith watched the man who was classically tall, dark and handsome. The fact that he had nearly killed May on several occasions through years of terrible physical abuse was neither here nor there; Judith could see the initial appeal. She waved at the three soldiers he had brought with him. They were presently posted outside the capsule and Judith saw the disdain on their faces at the revellers jumping up and down to the music in drunk and disorderly fashion.

'Okay,' Judith said, standing up.

Jarman immediately pushed her back down on to the seat. 'You'll get what's coming to you after what you did tonight, so I suggest you sit down,' he seethed, revealing his true nature. 'Please, May, you belong to me, I love you,' he pleaded.

Judith's eyes flashed an electric lilac and she leapt up, grabbing the general's head, and smashed it through the table. 'I'm sorry,' Judith said. 'We haven't been properly introduced.'

Three soldiers entered the room with unholstered pistols. Judith grabbed the first by the throat and drove his head through the glass of the capsule roof. She then knocked the other two unconscious and returned her attention to Jarman. 'I'm sorry, I tend to act out a little at times, just like these.' She grabbed one of his arms and snapped it at the elbow. Jarman screamed loudly and the sound bounced around the mini-dome. 'You see I used to be infamous, or is that famous? I always get the two mixed up.' Judith snapped his other arm and the general went into shock. 'I think he might die, for a change,' Judith said to May, grinning wildly then pouting. 'So, his name is Glynn Sharplin, and he's in charge of the Version programme at R&D where you work.'

'What?' May said, staring at the general who was now muttering something in a mess on the floor.

'Look, he's a bit shy so you'll need to take control.'

'What?'

'Ask Glynn Sharplin on a date!'

'Oh, yes, absolutely,' May said and nodded in fascination at Judith.

'I have to go now, I think I might have to leave the planet.'

Judith vanished and May turned her eyes to her husband. She picked up a large thick drinking glass from off the floor and broke it over Jarman's head. She looked around the club and at a few people who were watching with some amusement from outside the booth. May stepped over the unconscious bodies and left the glass capsule, moving through the partying crowd until she found the nearest fire exit and left.

*

The great wall reached as far as the shoulders of the Statue of Liberty and it seemed like an infringement on freedom rather than a defence against hurricanes and tsunamis. It was perhaps one of the worst atrocities of the war; a war for independence that doubled up as a testing programme for many weapons of mass destruction. The Prospect ships had destroyed almost all of Earth's defences: ships and orbital guns and long range rail cannons that were to be fired from the planet's surface. The great ships of the Prospect fleet were slow and cumbersome and yet they were unstoppable and laid down such terrible fire power. New York had been hit just as hard as Washington or Moscow. The city had taken as many casualties and its infrastructure destroyed as thoroughly as London or Paris, Berlin or Hong Kong. The list went on and on and the superpowers were left in flames.

'Colonel Young,' a voice went off in his head. He used a thought to activate his neural implant.

'Go ahead.'
'The team has assembled.'
'Received.'

*

Autumn was turning into winter and the sea breeze cut through him. His body ached not from the cold but was an indicator that his last few years of life would be agony. Young stood by a memorial plaque and watched the seemingly never-ending list of the deceased as they scrolled by on a weathered console screen. It had taken one specially designed bomb to be dropped ten miles offshore to create a tsunami that had engulfed much of the East Coast. The sea had surged and invaded everything up to twenty miles inland and had wiped out tens of millions within less than an hour and yet that still had not been enough.

Colonel Young walked down a long flight of steps off the great stone wall and towards the nearest train station. He then began the journey back to the bunker, all the while wondering what to make of Forbes and her theory on this visitor now doing whatever it was on the other side of the world. He had bouts of feeling depressed and thoughts that there might be no point to any of it any more until Forbes had brought up something that served as a reminder of how bad things had become, yet there was now something else. She had shown him a strange imaging device that depicted that this Logan was somehow linked to many energy cascades and that when the machine was pushed for more, an in-depth analysis had shown that all over the entire world there were millions of microscopic cascades opening and closing every second. She had pushed for an answer and the Pentagon had refused to give her the information, and for a good reason. The virus that continued to ravage the world was no ordinary specimen and it was already declared by some experts as unstoppable and that eventually every human being on Earth would die. Such information was classified due to the simple need for morale. There were ways of facing this end of ages. Some became aggressive while others sank into apathy. Many refused to face up to reality while most turned to religion that for the best part, and until the Prospect Earth war, had almost disappeared.

Young had considered taking his gun and shooting himself in the head on quite a few occasions over the past few months and yet somehow these past few days' events had made him persevere with a newfound conviction. This operation, Rashad, was pure madness and had come from the fact that the entire world was on the brink of despair. Rashad was an actual declaration of war except that Congress did not like to declare war. But by carrying out this most dangerous and reckless of acts, there arose a feeling of irrational hope. Someone had taken the trouble to traverse the distance of the cosmos and was now up to something. One last curiosity, one last chance of some intervention. Colonel Young sat back, pulled his coat around him and took some medicine to ease the pain. He watched the city pass by as a half-renewed and half-abandoned landscape of skyscrapers, and the few remaining mountains of broken rubble looked like tombstones left unkempt for an eternity. He felt sorrow change to something else as the task at hand began to take shape. It felt as though an unrationalised crazy optimism was coming back to him.

*

Judith had spent some time in her apartment cleaning up the mess left behind by the police. Eventually she swept the room for surveillance, locked the door, and took a shower. Judith then dried herself and pulled a tampon from between her legs, took it into the living room and threw it into a micro-incinerator. She checked herself and was satisfied she did not need to apply a new one, then dried her hair. Whilst doing so, she kept an eye on the vault door situated in her bedroom. It was exposed from behind fake cupboard doors and had scorch marks on the lock where the police had tried to access it. The apartment was smashed up pretty badly yet Judith was not disturbed by any of this. She had lived in many places and found that she was hardly ever home, wherever that home might be.

Walking over to the vault, Judith threw the towel she had used to dry herself on the bed. She knelt down and pulled a thread from underneath a solid plate on the vault's anterior surface. She inserted the thread into a tiny incision on the lock and activated the security code.

Judith then waited as the door made a clunking noise. She grabbed the handle and pulled the door open. There was a pause and some thought as Judith looked over the items the police had been searching for. Three second skins were crumpled up inside the safe as though a knot of snakes had recently moulted. She touched the first one of a navy colour, then the second of a lilac tint. The skins moved and wrapped themselves up and over on to Judith's naked torso, then arms and legs. Last of all there was a black one which had some significance to her other than the simple choice of colour. It, too, wrapped over her and took its place as Judith walked from the bedroom and back into the living room. She turned off the lights, poured a large straight vodka and stood at the large window lens looking out over the vast city ahead.

After a while in deep thought Judith returned to the vault and reached into a sack that had the logo *IMC Cargo* etched into the fabric. One at a time Judith retrieved two crystal-blue transparent blades and held them out. They were almost a metre long with a sharp cut-off end at an angle of forty five degrees. Judith swung them around in loops in order to test their weight again.

Returning to the window she scanned the buildings nearby. On the roof tops she spotted a sniper then winked at him, waiting for a reaction. *They think they can take what they want and answer to no one,* Judith realised. She had not fought, died and come back in over forty years until the Version had attacked her; she suddenly had to shake the thought of something that had happened all those years ago and took a deep breath. Judith took the bottle of vodka and drank heavily, leaving only a quarter of the bottle. She leant against the window ledge and fought to stay in control of her feelings.

A day had passed since the affair regarding the Version and the police, and causing General Jarman and three soldiers some considerable harm.

Two messages received on her secure domain were a mixed bag of news. The first was an old message from Hershal that the Spectra Prospect hybrid ships were now underway and headed for Earth. Hershal seemed paranoid that something felt wrong and, as with the most basic of instincts, could not quite place what the issue with the

Prospect Empire Military could be; she hoped it had nothing to do with her.

The second was from Glynn who was excited at being asked on a date by May; he did not need to know how that one had been achieved. Something bothered Judith, however, for part of the message had stated that Feng was at the Version facility and had demanded to be uploaded into the Version mainframe.

Judith sat cross-legged in her apartment. The crystal blades were attached to her back and she was ready, but ready for what? The room was quite dark apart from the city lights through the window, casting a reflected glow off the apartment walls. Acute hearing revealed two men posted at the end of the corridor to her apartment.

Traffic outside began to die off and its noise was replaced by that of revellers on the way to bars and restaurants, but many more were still protesting further downtown. A police siren, an ambulance, laughter, chatter within that marksman's ear piece, an argument, a street mugging, domestic violence. Judith could not decide what to do. She had to rationalise what Glynn had said from the perspective of someone who did not know of anything fantastical and someone who had not been exposed to the absurd or unbelievable.

A man wanted to become part of the machine network known as Version. In doing so he would gain an advantageous perspective into the unique mind of machines that perceive reality beyond the confines of this universe. That simple message had seemed out of the blue to Judith and according to the message Sharplin thought that if it worked, it would be a great achievement and something to be celebrated.

A man's mind is injected into the machine mainframe, Judith kept thinking over and over. A lifetime of other things had eroded one part of her rationalising capabilities and amped up another. It was as though a nuance of personalities had taken over through sheer time and decay and now a certain madness crept in from time to time. The fight with the machines had excited her and it had carried on so that she attacked Jarman and those men almost as though she had become a passenger letting go to some other person.

Judith tried to focus and gain some perspective on something burrowing through her mind. What were the fundamental problems with machines? First of all Judith knew that in order to get a machine to navigate through the world it needed what they called a neural quad consciousness. Apparently a machine, no matter how sophisticated, had to be trained to see and acknowledge reality, albeit terrain, objects or any movement. Then this artificial stand-in for a subconscious could learn how to negotiate what every other living thing had evolved to do; computers can number crunch but even a cyborg, robot or similar had to walk and furthermore know where it was going; they had to be fluently perceptive and reactive. This was all fine, although a machine had no real depth, never had any instincts, and it could never be programmed to have that inner life of never-ending needs and wants that came with feelings, that in turn allowed it to be smart, to be . . . alive.

Judith took a deep breath in sudden dread and realised why certain laws had been passed on Earth regarding AI many years ago. Some called it paranoia or the simple-mindedness of not wanting to progress, and yet there was some information that should not be transferred from the animate to the inanimate. *Foolish*, Judith thought, as though this tale of caution with machines had not already been told to death. Then again it might be as when people dreaded nuclear weapons; yet to date, and even during the Prospect War, only two nuclear bombs had ever been dropped in anger which thankfully was a very long time ago. Maybe some paranoid thoughts remained just that. Judith stood up in order to leave her apartment. She wanted to see the results of this thing that troubled her and it needed to be checked.

Judith sought information relayed to her brain from her second skin. Her craft was on its way and would arrive in a matter of days, although she now considered that leaving Prospect might have to wait. Wearing large cleavers and a three-tone second skin may have given off a certain aggressive vibe, but then again the damage had been done and it was time to act the part of an immortal with exceptional abilities. The utter decay of her convictions and even her personality had not yet been completed and it was time to get something back.

As Judith approached the door she noticed that the sounds of two policemen at the end of the corridor had gone. She glanced through the window and found no sign of the sniper. Something else outside her apartment was present though, and was almost empty and inanimate; inanimate like a puppet, like a Version.

The door to the room exploded and a crimson-skinned machine launched itself at Judith. It slammed her to the floor and crushed her ribs almost flat as it did so. Caught off guard and badly injured, Judith struggled. The Version drone clasped her skull and then twisted ever so gently, snapping her neck. The machine rose quietly and remained still, keeping surveillance over Judith's corpse for several seconds. It then flinched a little too slowly as Judith, now seemingly possessed by witchcraft, flung the drone across the room. She quickly cut off its arms and legs then threw the drone on to the bed and rapidly cut off its head. Judith stood back and held her neck. *Twice in twenty four hours!* she thought, regarding how stupid this was. She quickly headed for the apartment door as another drone leapt through and threw Judith out of the apartment window. She fell, hitting various cables and other antenna as she plummeted the thousand-foot drop. Hitting the street, she bounced and was hit by an oncoming truck that failed to brake. Judith was dragged thirty yards under the vehicle's wheels and sustained an extensive list of fatal injuries.

The driver leapt out and ran across to her. He gasped at the mangled corpse and immediately called for an ambulance. A crowd gathered and began to witness the grotesque as Judith's shattered corpse began to twist and move. Arms, legs and torso animated of their own accord and rectified themselves back into what became more of a human shape. Judith shot up as though gravity had disappeared.

Two Version drones, then a third and fourth, bounded towards her. At this point gunfire erupted and several people were in turn hit and fell to the street. Judith lashed out, hacking at one of the drones, then more gunfire, and a huge torrent of bullets mowed down everyone in the street. Judith carried on. Things were getting out of hand so quickly that she had no time to think. She ran and she fought, yet the going was far tougher than expected. The Version were now targeting everyone, everywhere Judith went. Chaos and the roar of panic filled the streets. An explosion rocked the ground, causing digital lenses to pop from every window. Crowds were now running en masse in all directions as Judith climbed a lamp post to avoid the stampede. Version were everywhere and it was at this point Judith realised the magnitude of the situation. This was not about her, this was now turning into a mass slaughter.

Something else was happening now where Prospect military were dropping into position. The soldiers were evidently not under the same orders as the Version and began fighting the machines. Fighter jets screamed overhead as an airship began to lay down heavy fire against the Version drones.

A Prospect soldier was killed instantly by one of the drones a few hundred yards from Judith's position. She sprinted hard to his location then disassembled three Version units on arrival. She grabbed the soldier's earpiece and configured it to her server chip. 'This is Judith Gibson. I need an evac from Denver Street now.'

'Acknowledged message, please stand by.'

Judith fought while she waited and totalled two more drones.

'Judith, this is Admiral Steiner. We need you to exit the city limits to Eighth Park west for a jack to the Version control complex. I say again we cannot enter the city, please respond, over.'

'What the hell is going on? Over.'

'We are under attack from all quarters. Sections three through five of the city are now lost, we need to get to the head of the serpent, understood? Over.'

'Understood, will meet for jack to Version control, R&D in twenty, over.'

Judith continued to fight her way through the streets. Version were fast and agile creatures that were systematically butchering anyone they saw. Judith took a sharp turn down a side street having spotted one of the tank units towering among the buildings. There was no time now for a protracted engagement and it had been so terrible that, as she looked around, she realised that where she stood there were hardly any people left alive to protect.

The tank Version spotted Judith and was now lumbering after her in relentless pursuit. She slipped down a narrow alleyway heading east out of the city and, as the tank unit followed, it smashed into the buildings and became jammed halfway down a snicket at its narrowest part.

Judith checked the navigation marker on her neural implant and sprinted as fast as she could. The carnage was deafening as all around her among the streets the Prospect military fought in vain against the machines. Tanks and other vehicles were smashed and now useless. Buildings collapsed and sent clouds of thick dust so that the remaining soldiers were disorientated and lost. As Judith ran she saw the bodies: soldiers, civilians and mainly those who had come out on this cold night to protest about the machines that had stolen their jobs, who had now taken their lives. One of the Version caught her and she flipped against the glass of a shop window. Its fabric dented and stretched under impact, then flexed so that Judith flew back at the machine with force. She chopped its head in half with one of her blades then shoved it with a boot to the chest to free her weapon.

The Version were now swarming on her position and Judith realised she had to move. The Version were quick, but she was quicker and managed to find the extraction point. The copter jet hovered a hundred feet above the ground as three other aircraft lay down suppressive fire. A loud noise, heavy calibre gunfire, caused Judith to turn and she saw that RA603 heavy bomber planes were now firing missiles on the city.

Judith sprinted to the copter jet and began climbing a thick rope that led to the craft's main deck. She reached the craft and climbed on board. 'Go!' she shouted.

Sitting on the copter jet's rear deck and hanging out of the open hatchway, Judith could see the true state of affairs. The entire panoramic view of the six cities from this distance showed that everything was on fire. Red specks laced at speed across the night skies followed by endless sounds of explosions and varying weapons' fire.

There was a sniper sitting next to Judith who seemed inept as only two out of his ten shots hit their marks as they scampered around below. 'Give me that!' she said, snatching the weapon. The soldier looked around at the rest of the soldiers hunkered down in the copter jet's rear compartment.

'Judith Gibson?'

Judith swopped the magazine on the sniper rifle with explosive tip rounds. 'Yes?'

One of the soldiers offered her a headset. 'Flag General Holloway wants to talk with you.'

Judith fired ten rounds into the fray below as the craft sped by. The soldier next to her had taken to looking through binoculars and was impressed at seeing an eight out of ten hit rate. Judith watched the Version and saw the true horror of these machines as they moved as though one large pulsating muscle across the ground.

She placed the headset on. 'Holloway, this is Gibson, go ahead, over.'

'Judith, we are monitoring you from the *Rising* and are unable to achieve a viable means of retaliation. There are now thirty ships that have been commandeered by the machines orbiting above the colonised locations of the planet. We need to know if you can reach the weapons research complex and deactivate the Version via the pilot units, over.'

Judith flinched as another copter jet whizzed by and she saw it was being flown by the machines. She fired a few shots at the rear stabilizing wing and watched as the craft spun out of control. 'We are taking a long berth approach from the south-west and trying to assess options for breach of the complex. It is likely that I will need to touch down and go it alone. Holloway, sir, I think we've lost everything. You shouldn't have allowed Feng to upload into the Version, over.'

There was a silence as Judith watched the world as it burned. In the distance she could see that beyond the research centre and military complexes, many of the Version were headed for space ships that were preparing to launch. As though a line of ants on the forest floor had formed to move back to their nest, the Version were stampeding their way for a ticket off Prospect.

'We have no active file on any authorised human interface with the machines, over.'

'Holloway, you are the Field Marshal for Christ sakes, refer to Huzima, over.'

'Negative, the government is gone, we can only hope to save the population now occupying the frontier. Judith do you understand? Shut these things down now!'

*

A jarring ride at two hundred and twenty knots had impressed Ologun. Jason had been quite engaging as long as the conversation revolved around his boat; a thirty-five-foot-long water rocket that was able to glide on the water's surface by releasing a stream of bubbles from beneath the hull. It had been a long journey for Ologun and he had paid for it handsomely. The route had taken a few precarious and exciting courses up the west coast and around to Tangier. Ologun had then taken a further long journey via another private venture by paying some woman named Nova to fly him by helicopter until they touched down on a mountain top at Debdou. She was interesting to the extent that she worked for a charity organisation that dealt with the provision of any essentials during what she had described as catastrophes or atrocities. Ologun had continued on by hiking through the new age jungles until the expansive farmlands of Aher were reached. The land had not changed. He had never known it as a dry dustbowl leading into a vast desert, although he remembered that the jungle was newer back then and more uniform.

Ologun's ability to hack various networks was now becoming quite proficient, however, and what he found and kept learning about the world to date was disturbing. Local issues within Morocco were bad, events in Libya and Algeria were building up to be even worse. Where could he begin with the mess left behind after the Prospect war for independence? Ologun knew nothing of Prospect or how things on that world were and could only learn of the atrocities that now existed as the legacy of that one event. Still, whatever was to happen, Ologun needed a starting point in order to find some equilibrium in his mind.

An oak tree stood not far from the house. Some things change and others remained the same. The tree was remembered as being half the size and had been planted by someone who simply liked the European countryside. Nostalgia crept in at seeing that a childish gesture of love still remained etched within the bark on its trunk.

'Hold it right there.'

A woman with a powerful-looking shotgun interrupted his introspective meanderings. 'Mister, you need to get off my property now!'

'Ologun, my name is Ologun.'

'I don't care if you're Jesus Christ himself, get the hell out of my back yard.'

The house was of a classical, environmentally friendly design with a large, sloping roof filled with digital lenses. The sandstone brick was still new in appearance and sturdy, giving off the pastiche of a French farmhouse. The stables and a dark wood extension were new and had replaced the swimming pool and patio that once took up most of the back yard. The fields were the same and ten acres south of the house had also been kept clear of jungle.

'Hasn't changed much. I used to live here when I was a teenager.'

'Mister, I'm going to count to ten.'

'I had my first real kiss under this tree, of course there was a swing that could sit three, maybe four people hanging from a branch that's been cut away . . .'

'Grace, get over here, Grace, Grace!'

Another woman came from around the side of the house. She was white-skinned and appeared to be scrawny and fragile with a permanent look of confusion in her eyes.

'What's going on?' she screamed at seeing Ologun.

'The ocean's that way. I suggest you go look for a surfboard before I blow a hole in you,' threatened the first woman.

Ologun checked himself and his second skin. 'Oh, I see what you mean. It's a terrible shame. It's all so wrong here,' he continued and scanned the sky for a moment. 'Someone's coming,' he said and as the two women looked west along the road leading to their farm they saw a car followed by a truck heading their way.

'Jasmine,' Grace said with fear.

'Get in the house, Grace.'

Jasmine then turned to speak to Ologun but found that he had vanished.

The car pulled up to a large wooden cattle gate at the end of the driveway where four men exited the vehicle. The truck pulled up shortly after and six more men alighted, armed with various pistols and rifles. They all made their way to the gate except for two of the group, who remained posted at the perimeter.

'That's far enough,' Jasmine instructed them. 'This is private property.'

Two of the men wore suits and ties and the remainder were clad in combat fatigues of no particular uniform. 'Official business, madam,' one of the suited men replied and continued his approach down the driveway. The remainder of the men spread out and took up tactical positions.

'What do you want?' Jasmine demanded.

'My name is Mr Wassab'e.' This seemed an unlikely name as every one of these men was Arabic. 'We are here under state law to search your property for illegal immigrants. We believe you have a person of European descent staying with you,' Wassab'e stated. 'Please allow access to the property for proper processing of the white woman you have inside.'

'We have all the correct papers so please stop wasting my time and your own time.'

'What about me?' a voice came from behind Wassab'e.

Startled, the group of men including Mr Wassab'e turned, with weapons raised. Wassab'e holstered his weapon under his suit blazer and began walking steadily towards a particularly scruffy-looking man who had what Wassab'e could only comprehend as an infected tattoo covering his whole body, arms and legs.

'Please, sir, if you would care to take a ride back to the office.' Wassab'e gestured with his hand.

'Sir is stretching it a little, Mr Wassab'e, my name is Ologun Jowett. Pleasure to meet you,' Ologun said, offering his hand.

Wassab'e refused the invite and glanced at his second in command. 'Please come this way, Mr Jowett.'

'How old are you, Wassab'e? Twenty five? And you there,'

Ologun said to one of the men dressed in dark green combats and shirt and wielding a powerful looking rifle, 'Teenager I'm guessing right?'

'Corporal, escort this man to the truck,' Wassab'e instructed.

Ologun released ten strands of his second skin and directed the silky strands until each found their way to a member of the hostile force and punctured the skin on their necks. The men simultaneously jolted and froze, with faces that appeared to twitch and contort in discomfort. Without a word, these men walked like zombies toward their vehicles, got in and fired up the engines. The car and truck sped off down the road until they were beyond sight.

'What just happened?' Jasmine asked. 'Who are you?'

Ologun made his way towards Jasmine until he stood way too close for her comfort. 'I mean you no harm, please believe me. I do not wish to be rude but I need a wash and a shave and I might even attempt a haircut.'

Jasmine nodded and swung the shotgun over her shoulder. She tried not to grimace at Ologun who smelled even worse than he looked, as though he had just crawled out of a rotting swamp. 'There's an outside shower near the barn across from the house and I have clothes that belonged to my ex-husband when he was still alive. I'll see if Grace can salvage the mess on your head.'

'Thank you,' Ologun said with the utmost sincerity.

Jasmine watched Ologun walk down the side of the house to the barn and wondered what the hell she was doing helping this strange little beast. She had to admit that whoever this man was, he had just bought her family some precious time and that this visit from government officials had come much earlier than anticipated.

'Ologun!' Jasmine shouted after him. Ologun turned to face her. 'You try anything and I'll blow your head clean off, you hear me?'

Ologun nodded and continued towards the barn for a shower.

*

The copter jet hovered as Judith demanded a stampede rifle from one of the soldiers. She retrieved a satchel from one of the compartments and began filling it with magma tip rounds for the weapon. One of the soldiers grabbed the drop rope and had begun to lower it over the side when Judith touched his arm. 'Don't bother.' She then spoke to the pilot via the head set, 'Get to the south and towards the frontier five hundred miles south. We've lost, so go and seek refuge.'

Judith took off the headset and replaced it with a small comms device that fitted in the ear. She jumped off the side of the vehicle and fell the three hundred feet to the floor. She picked herself up and checked her equipment then ran towards the perimeter fence surrounding the R&D complex to the military compound. It was not good news, she felt, when there was no hostile action taken against her.

Judith took one of her cleavers, hacked the wire mesh fence open, and entered the compound. Stealing from building to building within the compound she found it completely empty and deserted. Eventually she arrived at the door to the vault where the Version were produced and housed, but there was still no sign of the machines. There were no dead bodies and there were no signs of combat; in fact everything remained eerily calm and intact.

She tried her access code and DNA imprint on the door but the door read: *Access Denied*. Judith then began hacking at the joints of the heavy slab when something in her peripheral vision distracted her. Looking up and behind her Judith saw three consecutive explosions in the night sky as though crimson flares had been set off.

She ran as fast as she could to the compound's perimeter and took in the sight and magnitude of the city as though a wall of fire had been created across the dark horizon. 'Holloway, this is Gibson, come in, over.' She waited for a moment and saw another flash in the sky above the planet. Her eyesight was extraordinary but a telescope she was not. 'Holloway, are you receiving? Over.'

'Judith we are under heavy fire and are unable to repel borders. We don't . . .'

Another flash in the sky was accompanied by digital echoes on the comms. A loud thrum deafened Judith. A blinding flash followed and then a blistering wave of heat that burned beyond agony. Judith suddenly had a strange thought. The memory of Hina wittering on about time and motion and some strange negative outlook came to her as though relevant. "You cannot be God and you will not save this world."

An immense blast of energy hit Judith. Her body tore apart as though paper in a hurricane. The last thing she saw was the burning city being washed away on a flood of white heat.

EMPTINESS

The information Ologun had gathered became overwhelming. This small pocket of the world had not changed in over two hundred years. His vision was acute in the darkness and seeing the farmlands stretch out for many miles in front of him brought with it once again that certain kind of nostalgia. That was why he had come here. He had fought and avoided the disorientation he'd felt for the past few months since that rescue and his return to another reality. His wish to make sense of who he was had been side-tracked by what he should be doing. A memory of his last objectives in this reality resurfaced and he realised that it had been lost in the heat of the moment. Aliens were the enemy and a lifetime spent in contemplation had to be put aside, for there were other things to understand; there were other things that needed to be done.

A part of himself had been an onlooker this whole time back on Earth and he felt that some logic had to be applied and objectives chosen. He ran his hand under his freshly shaved jaw then over his now short-cropped dark hair. *They have done it!* Ologun reasoned to himself. Whatever mess had been left behind, the IMC had built the rainforest running across the north of Morocco and it now ran east across Algeria, Libya and all the way to Egypt. Of course he had been here so long ago that looking on a satellite image of the area within his left eye only reminded him of all that he had missed. Part of him was glad and part of him felt sorrow. His eye zoomed in on the image so that he could see Algeria and Libya with a clear infra-red view, and Ologun decided to cut the feed. He told himself to stop hacking technology and give it a rest.

'You didn't eat anything, are you okay . . . Ologun?' Grace said. She sat down on a sofa that was next to the rocking chair he had lazed in for the past few hours. Grace lit a candle and placed it on a table next to her. 'It's nice to be out here on the porch. I like it when it rains at night and when it bounces off the roof.'

'Yes,' Ologun said, nodding. The moon was full in the sky with no clouds to pervert the light. It was nice to have a pleasant moon on its own, for two and a half moons had been an impossible situation, especially as he considered himself to be a lunatic at times.

'My father used to grow grapevines here. You know the usual midlife crisis when you get to your sixties . . .' Ologun stopped talking in mid-sentence, remembering the terrible affliction now on this world. 'You don't seem to be growing anything at all here.'

'We have had problems,' Grace said and Ologun did not need to press her for the more elaborate answer. He knew that they were trying to find a way to escape this place and he began to work out how he could help them.

The front door to the house swung open. 'You need to start talking,' Jasmine said, bringing out hot beverages. 'You sure you don't want a tea or something?'

Ologun refused and continued to rock on the chair. He had not eaten in a long time and it did not appeal to him whatsoever.

Jasmine handed Grace a cup and sat down. 'What did you do today with those men? Who are you?' She became distracted by the sight of Ologun wearing her dead husband's clothes. Ologun was a little small for them and wore rolled-up black cargo trousers and a grey shirt that hung low across the collar; that too had rolled-up sleeves. Grace looked at Jasmine and grinned, trying to hold in laughter. Ologun's feet were too small for the men's boots they had so she had given him a pair of Grace's shoes instead: bright pink with blue laces.

Ologun saw the sly grin and checked his shoes with a raised eyebrow. He then contemplated Jasmine's question. 'It isn't who I am that's the real question.'

'What the hell is that supposed to mean?' Jasmine said.

'A long time ago it was decided that certain achievements were in need of an update. Antibiotics were too limited and were beaten by bacteria which led to the expensive development of phage modification. Viruses were always complicated and took too much time to cure, if at all. Then other drastic measures caused problems in disrupting ecosystems. For instance it turned out that we needed mosquitoes as much as bees rather than . . . Anyway someone at some point decided that it would be easier to make a vessel that could adapt and offer up solutions to the ever-changing world of microscopic hostilities. Primarily for off world . . .'

'What the hell are you talking about? Grace, I told you he was crazy, I swear to God . . .'

'Please!' Ologun vented at Jasmine.

She went silent and looked a little shocked at his outburst.

'I am an off-world sample and adaptation unit.'

'You're a robot?' Grace said.

'No, I'm not a robot. Look, I was made as a person in order to go to other worlds and to sample all hostile organisms and create harmony, balance between anything taken there by humanity and anything that might harm them in environments where humans are the aliens, if you see what I mean.'

'Are you telling us your job is to become ill?' Jasmine asked cynically.

'When you put it that way,' Ologun said, thinking about it, 'yes.'

Grace seemed frightened as Jasmine laughed long and hard. 'I've heard it all now.' Her tone hardened and she looked Ologun directly in the eyes. 'You Americans talk more shit than a sewage farm can handle. Whatever your real intentions are, Grace and I are thankful, but make no mistake, you need to be gone by tomorrow, is that clear?'

Ologun nodded and wondered why no one could ever place his accent. Jasmine continued to titter in bombastic fashion as she went back inside the house.

'I believe you,' Grace said as soon as Jasmine had gone.

'It doesn't matter, it all went to shit a long time ago.'

'You can help against viruses like the one that's killing us all?'

'I don't know,' Ologun replied after some thought. 'This is what they used to call a Coda code.

'I don't understand.'

'Ambiguous slang,' Ologun offered. 'Viruses are formations of DNA codes coated in protein that have no true life to them. This one is a sophisticated, well-designed, weapons-grade monster that reinvents itself and is intent on, well, the end of human life, or at the very least slowly thinning out the numbers. Look, Grace, I know what's going on here. Both of you want to leave this place but you can't. Many have evacuated because of the warrants and this is the main reason you have no crops in the fields and why the meal you ate tonight was so poor and basic. You have no money because you left it too late and you left it too late because there is a very sick seven-year-old girl in the house who cannot be moved.'

'How do you know this?' Grace said in horror.

'I can hear her fight for every breath as we speak, I can grasp everything from even the slightest groan she makes within that perpetual, feverish sleep of hers. Grace, I'm not impolite and I cannot force help on you in these circumstances. I can make her well enough to travel and I can pay for a flight to take you anywhere and fast, but you have to invite me, you know, like a vampire,' Ologun concluded with a wry smile.

His eyes seemed to flash emerald green in the moonlight and Grace felt nervous yet hopeful. In her desperation she felt that a chance had to be taken with this man. 'Those men from the government will be back soon and I don't think Jasmine can cope on her own, and if she loses . . . please don't be lying, I cannot take much more of this.'

'You need to talk to Jasmine.'

'I'll leave the door unlocked for you later. Do what you can.'

'I already booked you tickets from Oujda Capital Airport to Madrid. That's three days from now and there's a Hotel Gaza there booked for a week just in case. I need to hook up to your neural server to give you some money.'

'Please, I don't have any money,' Grace said.

'I don't want your money, I'm giving you money.'

'Why would you do this? I don't understand,' Grace said.

'Well,' Ologun said with a grin, 'I recently stole more money than I'll ever spend from a soft drinks empire, I just couldn't help myself.'

Grace felt that she was being foolish and that this was all too good to be true. She leant over and offered Ologun her neck as though he were a vampire and would suck the life out of her. He inserted a strand of second skin into her neural chip port. Within moments Grace checked her account and found that she was so wealthy she could afford to buy a small exotic island.

*

'Hershal, darling, you had better stop snoozing.'

'I'm meditating. Why aren't you using the ship's comms?'

'I think something has happened with our crew members.' The message whined as a vibration through his second skin. 'Hina, what are you talking about?'

'Got to go for now, ciao.'

Hershal stood up as though hoisted on a rope. He left the mattress-covered floor of his quarters and walked towards the lift that would take him to the bridge. He found an internal comms unit and was about to contact the bridge but thought better of it. There were ladders to each level of the ship so he took these instead. On each ascent he scanned the deck from the ladder. There was no sign of anyone. Hershal arrived at the top deck, climbed off the ladder and headed towards the bridge. He placed the palm of his hand on the thick bulkhead crash door to the bridge itself and was puzzled by it all. No sign of anyone as of yet and the bridge crash door, as thick as a vault door, was closed and locked.

Hershal went to a small panel on the wall further down the corridor. He accessed the security feeds on a small monitor and as he did so he tried to contact Hina via his second skin. 'Do you have any sign of crew members anywhere on board your ship, Hina?' The monitor showed a live feed of various decks and finally the bridge. There was no activity anywhere and even the officers on the bridge were gone. 'Hina, I need you to respond.'

Hershal then used the controls on the panel to manoeuvre a probe that was orbiting the exterior of the ship. He took a deep breath and switched it on. Hershal could not focus on what was being broadcast. Echoes and static and what Hina called phantoms came and went. Hershal cut the feed and went back to the bridge door.

'Hershal, you need to get to the bridge now.'

'Where have you been?'

'I have been busy, which is what you should have been.'

'Warning. Self-destruct initiated. Three minutes remaining, please evacuate.'

The pleasant voice repeated itself as Hina's voice continued to whine as a vibration through Hershal's skin. 'I just had the same problem.'

Hershal tried the access code to the bridge. *Access Denied.* He had no more time to waste. Hershal had a secret that he had never revealed to anyone, an ability that the others did not possess. He concentrated and visualised the atomic structure of the fabric of space directly in front of him. His mind began to move atoms of oxygen, compressing them together until he pushed them forward towards the bridge door. The string of compressed atoms were then forced through the door until they were in position. Hershal then pulled them apart so that they expanded with force. The door ripped apart from the inside out; a metre-thick asaronite-titanium alloy door peeled open.

'Warning. Self-destruct initiated. Two minutes remaining, please evacuate.'

Hershal leapt through the gap in the bridge door and went straight to the main computer. He found two cables within a large box underneath the deck plates, and attached them to the console. He then ran while releasing the cable as he went towards the rear of the bridge, opening another hatch within the floor and dropping down without using the ladders provided. Within this small room he found the Version pilot unit hanging from its own set of thick cables up and along the walls. Hershal attached the cables into the back of the Version among sixteen various sockets on its back. He then stood back and gasped with horror.

'Warning. Self-destruct initiated. One minute remaining, please evacuate.'

The Version had been shot in the head and was not functioning. Hershal had no other choice at this juncture and had to try something, anything. He bit off his thumb at the knuckle and grimaced at the pain. He stuck the stump directly into the wound on the Version's skull. Hershal thought it was over and that the whole ship was about to be destroyed by an anti-matter bomb; just about the only thing that might damage the shell and destroy the asaronite hull inside.

'Warning. Self-destruct initiated. Thirty seconds remaining, please evacuate.'

Hershal sat there with his mind filled with a vision. He floated off and beyond the ship and towards the nearest star, through masses of energy pinning one universe to the other, interchangeable information from one reality to the next and no way of being comprehended or measured. The whole of reality became a small point and could be seen as a set of grids and a dot-to-dot between the galaxies, some colliding as the rest moved apart. One universe expanded and cooled as another exploded and shrank back into nothing. Stars burned and then exploded as others withered and took information from one reality only to deposit it into another. The aether was a record of all that had been as though a negative to realities positive. A thought could be listened to here in this place and an idea stolen for better or worse. How was it that nothing can be until it is comprehended by thought? The universe did and did not exist until someone acknowledged or even imagined it to be true. Turn your back and the moon disappeared and the cat was no longer in the box. The elephant made no sound in the woods and the souls of the dead may never find the white light via the tunnel to salvation. A ship sat among the information of lives gone by. *Ryu Yo* drifted far from its intended path. Information was moving on the opposite tide as buttons made of light were un-pressed and footsteps rose rather than fell. Voices were heard and were misunderstood. *Htrae rof setanidrooc tes, og a si repaer tcejorp.*

Hershal's eyes flickered open and he looked at the Version. It was now functioning and had been brought back to what might be described as life. Hershal could not quite understand how he had healed the thing, but he had no time to think as the countdown to the ship's destruction had been stopped but he knew there was another plan, a failsafe.

'Project Reaper is a go, set coordinates for Earth.' Hershal had by now reversed what he had seen and heard. An impossible portrayal of events that had taken place perhaps hours ago had now led him to yet another desperate scramble to save the ship. He climbed the ladder out of the small room and on to the bridge, ran through the damaged door, exited the bridge and on to the ladder that ran the full depth of the ship. He stood looking down and wondered how no one had fallen from the top deck and dropped all the way down to the lowest deck by now. Maybe they had, but the design was ridiculous enough to allow him to jump all the way down to the engineering deck and make it a more viable option than taking the lift. Hershal jumped into the circular shaft and fell three decks before smacking his chin hard on one of the bulkheads. He bit his tongue in two and broke his jaw as he continued to fall. Battered back and forth as he went, each floor passed by at speed until the floor of the lowest deck was met with force.

Hershal's body righted itself from being broken in several places. He picked himself up from the floor and began running down the vast length of the ship from fore to aft, passing the enormous tanks holding Spectra blood and past huge transformer units that created the energy that were used in creating the cascade portals. He sped through a huge room where the fusion engines for power were housed at its centre and then beyond the long pipes of housing that held the laser fields that fed the fusion process. Within another large room filled with an ion engine was a large chest hidden beneath the grid mesh deck flooring. Within the chest was a very small atomic bomb with a massive yield that could potentially rip the ship apart from the inside out. Hershal felt giddy at having been linked to the Version. He tripped over a small trolley left in the middle of the deck space and flew into one of the bulkheads.

He stood up quickly but it was too late. He felt the chain reaction as energy was released. In reflex he made a bubble in his mind that surrounded the chest. Time was restricted in its wake as a dense chain of any type of atom available was formed into a sphere. The bomb exploded, creating a massive shock wave that escaped the mind-made capsule. Hershal's skin burned and blistered at the heat and his eyes evaporated. The energy of the explosion found the sphere's weakest point and blasted out and downwards through the deck. The flume of fire burst through the ship's hull via any conduit available and on to the inside of the black shell. The shockwave dispersed around the ship and out of the stern which was not covered by the black shell. The ship groaned and creaked while the vacuum sucked all the air out of the engineering deck within a millisecond. Hershal lay on his back, unable to breathe as his charred body healed. His eyes grew anew after a few minutes and he looked around the room. His lungs, having shut down, no longer required his body to supply oxygen by breathing. New energy pathways radiating from his mitochondrial cells supplied his regenerating body with the kilojoules necessary to proceed.

*

The bulkheads were hot and anything flammable on this deck had been consumed.

Hershal clambered to his feet as though fatigue from some form of shock had taken hold; it could have been much worse. He walked the way he had entered, through the fusion engine room and the rest of the fifteen hundred metres until he stood at the feet of the towering tanks of Spectra blood. He automatically went to climb the ladder and head to the deck above and as he looked, cursed himself for being only half-cogent when he saw an emergency bulkhead had activated to stop decompression of the decks above; he should not have been heading that way in the first place.

He ran further towards the aft of the engineering deck and found a computer console, then activated its monitor. The touch screen had unfortunately melted so Hershal had to crouch down underneath the console. Hershal ripped away a panel and, as he expected, the quantum computing keypad lay beneath. Yet more in depth design, as components were always shielded from electromagnetic interference. This had protected the battleship's infrastructure from the bomb's electromagnetic pulse.

He initialled a bypass so he could release a strand of second skin that would act as a neural cord to the machine. The skin was inserted into the badly damaged console and a diagnostic of each deck initiated. The pain of having his skin and second skin melt away and muscle fuse to his bones had finally gone. Ice crystals had begun to form on the console in minute patterns that glistened in the emergency crimson light. Hershal checked himself and found that he

113

too was now coated in a complex web of frost.

Continuing in his activities, Hershal found that the damage to the ship was minimal with only superficial charring throughout the engineering deck. He checked the Spectra blood and was satisfied that it was undamaged. He then activated the emergency seal chamber between engineering and the armoury on the next level. He walked quickly to the rotating room that would hold the vacuum in engineering at bay, made a checklist in his mind of what he needed to do, and then thought everything through. The crew had left the ship and boarded one of the other remaining four ships. Assuming that Hina had kept hold of the *Full Result*, he had taken those ships along with a further sixty standard class of vessel in order to reach Earth for an operation that sounded grim.

Hershal turned on his heel away from the seal chamber as a sudden thought struck him. Heading to a locked storage cabinet built into the bulkhead and next to the tanks of Spectra blood, he opened the door and dragged a large hose across the deck floor, unravelling its coils as he went. He pressed a few buttons and a deep hum vibrated through the deck floor even though it could not be heard. Hershal checked the temperature on the hose's gauge and plugged it into a socket on the tanks that housed the Spectra blood.

'Hershal,' a vibration in his second skin went off.

'How do you fare, Hina?'

'I had to rush around a little, but I managed to stop the carnage. You seem to be in a bit of bother though.'

Hershal took another hose from the cabinet and attached the pipe to the other side on the network of tanks. 'Luckily it's not too bad. How could you know that I've had trouble anyway?'

'Assumptions and of course *Full Result* politely letting me know that nuclear weapons are being detonated close by.'

'I see. And the *Result's* Version?'

'Dead, I'm afraid. Listen, Hershal, I think it's about time we showed our ex-crew mates who we really are,' Hina relayed.

Hershal switched the machine on so that it pumped the Spectra blood through a large heater. If the blood remained in such a negative atmosphere it would die and become unsalvageable, and in turn useless. 'I agree. They are headed for Earth.'

'Peaceful voyage?'

'Don't be sarcastic.'

'Do you think I could do some information-gathering this time? It's been so many years.'

Information gathering! Hershal thought as he headed back to the seal chamber. He activated a button that showed red on the panel next to it. The room oscillated so that a gap in the cylindrical shape of the room appeared in front of him. He stepped in and the room moved round again so that the gap to exit the room appeared on the other side. Hershal waited for the light to turn green and for a thick door just outside the seal chamber to open. He stepped out, walked over to a comms unit on the wall and waited a few seconds. Shortly after his first breath Hershal pressed a few buttons on the comms. 'Hina come in,' he said.

He waited for what seemed quite a while. 'Yes,' Hina replied over the comms.

'You really have to do that?'

'Do what?'

'Gather information.'

'This is the perfect opportunity, my brother.'

'Fine,' Hershal said. 'You can do what you like if we ever catch them. We need to get after them now.'

Hershal thought about the odds of catching up with the other four ships and the Prospect crew. He punched the bulkhead next to him so hard that his knuckles split. He looked down and saw that his hand dripped blood on the canvas floor while water dripped from his second skin, soaking into the material. The blood, however, died and dried quickly and then turned black as though stains of dirt. Hershal was angry. It had occurred to him that perhaps it was not a good idea to let Hina do what he called 'gather information'. It was a habit he thought had been kicked long ago and it was something that Hershal considered utterly distasteful. Still, if Hina wanted to eat the organs of those treacherous bastards then, for once, he would let him.

THOROUGH DEATH

The old stone house was approached with stealth as though gliding through the humid night air. The front door to the house was unlocked as agreed and Ologun slipped in. He could see the interior of the house with exceptional clarity, and its layout had not changed much in close on two hundred years. He crept up the stairs and quickly found the bedroom three doors down and to the left. A grin crept across his face, for long ago this happened to be his room and it seemed an extra nostalgic treat. Ologun opened the door carefully, but still made some noise and so held still in the doorway. He watched and assessed the young girl lying in bed. She was hooked up to various machines and intravenous drips surrounding her. He considered what he was about to do both necessary and intrusive, surreptitious and in some ways selfish.

Ologun needed answers and a challenge in order to do what he was designed for. He knelt down and watched carefully as the girl breathed. Her life had become wretched and filled with effort. Her dark skin was ashen and dry with wrinkled flesh around her mouth and eyes where some of the sleep mucus had not been wiped on a daily basis. Ologun thought for a moment and realised that he had forgotten to ask her name. This scrawny thing that lay on the precipice of death filled him with sorrow and he missed a breath.

Work beckoned and Ologun removed five needles, discontinuing the IV drips as he wanted no interference. He then released several strands of second skin from his shoulders and torso. As though plugging into a computer system the strands of skin inserted into the girl's neck, arms and shoulders. Ologun was careful not to connect with her mind, and concentrated purely on the disease. He was no doctor and had no true concept of where and what or how. This was a simple thing. The virus would be felt and it would be perceived as though an extra sense to all other senses. Why it had attacked one so young could not be deciphered but even though this was a cleverly designed and contrived encryption it had its flaws.

The pain of the virus eventually filled Ologun and it writhed through his body, reminding him of the first ten years of his life that he had forgotten for a very long time. The memories were not welcome and had been suppressed, and for very good reason. For him the pain was bearable as in his life there had been much worse to endure. His thoughts on someone so young having to suffer this made him seethe with anger. Ologun's bones ached and his stomach knotted causing agony; this thing had verve. Acute pains stabbed and pulsed through his face and head and his eyelids flickered without control. *Interesting*. The virus was changing and moving as though a conscious entity avoiding his own abilities to detect and destroy. By now much of the thing had been dragged into his own body and defeated, but unfortunately, Ologun felt that this battle might not yet be over. He did his best to cleanse and restore the girl's health, and boosted every system she had: lymphatic, nervous, integumentary, muscular, skeletal, respiratory, cardiovascular, endocrine, urinary and reproductive; the girl would be healthy for quite a while at least.

The door to the room slammed open and Ologun shot up, retracting the threads of second skin.

'You evil dirty—' Jasmine screamed. 'Get out . . . get out!' she continued, and pointed a shotgun at his face.

'Please, stop!' Grace shouted after her. Ologun did as he was told and left the room. He was marched at gun point down the stairs as Jasmine shouted after him, 'You sick man, you touch my daughter, she's dying, you sick . . . you are going to die!'

Ologun walked through the front door and stood on the porch to face Jasmine. Jasmine in turn had a look of utter despair and contempt as tears rolled down her face 'You molested my baby,' she said and pulled the shotgun's trigger. Ologun's head exploded clean off his shoulders while his body flew off into the darkness of the front yard.

'Jasmine!' Grace screamed. 'No, no, no, what have you done?' The two women fought over the shotgun, screaming at each other when Jasmine suddenly stopped and stared at the staircase.

'Mamma, I'm hungry.'

Jasmine rushed to her daughter, who was rubbing her eyes. The girl had no idea of the situation and was dazed and fatigued.

Grace ran to the front door and reached to turn on an outside light. She searched the yard for Ologun this way and that, returning to the house when she could not see him.

'Oh God, what's happening?' Jasmine shouted, holding her daughter in her arms. 'Get a shovel quickly. Get the truck!'

Grace was pacing the floor in the kitchen. 'I think we should pack our bags, we have flights to Madrid to catch and . . .'

'Grace, we need to hide the body, please listen to me!'

'Body?' Grace said as though she had seen a ghost. 'Oh, there is no body, he's gone.'

*

They lied and they cheated. They destroyed and they took what they wanted and they never had to answer to anyone. An image of a ship, the *Hollywood*, lands on the new world. It was an enormous vessel and even though new, it became one of the central buildings of power for over eight and a half decades. A figure stands on a walkway among thousands who had been taken away from their old home. They all complain about being exhausted as this new world places so much weight on them. The figure becomes a man and he is embracing someone whom she thinks looks familiar. Tears of joy and the man, a friend, has forgotten about things that have come to pass.

The feelings of abandonment and loneliness ripple on as a hundred lovers and failed attempts at normality come and go, countless missions to help those on the fringe of civilisation as they settle and forge a living out of sheer will; they will have their freedom no matter the cost. Faces buried deep within impenetrable hegemony scheme and take, yet every dog has its day and yet they are always replaced with worse than before. The world is seen from orbit and it has no arctic regions. It is a warm world, a new world with an amber moon. Vast lands of flora and more expanses of desert divide the one and only continent. They choose the deserts to avoid cross contamination and they set about cleansing the water and moving it across the void. A million flora and a million more fauna are learned and the old world fades from importance as a terrible crime is swept away and many values are rewritten. Goldilocks zones and the chance of conquering them are forgotten; one planet will do. The horizon floats near and a black shadow, a rhomboid, can be seen in front of the sun. It becomes a demon's eye, a cat's eye, until it tears a hole in the fabric of reality and moves beyond the universe.

The city can be seen below now and it is a cardboard city where a child plays with matches. The child is laughing and giggling as it strikes one match after the other; this is your legacy! The child succeeds and the flaming torch is dropped and it falls closer and closer towards an Empire.

*

Eyes flickered open to see a sky choked with smoke and ash. It was daytime and yet light could not find its way en masse. An alien construct sought its mark and continued to feed and project information. The damage has been thorough and it took time. One hundred per cent replenishment, but not all is configured. Judith Gibson sat up and absorbed a new reality. A holocaust peppered down from a sky of shadow. The world was black and white with ash, and in the distance there was a hole in the world, a crater that had once been the hub of civilization. Reflexively and without emotion Judith stood, then recalled certain protocols. She headed for the nearest control centre and passed through the military base, now flattened and scarred beyond recognition. She remembered that the cause of all this destruction was beneath the surface and a rectangular hollow was visible on the surface where a building used to be.

Judith made her way down spiralling steps that descended next to an empty lift shaft and to the lowest level. There were no multiple sets of objectives in this reality and each action only led to the next. Judith staggered the long distances of the vast hangar units and to the dais of Central Operations that controlled the Version.

She accessed a computer console and began a set of commands that would seek out and integrate in order to take control of any remaining computers unaffected by the devastation. Once full access was granted, Judith was satisfied that certain capabilities remained. She accessed the programme for environmental assistance and typed in the word 'conclusion'.

Around the crater that used to be a city and across the flat plains for hundreds of miles, many silo hatches opened. Within the silos were terraforming filters, colossal machines that if needed could change the atmosphere, although their use in this context could be found at the bottom of a long list. The machines were configured to the last atmospheric readings and a command was set to cleanse the air of impurities.

Judith checked the radiation levels via the pieces of apparatus positioned for many miles around the city's limits that were still functioning. The levels read as acceptable background parameters with only slightly elevated levels of neutrinos. Judith then accessed satellite control as it was better to use thermal imaging than to transmit them digitally at random and across such vast distances. The satellite image blinked on to another console on a desk that Judith recalled belonged to someone she knew. Her memories filtered through as she pressed for them and this information lag within her for now had rendered her a ghost.

She analysed the feed from the orbiting machine and saw a large gathering of thermal images along the Prospect frontier border. The image was enhanced where a whole ensemble of activity was observed. Many military craft had gathered and many people were actively setting up shelters. The clarity of picture was excellent as the information was assessed. The wounded and the confused, the frightened and the panicked were moving en masse from all directions in all manner of vehicles. Copter jets buzzed overhead in defensive patterns as many trucks and tanks were used to form a vast barrier around a makeshift military camp. As she observed the chaos, Judith accessed another satellite.

She continued to be systematic and wanted to see ground zero from an orbital perspective. The terrain of Prospect drifted by on another screen until Judith saw a black mark on the land that was spewing out a great plume of black smoke and dust. It looked tiny when considering the sheer size of this world and appeared more of a speck leaking ink, akin to an ocean hydrothermal vent. All data was cross-referenced. Wind direction and speed. Time of air filtration network completion. The planets' gravitational effect on such a level of air pollution.

Judith sat back as her emotions began to return to her. Satisfaction edged through; for all that had happened, and that was terrible, a WMD holocaust winter was unlikely. The dust was being blown north and the mass of the planet would pull much of the filth into the oceans north of the continent.

Judith sat for a while without finding the will to communicate with the survivors six hundred miles south of her. A terrible pain sprang from within her. Her chest felt as though it were being crushed and her throat tightened in yet more of an acute ache. She leapt up and began moving around the underground complex. She was looking for something but could not remember what or why.

Every corner and cupboard were checked. Every office and every inch of the warehouses. Judith checked the back-up vehicle storage facilities where every tank, truck and aircraft was sifted through. Another underground complex was accessed, and another until the star ship's developmental and construction facility that now lay as a virtually empty chasm had been examined. Mile after mile, through tunnels and through corridors and through half-built ships and docking warehouses, Judith searched and hoped it would come to her.

A specialist unit was reached and Judith felt frantic. She prised a door off its hinges and threw it aggressively. In this part of the military complex and deep within research and development territory there were contraptions and innovations galore. She spotted an older, less-needed form of tech within the gloom of a corner. Stasis chambers and cryogenic-sleep beds were still in development and housed in rows along an elongated room. Judith felt that this was promising and yet still could not decipher why.

She moved quickly and checked one after the other. On and on Judith peered through crystal window panes and into the cylindrical shape of sleeper pods. Empty casket, empty, empty until she saw a green light further down the corridor in the darkness. She was at the machine in an instant, as though teleported, and peered inside. A young man with brown hair was upright and asleep within this small chamber. In his arms there was a small woman with mousy blonde hair and pale skin. A tattoo on her neck, a flower, was visible through the frosted crystal of the chamber door. Judith thought for a moment and realised that this is what she had been looking for.

A month in summer, a utensil for cutting. No that's wrong. Elocution, can I go to the toilet, hungry like a beaver. No, no. Remember, you stupid bitch! May I, not can I, this knife is blunt! Sharplin . . . Glynn and May!

Judith collapsed to her knees. Her eyes welled but she did not submit. All that had been, everything that she was, exploded into the recently replenished, regrown engine inside her skull. Judith placed both hands on the glass of the cryo-pod and breathed deeply to gain control. Even at the total cost of the ultimate mutilation of being stripped to the bone and beyond; and even though something in the atmosphere that was invisible and moved through all matter had impeded her recovery, everything had now come back to her.

SWEET POTATO

Two craft with rhomboid wings attached to that of an insect's torso entered the valley via a luminous and viscous field. Beyond the exterior of the planet-sized rhomboid shell and below them was the legacy of another time when deals were made and an expansive jungle was created. One living craft of a deep crimson accompanied by another of a strong turquoise moved beneath the liquid sky of light that fed the vegetation below. Relics of another species were being excavated by the younger of the craft's own kind; the two craft remembered what had once occurred here and were fond of the thoughts pertaining to practice and victory. This place the craft flew through was once a circular basin that had now become a canyon that had been carved out for thousands of miles. The Shard had grown, the entity had grown and with it the number of craft bred to protect it had been multiplied. Amongst all that was new there was an old concave construction: a lake that had once been filled with water was now a spring where a small fraction of the entity lay; a shimmering light of tawny gas whose surface appeared akin to that of a star.

The two craft hovered at the north side of the lake of Spectra. They each released six legs from beneath their undercarriage and descended to land on the grass. There were others that remained around them although in their indigenous environment, they would have by now tried to flee from the two abominations of war that had intruded on them.

Zebra and lions, caribou and buffalo, sheep and cows, pigs and elephants were all together at this watering hole that provided an easy and mundane life. Primates of every kind, minus the ones who had initially built this landscape, watched with disinterest as did every other fowl, reptile and mammal. The predators were as passive as their prey and all seemed bored and complacent from their needs being automatically supplied; the garden could be called Eden but it seemed vacant of something, even tired.

The lake rippled and began to fill with energy until something broke the surface. A dark mound rose and grew larger. It became an island of marble black shell that continued to ascend as the plasma of Spectra ran, poured and gushed off the enormous behemoth. To any creature now staring at the island as it floated, it had no shape or structure that they would comprehend. But to those who had built this construct and had sent it into the depths of space hundreds of years ago, it would be recognised as a flat triangle – perhaps from a distance it was shaped like a guitar pick.

Modified and coated with the black Spectra shell the ancient exploration ship rose until it reached the orange liquid sky, passed through this layer and into the vacuum of space above. Another rose and then another, slowly and elegantly until eleven ships came to rest in formation above the great valley orbiting above its protective shield of Spectra blood sky.

The craft watched with curiosity and knew these ancient objects well; these things that had preceded their existence by centuries. They waited by the lakeside and were instructed by something from deep within the Spectra. Something had been spotted very close to one of the planets under supervision. A danger had been found and transmitted from a surveillance buoy not too far from Earth, if in fact fifty-three light years was considered to be close. The craft understood and were given instructions, the enemy had returned.

*

A noise echoed back at Hershal. Looking around for some time he finally realised that his fingers had been tapping the surface of the desk where he was sitting. He ceased the involuntary action as another sweep of the entire ship was in order.

Hershal glided around from deck to deck. The residual stench from different places filled his mind with images of past activities. Old locker rooms that smelled of soap and body odour and many fragrances that had been used to mask the scent of human flesh and all that it oozed. Dust and dirt, polish and grime were no substitute for the trees in the woods and the fragrance of a trickling brook. The soil after a downpour on a hot summer's day, the flowers of spring and all that the season could bring.

Cooped up, hemmed in and alone, Hershal traipsed on. An empty ship and a deceitful crew, a new set of objectives and a fresh attitude inadvertently quickened his pace. Hershal had at first thought it best not to disturb his brother, for when awake the man was not quite a man and seemed to be more of something else, something quite diabolical. When asleep, and on such an unusual occasion, the thing became a boy. Two sides to one being that swapped places and where dreams of Vanguard and a terrible existence could be heard in curdling screams from within a terrifying nightmare. A mistake had been made with Hina once at a time when it was thought that waking him from such horror was a good idea. Hershal shuddered at the memory, for as Hina woke and his mind was simultaneously both madman and boy, he shrieked like a banshee, a demon-possessed howl. Hina had ripped his brother to ribbons at that very moment and it was decided that from then onward it was best to leave things well alone.

Hershal found himself sitting within a space fighter jet on the second to lowest deck among many a military asset. He twiddled knobs and pulled levers and watched the outer skin of the plane's exterior surface flex and pull; it was nice to have controls that were so tangible in this day and age. Hershal's patience was wearing thin. He checked his second skin to find out when their craft would arrive. He sat back and felt somewhat worried and confused. Hershal had checked every deck of both ships that had been left behind and sabotaged by the Prospect crew, twice, and still Hershal could not find his brother anywhere.

*

An asaronite hull was a thick, dense-plated construct and, due to being stripped of all previous sound-absorbing layers for an austere refurbishment, noises bounced around as though in a twisted version of a concrete tunnel. The lag of a voice trailing off down the passageways or the barrage of simple movements would assault the senses. Someone screamed. The sound travelled along the starboard side of the ship on the interior of the empty stampede-turret operation decks, along various walkways, and through rooms that had once housed machines and control panels that fired enormous cannons that ran from aft to fore on both port and starboard.

The *Critical Belief* was an ultra-manoeuvre class vessel that had been modified by an alien entity and coated with a thick black shell. It sat among three other ships of exactly the same composition. The noise came again and was rejected by the density of bulkhead surfaces and passed around from wall to wall until its energy was lost somewhere on the way. On one of the longest passageways running throughout the ship, a wide walkway running the length of the ship's starboard, there appeared a blip on this otherwise spotless and shiny world of metal. The eruption of pain and sheer agony swept the passageway once again. The lighting along this elongated stretch of the ship remained dim and the sullied zone within this location was difficult to recognise. On closer inspection it appeared that an explosion of dark liquid had occurred. It dripped from the ceiling and ran down the walls until it pooled on the floor.

Neatly stacked on the side of the passageway were objects saturated in the same dark wetness. They were stacked five high as though elongated sandbags had been placed to absorb the aftermath of a flood. Beyond this area of mess and within another room with many operating consoles, three people were kneeling down on the flexible fabric of the floor's surface.

All three of them trembled and shook. Their hands and feet were bound and their mouths gagged. One of them had urinated and the fluid had soaked through the woman's trousers and into the flex fabric on the deck. The prisoners were fixated on the blue object that spun round and round and felt cohesively sure that it would not be too long now. They watched and one of them glanced at the stack of bodies that lay just outside the doorway of the room as though making sure that all of this was real and happening.

The blue object stopped moving abruptly and stomachs churned with fright. They looked at the man, if he could be likened to such a thing, and he in turn smiled before placing the blue object, made of a crystal transparent material, down on the desk next to him. The object, a long staff with a sharp blade on one end, rolled and fell on the floor.

The man smirked and he rolled his eyes and shrugged like a mime artist in mid-performance. The captured three thought they knew this man. The quiet one that never interacted with anyone. The shy one, the smallest one, the one to worry about the least; they had been so wrong! They had even joked that this one had a woman's name, an Indian name that had caused endless and amusing speculations.

Hina marched back and forth in the room directly in front of the last of the three crewmembers that existed across the four ships. It had been a long and pleasurable task and he had gathered as much information as he could, and yet Hina felt as though he needed to slow down and take more time when such an opportunity came his way.

'You know I always say a good system is where no one takes any responsibility,' Hina said and knelt down to address his victims on their level. 'A good company is a fascist company. A good killing is a direct killing, oh . . . but wait.' Hina stood up and made his way back to the desk. 'You people are all about the tactics. You steal our ships, sabotage and try to kill my brother, bless his soul, and then you take off toward Earth with the intent to kill all who remain there in their pitiful, short-lived hopeless existence once and for all. And I'm thinking, hold on a moment, that's all a bit spiteful don't you think?'

Hina moved across to the woman, dragged her across the room and placed her in another empty space. He did the same with the others and lined them up as he did before so that they now knelt on the hard surface of metal within the vast rectangular room. Hina moved back into the adjoining room and closed the door, then locked it by turning a large valve. He moved to a console and watched the three prisoners through a thick glass window on the bulkhead wall, scanning them intensely one last time. He read their names sewn on to their fatigues on patches and smiled a little and then grinned wildly. Colonel Wong, Captain White and the Colonel's sister, Corporal Wong.

'You know,' Hina said, with his hand hovering above a small switch located on the wall next to him, 'two Wongs don't make a White.' Hina screeched and laughed. 'The oldest jokes are always the best,' he cackled as he flicked a switch. Two enormous doors at the back of the room opened and Hina watched in fascination and smirked as all three slowly suffocated and froze.

*

More hiking through the old world that had been terra-formed. Once arid and open, beige and empty, it was now dark and full, moist and rich with activity. Ologun flinched as insects darted around; odd considering how he had spent the past eighty-odd years of his life. He considered that perhaps that was why he was agitated by the minute terrors that buzzed around in the early hours. They bit and drank from him, and his head and hands were briefly covered in bumps. The floor crawled with the mass of micro-life as a river of siafu army ants seemed intent on climbing over him.

He wandered on and south while occupied by all manner of thoughts. The women; a married couple in a crisis of trust who had lost their heads. Ologun had actually lost his. He grinned and then slipped and fell on an exposed tree trunk as something caught his attention. An opening in the tree line revealed a field of open growth.

Ologun picked himself up and walked into the opening. Ahead of him and at the centre of this exposed piece of land that was covered in tall grass, an object hovered. It was a large and odd-shaped construct that defied gravity and held position six feet off the floor. With a dull texture and a tan exterior, it seemed other worldly with its peculiarity. Ologun stepped forward and the thing reacted by manoeuvring up and away with an utter quietness that defied its size and bulk. Ologun stepped forward again and the flying boulder opened a small cavity on its surface. There was a pause as Ologun was more curious than cautious; this was not the strangest thing he had ever seen, although it was quite unusual: organic, fat and elongated like a tuber, like a sweet potato.

The object then fired something across the field and it hit Ologun. It was a long string of what seemed to be flesh that was gelatinous and pink like the shoes he wore. As it hit him, it penetrated his shirt, second skin and deep into his body. Ologun doubled over as pain burst through him. It burned and ate at him and crawled through his veins. He reflexively ran away and to his left, yet the flying bulb followed him. It glided over the treetops of the jungle and searched for him while Ologun ran and fought this internal intrusion.

The virus he had taken from the young child had by now erupted and multiplied and Ologun felt overwhelmed as he stumbled and scampered in the undergrowth. He hid behind a tree where another string shot down from above and missed. It hit the floor and crawled around like a tapeworm had been ejected from some orifice. It died on the dirt and turned from a fleshy pink to a dull grey. The horde of ants was ever present and en masse dragged the thread away.

Ologun waited until he regained much of his strength and was sure that similar attacks of this kind would fail. He ran to the tree line and the thing came back into view. It fired many threads and they bounced harmlessly off Ologun's second skin. *You're ruining my new shirt!*

Ologun released hundreds of thick strands from his second skin, giving the impression that he now had many arms, a strange parallel as though he had become a rhizome attacking a tuber. The thick strands of second skin shot across and over the top of the grass and up towards the enemy. The skin wrapped around the alien object and tightened its grip. Ologun held on to a thick tree for some purchase as he reeled the skin back into himself. The hovering boulder lurched and tried to pull away. Several strands of second skin snapped under the pressure, yet the rest adapted. The tree Ologun held on to and around which he had wrapped yet more skin lurched heavily under the bulb's strength: tuber versus tree.

Ologun pulled harder and the thing hit the ground as it was dragged ever closer. It released more strings of flesh as its mass was dragged across the field, churning up the soil as it went. Then, without warning, it fired an intense invisible thin beam of energy at Ologun that sliced him down the centre.

He let go of the tree and was now hanging like clothes peg on a washing line between the tree and tuber on his second skin. The object yanked and pulled as Ologun bobbed up and down until finally the thing broke free and shot up and away into the night sky at great speed.

'Come on!' Ologun shouted after it. 'We're not finished!'

His body pulled itself back together from his stomach all the way to his shoulder. He staggered, breathed heavily, and his body shook.

He was totally preoccupied thinking about what he had just encountered. He then realised that he was headed south and had not been paying attention to what he was doing for some time.

Eventually Ologun found himself in another clearing and at yet another farm. He jogged his way across the field and towards the house. All was quiet and there was no sign of activity. There were no lights on in the house and, looking around, Ologun saw that the fields had no crops but were covered in indigenous plant life, and that there was also no livestock to be seen or heard. A quick inspection of the farmhouse revealed that it had fallen into disrepair, with torn surfaces within the digital lenses, tiles missing from the roof, and the wood that was fixed into the stone of the walls was in dire need of painting; the place had been abandoned some time ago.

Ologun paused as he came to the dirt track just outside the house. He walked closer and searched the sky and found no sign of the giant tuber. Ologun stopped walking and thought for a moment, deciding that the derelict, run-down house seemed a good place to stop. He sat down on the dirt path outside the house and checked every device that he had hacked. Surveillance cameras, satellite feeds and various other tools were considered in turn in order to keep an eye on things at the north of the continent and then further to the south. As long as what he had been watching in the north did not start moving south it would be all right for now.

Ologun then received a flag to check another satellite feed. The tech belonged to the Chinese and they were monitoring the Atlantic Ocean seven hundred miles west of Africa. Another feed had also flagged for a response and Ologun accessed another satellite belonging to a private news firm. His heart leapt as he saw an infra-red visual focused over the western provinces of Nigeria. There was no time to lose and Ologun jumped up, heading for what he thought was a garage; a vehicle would be the best thing to find right now.

This plan was short-lived, however, as a sharp slap to the back of the neck brought Ologun to his knees. He turned and fell on to his back, and was utterly surprised.

'You've been busy,' a voice said.

'Ray?'

Ray smiled and crouched down. 'You looked a bit ridiculous so I gave you an upgrade.'

Ologun scanned Ray in the dark and was at least happy that the man was not naked. Ray wore a linen cream suit with a black shirt and dark brown shoes. Ologun stood up and then realised that something was quite off with Ray, who was now extremely tall and towered over him. 'You are . . . bigger than I remember, Ray.'

'Yes,' Ray said and sat down on a bench he found up against the side of a wooden shed. 'You're welcome, by the way.'

'Welcome for what?' Ologun asked, and then fell over as terrible shooting pains pulsed through his body. 'What did you do?'

'You are too short to go unnoticed and the wrong colour, but we'll get back to that in a moment.'

'Colour?' Ologun vented as the pain became worse. He looked down and saw that his legs were growing out the bottom of his turned-up trousers and that his arms, chest and shoulders were beginning to fill his shirt. His pink shoes had by this point ripped open at the seams within the fabric and fallen off as his feet became longer and wider. It all hurt like hell.

'Enough!' Ologun screamed and at that the pain dispersed.

'Now for the other treatment.'

'Get off me!' Ologun shouted and smacked Ray's hand away so that a small, flat patch of gel flew out of his hand and landed in the dirt, grew legs like a centipede and ran off into the long grass.

'What's the matter?' Ray asked in confusion.

'Do you know how much pain I've been through for the past gazillion years?'

'You cannot go around this part of the world being white. You need to be brown or black.'

'Do you know what the hell you're saying?' Ologun said in anger. 'I'm not having these stupid conversations with you.' He stood up and then fell. It was like the strangeness of inhabiting a newly constructed avatar. 'What have you done to me?'

'I made you an acceptable average size rather than a munchkin.'

'What the hell is a munchkin? Look,' Ologun said, crawling away and sitting next to a fence on the other side of the dirt path, 'it's been a rough week, so leave me be.'

'You need to be black.'

'I need to sit down,' Ologun replied. 'I was okay at six feet and I'm okay with being white.'

'Exceptionally white, even whiter than a ginger.'

'I don't need to be ginger either.'

Ologun sat watching light as it rose above the treeline a few acres away from the west. 'The sun is coming up.'

'So,' Ray nodded, 'you've been here only a few weeks and are already causing a shit storm. I'm thinking that book your father wrote, you know the one, *The Almagest Intersection*. He must have written it about you because there's no way you can always turn up here and there and somehow always manage to arrive . . . You're a shit magnet.'

'Ten billion,' Ologun said, glumly.

'Before we go down that path and trudge through what I think we're about to, can I just say that a peace envoy is on its way and will try to establish . . . well, peace between Prospect and Earth. Hershal and Hina are on their way.'

'You know, whenever it was imagined that the world would end, people always thought it would be some nuclear holocaust and over quickly with utter devastation,' Ologun said with his head hung low. 'But what have we got instead? A slow, creeping inevitability. I tried to intervene, but I'll need more time.'

'More time for what?' Ray asked. 'You know everything that has been done was part of a sound plan to reduce numbers. It was an efficient cull in order to promote sustainability.'

'Cull? People aren't cattle, Ray, mass murder can never be justified . . . ever,' Ologun fumed, looking at Ray in disgust.

'Twenty two billion people could never be managed no matter how sophisticated the solution. Anyway I thought I'd meet up with you and make sure you don't get involved any further.'

'I need to head south, and soon,' Ologun said.

'Here we go,' Ray sighed. 'Let me tell you something. What's done is done and what is about to happen is being managed so please don't just come back here and think you can throw your weight around.'

'Operation Rashad, Ray, the world is about to go to war,' Ologun said, picked up a stick and began etching something with it in the dirt. 'American and German allied naval forces are about to attack from the south and west of Africa. Polish and Italian armed forces are going to attack from the north-east via Sudan and into Ethiopia, and more American forces along with Serbian forces . . .' Ologun raised and dropped his hands as though giving up. 'This continent is about to . . . Ray, do you know what will happen if this goes ahead . . . and what the hell for?'

Ray sat back and thought about the question. 'Three Prospect ships commandeered during the war. Although I suspect it's for the cascade engines. Idiots don't realise you need a Version pilot, wait a minute, yes, I think this in fact is about . . .'

'Ray, it was a rhetorical question.'

'I see.'

'This is going to lead to a nuclear holocaust.'

'Technically,' Ray said, 'yes. But as I say, it's all in hand so don't get involved. There's a temporary inter-dimensional pocket of space been created within the solar system. Anything that gets launched gets plucked and stored without reaching its intended target.'

'That's good,' Ologun nodded in thought. 'Even so, there is going to be a world war over this and it's going to be protracted, which in itself will cause countless deaths.' Ologun stood up to walk and fell over again. 'Damned legs!'

He then noticed something slithering over the ground towards him and watched as it sped closer. It came within a few feet and Ologun was relieved that it turned out to be a snake and not fired from that other thing. The snake, however, seemed intent and launched itself at Ologun and bit him on the face. Ologun prised the creature off and injected a strand of second skin in order to render it unconscious. He then gently placed it on the floor.

'See, a complete and utter shit magnet,' Ray mused.

'I should have known it was a black mamba,' Ologun said, cursing himself.

'If you get involved in this,' Ray said, amused at seeing Ologun's face swell up, 'you will only A, mess this thing up because you are not able to stop a vast army from attacking on three fronts, and B, reveal yourself and therefore Hina and Hershal along with the Prospect envoy as hostile or even alien.'

'We can draw on the craft, Creed will help.'

'Not a chance, our craft are under strict orders not to get involved. It's bad enough that the two of you came here as though . . . well, the whole world is extremely nervous over such an entrance.'

Ologun stood up for the third time and began to balance on overly long legs that felt alien to him. He began walking around the yard, up the step to the house porch, and then back again towards Ray. 'Maybe, although I did an entire sweep and checked out the military tech and I'm sure someone, possibly the South African Government is hiding something that may help them.'

'Oh,' Ray said. 'What would that be?'

'Some strange organic weapon that looks like a big potato, a sweet one at that. It attacked me a few hours ago. It has some gravity-defying ability, pretty impressive.'

'I see. I think you'll find it isn't South African.'

'Who then?' Ologun said disappointed. 'The Chinese, Israel, a new American drone that I missed, or rather Creed's scan missed?'

'Alien!' Ray said, with eyebrows raised.

'The enemy,' Ologun replied and began heading towards the garage as though even if he found a vehicle it would actually make a difference.

'No, not them, another race.'

Ologun stopped and spun round to face Ray who had followed close behind him. 'More aliens? Jesus Christ!' Ologun shouted.

'Calm down, it's only one more,' Ray offered, rolling his eyes.

'Is this how it is now?' Ologun said, voice still raised. 'We sit on Mount Olympus chatting about people and their lives and intruders, oh it's all right it's just more aliens floating around being mysterious and shooting bits of flesh from oh . . . I don't know, its arsehole. Oh, it's okay, the human race is about to have another world war but we still have the numbers, ten billion dead in less than a hundred years, but we still have it all under control. You're an arsehole yourself, Ray, and I never wanted to be taller and I don't want to be black because

I'd look like you and you're the biggest prick I ever met.' Ologun stood, breathing heavily, and realised he had lost his temper, yet Ray seemed completely disaffected by the outburst.

'Feel better now?' Ray asked. 'As I said, those intruders have been around for some time hiding out here and there since, well, a while. I think they're waiting for something, maybe perhaps they want to move in when humanity finally destroys itself, on this world at least.'

'Well, that's fantastic. Anything else, a swarm of locusts perhaps? Krakatoa or Yellowstone Park erupting? Maybe the sun will go super nova or the poles will shift while we're at it,' Ologun ranted. Suddenly, he got a message from his second skin regarding the situation in western Nigeria. The news satellite keeping tabs on Nigeria continued to play surveillance into the vision of his mind and what he saw disturbed him to the core. 'I have to go.'

'I told you not to get involved,' Ray said, grabbing Ologun by the arm.

Ologun shrugged off Ray's grip and began heading towards the garage. 'What the hell are you doing here, Ray, since when did you go anywhere or do anything?'

'I'm on a mission.'

'Right now?' Ologun said, turning to Ray once more. 'There's an army of mercenaries or so-called terrorists moving from town to town across Nigeria from west to east. Do you know what happens when this kind of thing takes place?'

'Yes.'

'Again it was a rhetorical question and I don't give a shit about what you want.' Ologun reached the garage door and went to turn the handle.

'Wait,' Ray ordered.

'People are dying and are going to die, everyone is going to die. I need to do something that shows some force, I mean I can't just call up Chancellor What's His Name in Germany or the President of the United States and say, look you need to start thinking about the fact that not only one, but two alien races are out there and they may or may not attack.'

'There is no vehicle in the garage,' Ray said.

Ologun yanked on the garage door, found it was locked, and turned to face Ray. 'I'll go and at least try to stop this fake military coup from happening and then I'll intervene and try to stop the allied forces to the north and then send a message, the kind that those in power listen to if they see exceptional force, no, no . . . power,' he said, yanking hard on the door and breaking the lock. 'I think the navy off in the south and west coasts is a ploy in order to thin South Africa's military and cause them not to come to Nigeria's defence, and as for the terrorists . . .' Ologun had by now turned his head to see a vehicle. 'No vehicle, idiot?' He then saw something in the corner that he very much recognised. 'Ray,' Ologun said, his voice suddenly small and quiet, 'what the hell is going on?'

REPUDIATE

'We got something.' A group of so-called specialists had assembled within the underground bunker west of New York City several hours ago and had achieved little by this point. Colonel Young watched the proceedings from the other side of the room. The first candidate drafted in was Martin Banks, the IT expert, and he had found something of interest.

'I'll run it through the heads and see what we get.'

Natasha moved over to his terminal to see what he had found. 'I don't think so, he's six foot five for a start.'

'Where is that, exactly?' Young asked.

'North-east Moroccan district,' Martin answered.

'A white male?' Young asked.

'Yes.'

The colonel could see the reversed image of the hologram and became intrigued. 'Being white in that region is, shall we say, dangerous and the man is clearly out in the open without caution.'

'I thought we were looking for someone from beyond space? If you like I'll move the configured satellite over the area and set it to scan for cascade activity,' Natasha said.

'Could someone please tell me what we are doing here exactly?'

Colonel Young glanced at the two men and a woman sitting at the other side of the main conference table. Martin was just fifteen years old and a very good analyst who was apparently brilliant at hacking surveillance systems regardless of quantum encryption, and could work the holograph recordings with exceptional ability. The three new team members sent by the General remained perplexing to Young. Doctor Douglas Francis, who was a leading biologist, already had clearance as he worked at the classified antiviral research facility in Northumberland, Pennsylvania. He was an obvious choice due to the odd nature of the unusual superhuman attributes of the thing or person they were attempting to track.

The psychologist, Doctor Violet Amber, whose name alone had managed to lift the colonel's spirits, and a professor of specified history, Edmond Higgs, had also been sent. All three were now waiting for more explanation for having their lives interrupted and being dragged to this classified location.

Natasha Forbes looked at Young as though it were about time they were briefed. The colonel thought about this for a while as he watched Martin working away on his computer. 'All right,' he said. 'Martin, you carry out the search on the man you spotted, we might get lucky with something, anything, at this stage. You three and Natasha come with me please.'

Colonel Young walked across the room and placed his hand on a scanner device on the door to the dead room. Cleared for access, he entered and the other four followed. Young sat down on the seat at the head of the table and watched as the others took seats, apart from Natasha who remained standing.

'Well this is all quite a mystery don't you think, Edmond?' Douglas said.

'Quite the intrigue,' Edmond replied.

Violet said nothing and simply folded her arms, sitting back in her chair. She had already tired of the two men sitting next to her and wondered how two British men, men who seemed idiotic and almost identical in their every demeanour, had managed to reach the top of their respective fields.

'Have you all accessed your carbon blocks and read the files?' Young asked.

'It was empty,' Douglas said, and the others agreed in a disgruntled fashion.

Colonel Young felt embarrassed at this and automatically began to fib his way out of the situation. 'I apologise for the delay in this briefing. Protocol demanded that we wait for further developments before briefing you at all, um . . . so at times we blank the boxes.'

'Have there been?' Violet asked.

'Sorry?' Natasha asked.

'Any developments?'

'No.'

'Then perhaps we should wait until there are, then,' Violet said with sarcasm.

'General Dean sent you,' Colonel Young said, 'so I doubt you will be going home. She chose you for a reason that I am sure will become evident. Please, Natasha, continue as you were.'

Natasha used her neural implant and activated the holographic projector on the room's long conference table. 'This is an image of an object that burst into our universe three weeks ago. It descended on Earth and began, we believe, to scan . . .'

'I'm sorry, Ms Forbes, did you say burst into our reality?' Violet asked.

'Oh dear, Edmond, we have an interrupter on our hands.'

'We certainly do, Douglas.'

Young placed his hand over his mouth in dismay as Natasha continued.

'Energy cascades are difficult to explain and are even more difficult to achieve.'

'Impossible you mean,' Douglas interrupted.

'This is a three-dimensional image of the craft. We monitored it until it cloaked itself as it moved over the southern coast of . . .'

'My God, it looks like an insect,' Douglas said.

'No, I think if you take away the mid-section and add the front torso to the end it becomes a headless dolphin, or a shark perhaps . . . no, if you put all the wings together it's a rhomboid, you know? Like an African Zulu shield,' Edmond said.

God's sake! Colonel Young thought. There were similar teams doing this same job all over the country and no doubt the world. The CIA alone had intelligence operations that made this small ensemble appear utterly pointless. Still, this is what General Dean wanted, there had to be a good reason.

A further interruption occurred when a noise indicated someone was at the door to the locked room. The colonel decided this was an apt moment to adjourn the proceedings. 'There's a file under the local domain called EX1, I propose the three of you just read the no-frills version of the briefing from there,' Young said as he made his way to the thick metal door. He realised that this would take all day at the rate they were going and felt it would impede things further if he tried to instil any kind of draconian order into the group. He opened the door to see Martin looking agitated as though he were in desperate need of the lavatory.

'You wanted luck,' Martin said. 'You are not going to believe what the head units have found.'

*

The cryogenic casket was lying flat on the floor. Judith, after such a devastating attack, had become stronger than she thought possible and had dragged something which was at least a tonne in weight through the entire underground military complex and up the narrow set of steps to the surface. She waited and watched the horizon and knew that it would not be too much longer. Glynn and May remained in the stasis bed and would stay there until Judith could deliver them to the ever-growing camp of survivors six hundred miles to the south. The smouldering plume in the middle distance continued to pour upwards into the sky and flecks of ash still fell softly on the world like a noxious snowstorm.

Judith kicked the ash beneath her feet; it was now two inches thick and getting deeper. Her gaze was drawn by some feeling that went beyond her usual six senses as something came closer. Out of the cloud and hovering low, a craft the colour of ivory slowly made its way. It would usually have jumped from seemingly nowhere but instead it had made its way towards Judith at an unhurried pace. Its lungs were of a blue energy that pulsated as it turned back and forth to scan the area. It then pitched towards Judith as it came to hover steadily twenty feet above the ground.

'Grab this,' Judith said, referring to the casket. 'I need you to take me south to the camp of survivors along the six canyon divide.'

The craft made a grumbling noise and extended two long tentacles. One wrapped itself around the stasis unit that was in turn deposited inside a compartment in its undercarriage, while the other held on to Judith and placed her inside a hood that opened quickly as though a clam shell and closed again when she was seated inside. Inside the hood, Judith received three threads that injected themselves subdurally into her skull. She interfaced with the craft and saw what it saw as it moved south at great speed while ascending higher into the atmosphere. A message was sent to the crisis control camp to the south and Judith informed the craft that it should undertake a flyby of the entire area.

Judith saw through the craft's eyes: a strange, extra-dimensional version of reality so that the planet's surface became a more hyperbolic representation. Judith felt peculiar at this and requested the transformation of the visual into something she could comprehend. Prospect's surface came into view and the vast singular continent could be seen as an enormous expanse of mostly desert until the outer perimeter was reached. A thousand miles from the former Prospect city limits, now a smouldering crevice and running in one large vast circle around this epicentre, the last man-made jungle remained. From such a height the ring of green, as with most Integer-Project-inspired designs, was akin to a large target.

The dark blip that was the city still spewed blackness across the beige interim before the emerald divide and then outwards for another thousand miles across the arid planes until the indigenous life began to show up as a wild, unkempt and non-designed explosion. Deep forests of green and red, roaming hills with snow capped peaks. Unending lakes and shallows of water containing a world of coral and marine life that had yet to be catalogued; perhaps nothing had been lost after all.

Judith saw this spectacle of difference between three worlds colliding and felt that right now and at this moment, it was the only thing that held her sanity in place. She knew all too well how strange and difficult it had been to cross-exchange the flora and fauna between Earth and Prospect; names of planets and those who had come from one to invade another meant little to all that had evolved here. No one ever really owned anything and it was all just a perception, an illusion that had been found wanting by recent events. Judith had not just helped the people, she had spent many years helping all manner of life here in order to help adaptation as evolution was too slow. When all was said and done, nature would still thrive long after the demise of the human race on this world. Trees and birds, insects and so many other animals had been taken from Earth, introduced and managed, and would be a fair legacy.

The Prospect Empire was dead and along with it that famous and exulted department: the house of ecology. Vast pipework fed the human jungle from the oceans whose water had evaporated into humungous glass domes on the coast. The engineering had been tried and tested so many times with materials that would last for hundreds of years and by then it was hoped mankind's true legacy here would self-sustain.

Judith instructed the craft to head south towards the planet's equatorial plane and to the survivors of this catastrophe. Six billion people had died in an instant when the city and its surrounding districts, the size of a country such as Belgium, was wiped from existence in an instant. Not much remained yet there was no time to stop and there would be no time to grieve.

*

'Hina hates you because he's jealous, I think. You and he were the first two, and the rest of us came into existence much later. I mean you both went through the same ordeal, but then you had a father who loved you and had a life and, even though you messed up royally, it was still more than he had. And then there's the envy because you got picked to become an assassin which you also messed up. And then the last thing you did before you left Earth, Hina thought was some sort of masterpiece, a work of art perhaps.'

Ologun listened to Ray as they drove south in a truck taken from the garage five days earlier. Much of the conversation had come from Ray, who had insisted on coming along for the ride as he was sure he could change Ologun's mind.

'Yes well, you didn't have to fill my head with nonsense from one of those gel pads, I mean I didn't know anything and you took advantage,' Ologun said.

'What exactly do you consider to be lies?'

'I misread everything.'

'Like you're doing right now,' Ray said.

Ologun put the vehicle back on to cruise control and took his hands from the steering controls. He looked in the rear-view screen and saw the passenger in the back seat. What was going on exactly still eluded him as he looked her up and down.

Beneath the burka that Ray had given her, Ologun could see large cobalt eyes that had no eyelids and no pupils to indicate where or at whom she was looking. Others of her kind, the mysterious species of which he had killed many, and the reason he had lost over a lifetime stranded, had blue marble eyes and very white skin. Perhaps she was different in some way, or perhaps she was from another region on their home planet. As different as Ray was in skin colour and feature to Ologun, this thing was as different to the others, and of course exactly the same.

'I can't believe you brought her here.'

'No need to be rude, she is right here,' Ray insisted.

Ologun watched the road ahead and thought about things. He considered that she might be a weapon or maybe something else entirely, yet all he could really fathom was that the Spectra must have taken the fallen soldiers of the enemy and made this. All other facts regarding her were beyond him.

'They told you to bring her here,' Ologun said.

'Yes, once again, I was told to bring her here to Earth.'

'And they never said why?' Ologun quizzed him further.

'The Spectra doesn't speak to you in a usual sense of the word, it's very difficult to grasp what they mean at times. Like for instance, the week before the enemy arrived, I was told that something was likely to happen, yet I had no idea what except that it might be bad, and so I tried to tell the captain, that Frank, to leave. All I knew was that the Spectra imparted dread to me.'

Ologun looked at her one more time. She was tall and slender and yet much smaller than the ones who had attacked the basin. By all accounts Ologun had at first presumed that it was because she was female. It turned out that all that were killed in the basin were female.

'The leader of the militia army is Colonel Lou Armistead,' Ologun said, changing the subject. 'He's ex-Algerian Special Forces, trained by the French, and spent the past ten years working for them. Someone from an American firm paid him a vast amount of money for this operation of his and he didn't go straight for the capital, so I'm thinking it's absolutely not political or ideological in the usual sense. This is a distraction. Anyway, the reports from inside the country are confusing. This terrorist group initially attacked several towns and then disappeared so I'm hoping they've stopped. Still, whatever's going on, this army or whatever hasn't hit the capital.'

'Yes, I'm sure,' Ray sighed, tilting his seat back. He watched the world go by at speed and was happy to travel and to observe. Fields of digital lenses that were bright orange in the midday sun whipped by and were replaced by town on village, and mostly forest filled the interim. The whole continent seemed frozen as though the world was holding its breath. There were few people to be seen and the roads were empty apart from the odd vehicle headed north; no one was headed south.

The travel arrangements so far had been an odd affair and Ray had been impressed by Ologun's resourcefulness, even though Ray hoped the fool would fail to get so far so quickly. Ologun seemed to have become quite the thief and kept hacking major corporations for loot. He had in fact in the past few days paid for some contact that he had made, a woman named Nova, to meet them at Oujda airport in Bouarfa.

Ologun had already bought an old British Hercules Reincarnate class mark eight for the woman to fly, although it turned out she could not fly the behemoth at all. Still, she had clearances for air space intrusion from essential contacts in order to fly the plane south and to Tanout in Niger. Ologun had flown the plane in the end and had instructed her in the process. He had done this by hacking her mind and instilling the information that he had learned from acquiring quite an expensive passive-induced training programme. They could have landed at an airport yet Ologun, being a bit insane and full of better ideas, insisted on a T-load drop inside the truck that would be attached to a heavy duty parachute from ten thousand feet.

It transpired that Ologun was better at reading Ray than the other way round. Ray had screamed the whole way down to the ground while the alien he had in his charge seemed unbothered, which had amused Ologun and embarrassed Ray. Luckily Nova was happy to do anything for assistance for her charity organisation and had a new plane for her troubles. Nova had not noticed the seven-foot woman in a black burka as anything unusual, yet then again they were not in France or Italy where such a thing was not allowed. Nova was mainly concerned with her charity work and heavily involved in some aid organisation called the International Red Cross, and had really done this whole trip on the basis of transporting aid to those in dire need. Right now the truck had crossed a huge distance and was close to the northern border of Nigeria and south of Maradi, which made Ray nervous.

'So the main objective with all of this, is getting to Abuja before the drones. Have you seen these things, Ray?'

'Not sure I have, no, not interested. You need to drop us off before you cross the border.'

'I'm not entirely sure what these drones are as they all have numbers and for some reason when I search the Net I can't find any visual references to many of the drone types. Maybe there's some extra level of classification I can't hack, and I can't seem to find anything from Creed's scan and none of it makes any sense to me,' Ologun continued. 'If we can cross this border in good time it puts us equidistant I think, as the army has just taken Lagos. Shit, Ray, I hope the Republican Army can hold them off before we get there, I mean it's all we can do.' Ologun shook his head and tried to banish the reality of the situation and the potential horror of what might be encountered.

'What's with the "we" business?' Ray said. 'We're getting off this merry-go-round of yours as soon as we hit the border . . . and I'm taking this truck so I suggest for the millionth time that you listen to me.'

A road blockade appeared in the distance where the army were deterring anyone from going any further.

'I can't believe you're still going,' Ray said, annoying Ologun who had heard hardly anything else from Ray the whole journey. 'No wonder Hina had the Spectra hold off freezing Deceiver until you arrived.'

'He did what?'

'Well, it was part of the deal anyway so that mining for minerals became easier, sort of killing two birds with one . . .'

'Are you out of your mind, Ray? Thousands died, too many people have died so far and all you ever do is talk about it as though it were some average deal like the weather or buying a pair of socks.' Ologun stopped the vehicle and got out of the truck. 'Wait here,' he instructed Ray and made his way to the soldiers standing by their large trucks, blocking the road.

Ray watched as Ologun was shot due to ignoring the soldier's orders, and in some amusement as Ologun got back up and rendered all of the soldiers unconscious. Ologun checked the soldiers, holding up a soldier's leg here and another soldier's leg there until he found what he wanted and stole a pair of boots. Running back to the truck, he threw the boots in the back seat next to the alien woman and then ran back over to the soldiers.

He picked them up one at a time and loaded them into one of the trucks until they were off the road. He then jumped into the driver's side of the truck that blocked the road before jumping out again in order to enter the rear of the truck where he had placed the soldiers, subsequently re-appearing from behind the truck holding an ignition key. He smiled at Ray, giving a thumbs up. Ray rolled his eyes and sighed at the buffoonery as Ologun finally moved the army vehicle out of the way. Ologun eventually got back in the vehicle, sat next to Ray, and started the engine.

'Why didn't you just drive us off the road and around the road block?' Ray asked.

Ologun took the controls in his hands and the vehicle sped on. 'Um, I see what you mean,' he said.

OUT OF CONTROL

They reached the border and Ologun stood by the truck looking at a great wall that divided Niger and Nigeria. For hundreds of miles in either direction this thirty-foot barrier had been built as a replacement for human security. It was constructed entirely of heavy stone, and along its top surface barbed wire and retractable turrets were installed every thirty feet. Carcasses of wild animals that had strayed too close were scattered on the dry sward. The vultures who had joined them, unable to resist such an abundant opportunity, also lay at the bottom of the wall.

Ologun went to the truck and retrieved a piece of rubbish from the trunk. He walked to where he believed the perimeter range of the weapons would be and threw garbage into the air and towards the wall. At remarkable speed, one of the turrets sprang to life from beneath a metal hood and shot at the flying fabric, blowing it to smithereens.

'I can sort this problem out for you,' Ray said.

'No, I got this.'

'Yes, but can you do this?' Ray offered and rolled up the sleeve of his shirt. He raised his right hand and it began to twitch and pulsate and contort in a hideous fashion. The fingers fused and the hand became elongated until it had morphed into a phallic shape.

'Christ, Ray, what did you have in mind?'

'Watch this,' Ray said, boastfully, and aimed the tip of his mutated hand at the gun on the wall. The skin on the limb began to pulse with light from beneath the surface, then rushed in random bursts to the tip until suddenly a burst of white energy exploded and hit the gun, annihilating it completely. Ray doubled over and held his arm in pain. Where his hand had been was now a mess of flesh that had been ripped to shreds.

'Well that's great, Ray, maybe next time you should attach one of those to your head.'

'Teething problems,' Ray said and relaxed as his hand grew back.

'All right, big shot, watch this,' Ologun said and walked thirty feet to where the next embattlement was. He focused and watched the gun, then made a gesture at which the air a few feet in front of the wall compressed and moved. The gun launched into an attack and fired in all directions at nothing. Then Ologun used his ability to smack a chunk out of the wall next to it. Having missed he tried again and on this attempt ripped the turret clean off the wall where it flew backwards and out of sight.

'What was that?' Ray asked.

'Just a little something I learned over the years.'

'Really, well you need to practice more.'

'Better than your dick gun, Ray.' Ologun grinned, then his expression changed to concern as he heard something moving in the distance high above. He should not have been able to hear it at all and what approached was almost impossible for the human eye to see. 'Ray, we need to get to cover, get her to cover.'

Ray and Ologun rushed to the truck. Ray held his hand out to the alien and she stepped down from the vehicle. 'Come on!' Ray shouted to Ologun. Weapon fire rained down from above and Ologun saw a drone flying around as a small speck growing larger as it approached.

'Get behind the vehicle!' Ray shouted as bullets hit the grass floor, churning up reddish dirt. Ray peered from behind the side of the truck and saw Ologun on his back. 'I told you, I told you!'

'The rounds would have passed through and killed her, Ray, unless she's like us, is she?'

'No,' Ray said and noticed the wounds on Ologun's chest and legs healing as he sat up.

'It's coming back so stay there, Ray, it's got a thing for me now, I can tell.'

'Of course,' Ray said without any intention of moving. This time, however, the drone flew closer and fired a missile that hit Ologun. The projectile exploded and threw Ologun within range of the border wall's defences. A turret gun then released from under its hood and fired at him relentlessly as he lay there as a bloody, mashed-up pulp of mess. The drone returned and fired another missile and this time blew Ologun through the wall to the other side. Ray squeezed the alien's hand and looked at her. 'Don't worry, it is all part of the plan.'

Ologun was now running across the grass. 'Get in the damned truck, Ray!'

Ray pulled the alien into the truck and she sat down on the back seat. Ray got in the driver's seat and saw Ologun trip over, only to hit his head on the truck's bumper. He got up and leapt to get into the driver's seat. 'Move over.'

'No!' Ray yelled. Ologun shunted Ray out of the way with great force and sat down. 'There's three of them up there, we have to go.' He drove the truck erratically and managed to steer the vehicle through the hole in the wall made by the drone.

'Idiot!' Ray shouted. 'We can't come here with you!'

Ologun kept driving at speed and headed over more grassland. The truck hit a banking and jolted wildly. It sped up and over the bank and down the other side towards a road that ran parallel. Ologun could see what he took to be a mountain straight ahead and he hoped they might find the cover of trees. Soon the truck reached the jungle where Ologun was unsure whether the canopy of trees covering the road would mask them from the flying machines.

'Turn the truck around! Turn the truck around! Turn the truck around!' Ray continued to shout hysterically.

'Shut up, Ray, shut up, shut up. *Shut up!*'

An explosion knocked the truck sideways and Ologun managed to regain control. He then noticed in his rear-view screen that more machines – land drones – were on their tail.

'That's great,' Ray said. 'What now?'

'Are you bullet-proof yet?' Ologun asked.

'No.'

'Well stick your head out the window then!'

The land drones were four-legged machines similar to headless horses that galloped after them in a nightmarish stampede of metal, mimicking the real thing. 'We need to cover her in second skin now!' Ologun shouted. One of the land drones opened fire and hit the truck, blowing a hole in the fabric of the rear window.

'I don't know what you mean,' Ray said.

Ologun released many threads of skin that formed into a thick blanket to cover the alien woman. 'What the hell is this, how the . . . ?' Ray asked in disbelief.

'Get down,' Ologun ordered the woman.

A fork in the road appeared. 'Turn right,' Ray shouted, punching Ologun in the shoulder several times.

Ologun did as he was told and turned right.

'What the hell are you doing? I said right!'

'This is right!' Ologun shouted as Ray slapped him across the head.

'Not that right, the other one!'

'Get off me, Ray, get off me!'

The road rose in a steady incline that began to spiral around the side of the mountain. Ologun looked in the rear-view screen and saw that the land drones were closing in again. He then saw a quick flash of another drone as it flew at an angle to gain a better aim.

One of the land drones galloped up next to Ologun and turned a machine gun from its right shoulder to aim at him. It opened fire and shot him in the face repeatedly, making his head bounce around. *I can't drive like this!* Ologun produced more arms of second skin that began to wrap around the drone's torso. He held on tight to the controls and yanked them to his right, pulling the drone off its legs. The machine stumbled and fell front over end and tripped up four of the five remaining drones that galloped in close pursuit.

The truck surged forward, onwards and upwards and Ologun finally realised what this place was. They passed the canopy of trees now beneath them to the left, and the world around them came into view. As the truck climbed higher the forest below began to shrink into the distance.

Man-made mountain! 'Oh no,' Ologun said to Ray.

'I know, you moron.'

One of the flying machines continued to fire at the truck that was now sustaining severe damage. Behind them and on the back seat of the truck, the alien was still covered and being protected within second skin that had formed around her as a blackened chrysalis. On top of this and behind the cocoon of flesh, the bullet heads had mounted up into a pile.

A land drone was now at Ologun's side and was yet again trying to fire at him. He yanked the truck into the thing and smashed it off the side of the road where it fell away into the distant canopy below.

The truck reached the summit and broke through a metal mesh gate as all four wheels left the ground. The vehicle hit hard and bounced around until it landed on a level, smooth concrete surface. Ologun pressed the brakes which seemed sluggish and unresponsive. When the truck eventually stopped Ologun got out and ran to the back. He knelt down as the remaining horse drones stampeded through the same gateway after the truck. He made a gesture with his mind and, as the machines advanced, they crashed heavily into an invisible wall with such force that one of them flew up and over into the air and splash-landed into the deep waters of a reservoir.

Ologun stood up, satisfied by the crumpled mess of destruction of land drones, and turned his attention to the sky. In the distance he could see three specks regrouping and heading their way. Ologun rushed to the truck and sat in the driver seat. 'We need to get out of here.'

'No shit, you cretin.'

Ologun pressed the ignition and found that the engine would not start.

'Great,' Ray said. 'Why did you switch it off?'

'I didn't, it stalled.' Ologun tried again and again and could see the drones coming closer.

'Why did you bring us here?' Ray demanded.

Ologun quickly looked around for options. To his right was the front end of the reservoir and in front of that was the massive horizon of a man-made structure: a dam wall. It was a drifter damn which brought back memories of childhood where the odd dare might prove fatal. The kids used to bring all sorts of objects to ride the anterior face of the dam wall, or should it be said the first thousand feet that sloped off at a sixty degree angle. At that point there were slipways that ran at intervals and into small pools of water where the fun slide should end, and failing that there was a wall with gaps along it that lead to an ever-increasing decline until it reached a vertical drop off.

Ologun tried the engine over and over but it was too late as the drones in the sky were almost on them. Ologun got out of the truck and ran to its rear. He began pushing the vehicle across the concrete flat behind the dam wall and towards its edge. He grinned to himself, for nothing good had ever happened to him at one of these places.

'What the hell are you doing?' Ray shouted.

'We can outrun them this way.'

'What, down there, down the front of a dam?' Ray screamed.

Ologun jumped back into the driver seat and used his special skill to knock gently at the back of the truck.

'Release her from your skin,' Ray demanded. 'We're getting out.'

'No,' Ologun said and knocked the truck again.

The truck teetered and rocked and Ray felt giddy looking across the concrete expanse that went downwards and into oblivion. 'If you think . . .'

An explosion hit the ground next to the truck, tearing the roof off and shunting the vehicle forward. Ray was wounded and had a piece of shrapnel in his head. He slumped forward against the dash and was temporarily quite dead. The truck was now rolling slowly down the face of the dam as it became steeper. Ologun pulled the shrapnel from Ray's skull and sat back, getting ready.

Ray's deep wound healed within only half a minute; he gasped loudly, jolted upright, looked around and took a few seconds more for reality to hit his senses. 'What's happening?' he said and looked at Ologun in confusion.

Ologun turned to him and grinned. 'Hold on to your underpants, Ray,' he said, and his eyes flashed green as he winked.

The truck's pace increased steadily and Ray jumped on Ologun while trying to hit the brake with his foot. The truck slowed and Ray sighed with relief only for a clunking sound from somewhere at the front of the vehicle to send him into a further panic as the brakes failed.

'You're going to get us killed, she can't survive this, you bastard. Let her go!' Ray yelled, punching Ologun in the face over and over.

The truck accelerated as it rolled down the dam surface. Two drones appeared at their flank and both fired a sustained burst from their heavy machine guns.

'Good news, Ray, they ran out of rockets.'

The truck sped on faster and began to slide sideways out of control. 'Fire your dick hand at them, Ray.'

The truck then slid around until it was facing backwards. 'Hit them with that thing you do,' Ray said, configuring his right hand. He held it out and waited for a drone to come within range, then fired bolt after bolt of energy.

Ologun yanked the controls and fought to get the truck facing forwards. As it spun round, the vehicle nearly flipped over and Ologun made a barrier to smack it back down hard into the concrete plane. The truck now faced forward and was racing towards a filtration wall that ran horizontally across the face of the dam. 'Use it to stop us, please!' Ray begged.

'No!' Ologun shouted.

Ray continued to fire his weapon over and over and began to feel dizzy and slumped. The door to the truck on his side flew open and Ologun grabbed him just before he fell out. Machine gun fire hit the cockpit of the vehicle and smashed the dials.

Ologun lost control and the truck spun around and around as it descended. He grabbed Ray by the ankle, who was now hanging with his body halfway out the vehicle as his head slid across the wet concrete of the dam surface. Ologun flinched as he saw the chicane was fast approaching. He tried to concentrate on several things at once as the truck spun around. Ologun was stressed and knew he had to get this next bit right.

He made a compressed field of atoms so that they created a solid surface up and over the divide. The truck slid at tremendous speed and half-missed its mark. It slid up the invisible ramp and flipped over while travelling through the air. Ray fell out of the truck altogether and Ologun hung on to the steering rods. The truck crashed on to its wheels and bounced several times before it continued onwards down the slope.

Ologun crashed down on the bonnet and used his second skin to drag himself back over and into the driving seat. He searched for Ray but the speed he was travelling at made it difficult to see anything. Ahead and only a thousand feet away, the dam wall stopped being a slight decline and was about to become a sheer drop. Ologun braced himself yet again as the truck arrived at the junction at colossal speed. The truck flew over the edge of the cliff and at quite a distance away from the face of the dam and then fell. Ologun held on to the steering controls once again as his legs flew up and behind him, followed closely by the alien who was still cocooned and being dragged through the air.

Around him and now in some strange tranquil moment, he saw the world open up with a sea of green below him. Tree tops could be seen for miles and the sky was a glorious blue, while behind him the massive surface of the dam wall seemed to be the face of Earth itself and it was as though he was falling in the wrong direction over it rather than towards it. It then occurred to Ologun just as he hit terminal velocity that he had a simple solution.

He let go of the truck and released eight strands of skin from either side of his body that moved upwards in order to meet in vast loops above him. The skin then flattened out and caught the air to become a multi-ribboned parachute. *Genius!*

The sudden force of slowing yanked Ologun hard and the cocoon flew past at speed causing a further violent yank that hurt Ologun's lower back, knees and ankles. He floated down in front of the face of the dam as a peaceful and slow atmosphere presented itself. The drones flew by and had seemingly run out of ammunition as they failed to fire at him, while the alien woman cocooned in a large sack swayed gently as she hung several feet beneath him. A crashing sound indicated that the truck had hit the jungle canopy. A loud scream that whizzed by at speed indicated that Ray was about to do the same.

*

A shuttle entered a small chamber and hangar doors closed behind it. The chamber was pressurized and two large doors at the front of the shuttle opened. The shuttle was brought forward into a vast room where many types of flight craft designed for either vacuum or atmospheric combat sat in long rows at either side.

Hina exited a shuttle craft on the flight deck of the *Ryu Yo*. He walked the distance to the flight control room at the anterior of the hall where he was met by Hershal. 'Where have you been?'

Hina grinned and carried on past his brother and down a long corridor.

'You think this is funny?' Hershal said with anger.

'You failed to find me didn't you?' Hina said, walking off.

'I'm talking to you, where have you been?'

Hina stopped to face Hershal. 'I was trying out some new tricks, a sort of stealth test to see if you could find me.'

'Hide and seek! You spent eight hours playing hide and seek,' Hershal said, raising his voice. 'I don't know what kind of excrement that excuse is, but I don't believe you.'

'We all have our secrets and we all have our lies,' Hina offered with a dead-eyed stare. He turned around and began to walk away.

'Funny how the tracking beacons on board the commandeered ships suddenly came online ten minutes ago,' Hershal shouted after him. 'You need to come with me now . . . Hina!'

'My name is pronounced Hi-ena, three syllables.'

'Maybe then you should have learned how to spell.'

Hina walked up to his brother and came nose to nose with him. 'At which point did I ever write what my name was or indeed at which point did I say it in all these years? You think that that craft Creed actually called itself, Creed? These things are gestures in the dialect of the mind that are translated to the likes of you as hopeless horoscopes where you apply your own pathetic presumptions.'

'You smell like blood,' Hershal hissed.

'You smell like fear,' Hina replied.

The two of them stood staring at each other for quite a while as though things would get ugly. In the dimness of the flight deck and reaching up to its ceiling a hundred feet above, a static charge was building.

'Enough!' Hershal ordered. 'You need to come with me, you want something to do, then you need to see this.'

Hina stood back, intrigued. Hershal walked off down the passageway and entered a lift at a junction that led off in three other directions. Hina followed until they were at the mid-deck of the ship.

They disembarked and found themselves on yet another similar corridor except that this time the walls were of a different design with handles on a rail and where there was a standing platform. The two climbed on to the corridor wall platforms and held on to the handles. Immediately the platform began to move at speed and down the passage until it arrived at another junction. They both got off the conveyor and stood outside what was referred to as the B-plus room. Hershal entered a code on the vault door to the room and pushed its heavy plated bulk inwards to reveal what looked like another bridge to the ship. It was a circular room with consoles and flat screens in a large formation the full circumference of the singular surrounding wall.

Hershal keyed in a few commands on one of the consoles and the adjacent screens switched on to reveal the universe around them. Then, as Hina looked at the 360 degree image, he saw something that was far enough away from the ship to make out but not near enough to identify.

Hershal typed in yet more commands and adjusted the imaging so that the object became clearer. Hina's mind processed the image and he took a step back.

'I know,' Hershal said. 'These things came with our craft just under an hour ago.'

'They are . . .'

'The human ships that were sent to Deceiver over two hundred years ago.'

'Our parents,' Hina said softly as he watched eleven ships of colossal size hang motionless in the vacuum. The *Ryu Yo* and even the newer bombardment class of ships were massive, and yet these things were larger. Hina liked them for they were not just uninspiring long, rectangular shapes; to him they were like stingrays or at least something better with more curvature and had an intimidating vibe.

'The Spectra sent us these in order to create better numbers. The craft have relayed that something is coming, something they called the Almagest Intersection,' Hershal said.

'Intersection.' Hina nodded as though he understood.

Hershal typed in something else and the surrounding screen

became an elongated representation of the Milky Way. 'Here,' Hershal said, pointing. 'There's Earth, then eight light years to your right is Deceiver, well beyond that still is Prospect. All other markers are colonies that are either abandoned or have been marked for future interest.' He typed again on the console and the screen moved in to a navigation marker.

'This is buoy three-six-five-three-six-seven-three. It sits eighteen light years from Earth . . .'

'What did it find?' Hina asked, impatient.

Hershal looked around the room, wondering how to articulate the answer. 'I think you know what I'm going to say.'

Hina watched as the screen marker pulsed a red blip over and over. It had done what it was designed for and would activate for only one particular find, one kind of movement. It had kept surveillance of an entire solar system for over seventy years, camouflaged as a lonesome bit of rock. Now the thing had spotted and identified that for which it was designed; the enemy had finally returned.

*

The old admiral watched from an elevated position as the crowds below assembled in very long queues that felt slow and fraught. These people were waiting to be given food and water rations, blankets and a reference number. The woman that had retired in this district, who had been in charge of an entire fleet at one stage, felt a sharp pain shoot through her body. 'Are you all right, Admiral?' a voice came from behind her.

'I'm fine.' She checked a pad she held for information as it was transmitted. So far nearly fifteen thousand people had made it to this location and things were becoming difficult. *I need you, come on!*

Beyond the queues and the rest of the crowd, beyond the tanks and trucks that acted as barricades, was an endless sea of vehicles as far and wide as the Admiral's eyes could see. The injured and the elderly, the young and the lucky had responded to the beacon of this camp and would now have to be managed and they would have to be saved. The combat hospital unit vehicles to the east and five thousand metres away at the edge of this camp had become overwhelmed hours ago and things were getting worse. Supplies were running low and it was hoped that two possible solutions could be found before things got out of hand, for there were not enough military personnel left to control a crowd of this magnitude if things turned bad.

'Admiral Langmead,' a voice said.

The woman turned to see a young man in full frontier combat gear had climbed the stairs on to the platform where she stood. They were on a vehicle, a tank known as a sloth block vehicle, which was a huge beast of a machine with wheels three times the height of a man and whose top deck stood thirty feet above ground level. Langmead acknowledged the man and made her way down to the open-cast control room on the bottom floor of the tank. 'I need a sit-rep . . . Sergeant?'

'Sergeant James,' the man said, following her and she turned to glance at him.

'I know very well who you are.'

'Right,' Sergeant James said. 'The engineering crew cut a track through the ring of forest and laid a bridge mesh the way through, although I checked the satellite feed and the thermals indicate there aren't many more survivors. We set up a transmission on a loop to let them know to come that way.'

'Very well, Sergeant James, and well done. A hundred miles in less than thirty six hours is excellent,' Langmead said of the endeavour. 'We will most likely need it for the future so congratulate the engineers for me.' Langmead sat down on a vacant chair in front of a set of control consoles fixed in a rectangular formation on the deck. 'We have over three million survivors on the frontier and a million more a few thousand miles south within the province of new Shaanxi and the Amoonguna wetlands five hundred miles east. We need to think long term and begin collecting genetic samples from everyone down there.'

'Excuse me, Admiral?'

'I'll need to relinquish command to someone soon and you are the best option I can see, having checked a few files.'

'I'm not even an officer, ma'am . . .'

'Listen to me, Sergeant, we are now in a very difficult position and are as a nation on the brink. The people that have retired or are on holiday down south are not going to repopulate this world.'

'Why would you say that?' the sergeant said.

'Everything is gone,' Langmead said and checked the surveillance feed that watched the crowd thirty metres away in front of the tank. They seemed passive enough, yet the din of many voices was becoming louder. 'No more city, no more hub, and no more life span treatments. It's like a karma that has hit this world, son, and a further half million will be dead in the next week simply because they were meant to be dead years ago. Get samples and we can use the genetic code variables to keep things going, to repopulate from a wider range of stock.'

Sergeant James was horrified and dismayed at the Admiral's attitude to all of this but simply nodded in compliance.

The Admiral stood up and made her way to the stairs to climb back up and see the crowd from the top deck. She then turned quickly to view the monitor on the console as noise from the crowd erupted. Gunfire was heard from outside the tank and soldiers began firing into the air as the crowd began to bunch up and grow hostile.

'Close the rear shield door,' Langmead instructed and decided to remain where she was to monitor them on the screen rather than risk being out in the open. People were now kicking and punching or running away to find cover as the mass of people started to riot. The screen the Admiral was watching changed its visual representation into a tactical analysis of the crowd.

Gaps appeared as people spread out, moving around in patterns back and forth this way and that in order to attack and retreat. Watching it on the visual representation was almost like watching a flock of starlings darting and weaving through the open sky. The soldiers had deserted their posts at the supply banks and had found protection in various armoured vehicles close by. People pillaged and ran, threw anything at hand all over the place and at each other, and at the military vehicles where the sound of pelting could be heard from within the sloth block tank as the pinging sound of metal echoed around the interior on all decks. Langmead watched the screen as many people now lay in the dirt, bloodied and still. *Where are you?*

The gunfire had increased as this had now become a fully blown and savage riot; people were now trying to kill each other. The Admiral closed her eyes and desperately hoped for the element of surprise and the fear of God to stop this madness in its tracks.

'We need to do something, open fire above their heads, anything,' Sergeant James insisted.

Then, and as things seemed to be beyond salvation, a number of screams prompted by a certain kind of sheer terror sounded in the distance and became louder and louder that became a synchronised harmony. *You made it!*

With the wave of increasing sound, the crowd changed the rhythm of movement from that of riot to that of cowering or fleeing. Langmead made her way to the top deck and was greeted by a scene that took her breath away and frightened her to the core. There, only twenty metres above the fleeing crowd, hovered a massive craft with an enormous wing span. Its bone-coloured marble glistened in the fading daylight and its engines beneath its wings flashed and flickered a brilliant neon blue like that of a police vehicle. It honked a deafening sound as it spun slowly around as though searching for something or someone. Some idiots were firing weapons at the abomination from behind parked cars and other hidden positions. The craft spotted them and released a spark that sent a mild electric shock to each and every hostile, rendering some of them soiled and all of them unconscious.

The Admiral knew what it was and felt a mixture relief and consternation. She quickly made her way down the stairs and pressed a button for an emergency opening of the doors to the rear of the sloth block. Langmead jogged down a ramp and around to her left to see Judith Gibson standing there waiting for her.

'Sam.' Judith nodded.

'Judith,' Sam Langmead replied.

'I thought you retired.'

'A week ago,' Sam said with a hint of sarcasm.

'I have your son with me.'

'Thank you, Judith. Tell your machine to place the cryogenic pod to the rear of the sloth unit.' Sam then turned to Sergeant James who had taken up a tactical position near to her. 'The ship will lower the casket to the ground and I want you and a few others to take the stasis unit on to the tank, is that understood?'

The sergeant was obviously afraid as he stared at the thing hovering above them. 'Yes ma'am.' Judith watched as Sergeant James ran off, the craft following above while it, too, watched him.

'We need to talk urgently,' Sam said and began making her way back to the sloth tank. Several men struggled as Sergeant James barked orders. Judith walked right up behind the casket, slanted it up at an angle on its wheels and pushed it all the way up the ramp. She laid it to rest within the confines of the lower deck of the tank. The soldiers looked on in astonishment as Sam peered in through the frosted glass of the stasis bed. 'Who's the woman?'

'Your son got himself a girlfriend.'

'I thought he had a boyfriend.'

'No, that was his best friend, Glynn is straight.'

'Really?' Sam said with surprise. 'James, this is my son, Glynn Langmead.'

'Sharplin,' Judith interjected. 'He took your maiden name.'

The Admiral nodded and understood even though when they last met, when they met Hershal, Glynn had used Langmead as his last name; perhaps he had lied to avoid offending her. 'Leave them both in the chamber, it will be safer for now. Come with me, Judith, if you please.'

Judith followed the woman up some metal grid stairs to the second floor and into a small office at the anterior section of the tank. Judith closed the door behind her as Sam took a seat behind the desk. 'What happened, Judith?'

'I'm not sure, you're best off asking Glynn.'

'How did he survive, was it you?'

'No, the little blighter somehow got himself to safety. Listen, from what I can ascertain, your son helped General Feng upload his mind into the Version system. Obviously it didn't go well.'

Sam placed her elbows on the desk and her face into her hands as though hiding from this news. She then sat back and sighed heavily. 'How are you, Judith?'

'I don't know. I think it will all catch up with me soon and I can't face all of this right now.'

'We're too old for all this,' Sam said in sympathy.

'I've still got it,' Judith quipped with a strange emptiness to her tone.

'Nonetheless, you spent so long being a nurse to so many I have to ask you, are you combat efficient? Can you fight?'

'Yes.'

'Then we need to crack on. Two thousand miles south and to the eastern province of Olonge, there's a valley that has been digitally camouflaged to house thirty five varying type combat ships in hibernation.'

'Hibernation?' Judith asked.

Asaronite is an element that shouldn't be here in our reality, Judith, it belongs in another universe. Any hulls made of the substance have been dissipating, evaporating very slowly. Radiation brought on solar winds has, after so many years, placed the ships in a state of decay. The only way to stop this reaction is to hide them in complete darkness, although no one has yet concluded whether this actually stops this process, due to other forms of radiation.'

Judith nodded, fascinated. 'What do you want of me?'

'I need you to take that warship of yours and a handful of soldiers to the location and secure the ships. There is no indication where the army of Version went, they left the solar system and there has been no sign since. We need to make sure, in case some were left behind, that they do not acquire any more of our ships. Also, we need to utilise these ships for everything from hydroponic farming to defence of the survivors. I'm proposing that maybe ten to fifteen ships land to provide room and shelter and the rest go into orbit in order to act as defence. There are other options, another classified facility is available, but I need to think about it first. One step at a time.'

'When do you want me to leave?'

'Immediately.'

SAVAGE

Ologun sat on a large boulder as the river from the bottom of the dam roared past. He glanced at the truck in the distance, wrecked and marooned on a tree top. He shook his head. 'We're screwed.'

'You mean you are,' Ray said, and once again checked the alien woman for injuries and general well-being. She was sitting beneath a nearby tree. 'Are you okay, did he scare you?'

'It's not a dog, Ray,' Ologun scoffed at Ray's tone.

'Her name is Amina,' Ray spat back.

'Since when, and what kind of name is that anyway?'

'You really are an ignorant beast aren't you? Amina was once a legendary princess warrior of Nigeria. The name means truthful and trustworthy.'

'Well, I stand educated.' Ologun smiled. 'It's a good name, but I hope for all our sakes that the name doesn't become some sort of irony.'

'Irony?' Ray asked.

'Her being here disturbs me. She might be the opposite or represent the opposite of the name you just gave her.' Ologun stood and jumped down from the rock. He thought about how he could get to the capital in time to stop the terrorists.

Ologun flinched as one of the alien craft, a tan-coloured one that he remembered belonged to Ray, appeared above the river. It hovered and whipped the area into a frenzy of movement as trees swayed and leaves were blown around. The river frothed in expanding circles beneath the behemoth as it pointed itself towards Ray as if waiting for instructions. 'We're leaving now.'

'Wait, I need a lift south,' Ologun stated.

'How about you go for a long walk and think about your actions.'

The craft extended two large tentacles and grabbed Amina and Ray. It gently lifted them up towards the hood on its back.

'Wait!' Ologun shouted. 'You can't just leave.' He watched and

163

waited. The craft turned and pointed to the sky, then was gone in the blink of an eye.

Ologun was fuming and clenched his fists. He also felt desperate and began to search the mainframe for an idea. *I can't do this on my own!* He frantically went through ways to get in touch with Creed. He found a laser dish situated in South America that belonged to an organisation called S.E.T.I. and made the machine disperse a message on a specific and wide band width that would cover most of the solar system. Ologun waited impatiently. *Come on!* As before, and a good half-hour later, a craft appeared above the river sending the wilderness into chaos. This time the craft had a jet-black marble sheen that was larger and seemed more ferocious in its attitude. 'I need your help,' Ologun said to it. The craft grumbled and turned to leave.

'You're pathetic, Creed, you haven't practised in nearly a hundred years.'

The craft turned to face him. 'There's an army headed this way; they have machines that I don't think you can handle, I think it might be good practice for you. It is what you do isn't it, fight?' The craft made a sound that Ologun realised had translated into something unexpected. Creed was a name he had misunderstood for it did not reflect a set of beliefs but rather arrogance and superiority. The thing indicated that it was far too great to get involved.

'Afraid of the challenge?' Ologun taunted it. 'I'm saying that you can't destroy every one of those weapons of war while not killing a single human being, you can't aim for shit can you?'

The craft indicated that it could and that it would prove it.

Ologun smiled wickedly at manipulating the thing. 'Before you do, I need a lift . . . oh and I need to be prepared, so injure me a little.'

The craft tilted back and forth then fired a tentacle at Ologun. The harpoon smashed straight through Ologun's chest and opened up into a fan shape gripping into his back. The tentacle then swished around smashing Ologun into a tree then a rock, back and forth, up and down, beating him to a red pulp of mush. Ologun's body pulled itself back together until finally he sat up. He looked at the craft. 'I said injure me a little, you dumb shit!'

*

'Are you getting this?' Young ran through several rooms until he reached the operational room of the bunker. Natasha, Martin and the others were watching the main holographic monitor high up on the wall at the front of the room.

'Jesus Holy Christ!' Young blasphemed. The monitor showed an image sent from a satellite feed that showed the black craft akin to a hideous marine animal, or was it an insect? The thing had hovered at the foot of Apollo Dam on the north-west border of Nigeria and had flown south to the city of Abuja, stopped for a few minutes, then flown north towards Chad. Young tried his server chip to get hold of anyone for more information. He tried the comms box and every domain to get anyone above his rank to give him some clue as to what was happening.

'We have something!' Martin shouted to Young.

The colonel ran back to Martin's side and watched the monitor. 'Who else is watching?' Young asked.

'We have eight hundred addresses hooked up to the satellite, I'd say everyone in Washington, I mean anyone with clearance is watching this,' Martin said.

Young saw movement from the south as jets were launched from Kenya and flew north. Then more movement as jets were launched from Iran and Afghanistan.

'We have over eight hundred bogies closing in on Chad.'

Young watched as the mass of vehicles on the ground headed south over the border into Cameroon.

'We got Chinese, Russian and Iranian Jets closing in,' Martin informed the room. All of the staff at the base had gathered in silence as many angles and representations of these movements unfolded across large monitors hung on the anterior wall of the room. The middle screen zoomed in and focused on the alien craft. It hovered a few miles south of the American and European allied forces. Rows of hundreds of tanks and many other forms of land vehicles pushed south. In the sky above, over a thousand jets and heavy bomber planes moved in defensive patterns, and above these a mighty airship moved slowly as the convoy's ultimate firepower. A small drone jet broke the formation to head towards the alien, and came to a halt hovering directly in front of it at quite a short distance.

'I don't like this at all,' Young said.

The alien fired an energy bolt, destroying the drone. What happened next sent shivers down the colonel's spine as the craft attacked everything at once. It zipped back and forth, up and down while the projectiles of white heat it fired moved as though independent living entities.

Missiles and stampede fire from sixty calibre rounds found their mark and failed time and again to deter the thing. A laser blast from an orbiting weapons' platform hit it from above as an invisible force and still, the thing took the punishment as though nothing had happened at all. The room was silent and everyone watched. The atmosphere was thick with anxiety and Young could see that Martin was shaking like a leaf. Young placed a hand on his shoulder and continued to watch what he considered the end of the world unfolding.

The alien ship flew over the entire army of American and allied forces once again at great speed and then stopped. A pause that seemed to last an eternity ensued and then it opened fire, hitting the airship. One woman somewhere in the room screamed as others gasped. Young closed his eyes in terror as the screen showed an unbelievable display of force. Thousands of energy bolts streaked the sky as they were released by this creature of utter destruction. Jet after jet, drone after drone, bomber planes and heavy artillery planes were hit and fell from the sky. The craft then changed angle and strafed the military below. Tanks, trucks, land drones; everything was pounded by varying types of alien weaponry whose energy wriggled or flipped end over end and moved as though conscious, changing direction mid-flow, searching and destroying everything in its path.

The Chinese, Russians, Iranians, North Korea, and Afghanistan fighter jets arrived en masse. Thousands of jets began attacking the now immobilised troops on the ground. Then something else happened. The alien craft took exception to this attack and released an even more intense bombardment on the incoming jets. The sky and the ground below spewed black smoke as the carnage intensified.

A swarm of glowing balls had erupted from the alien vessel as it hovered so that now drones and fighter jets alike fell from the sky as though literally a metal storm.

They all watched as the craft hovered and turned from left to right as it presumably scanned the area. It was all over as thousands of parachutes descended like a shoal of jellyfish. The devastation was by now complete; there were no more jets in the sky and no more vehicles moving on the ground.

Martin looked up to his right and checked another satellite feed. A secure military imaging system followed the naval fleet as it approached the South African west coast. At two hundred miles distance from the navy's intended target, over a hundred ships turned starboard and in unison to go back the way they had come.

Flashes of gunfire erupted on the ground where the Allied forces had been destroyed. A maximum close-up showed that the pilots that had attacked – the Russians, the Chinese and their allied forces – had landed via parachute and were being shot at or rounded up.

'Thank God we only use avatar drones,' Martin said.

'Tell that to the families of the crew aboard the *Shadow Light*,' Young replied.

Young watched Martin as he manipulated the visuals of several recordings taken from various satellites. 'Why? It attacked us and then it attacked everyone else when they attacked us. I don't understand.'

Natasha stood in silence and was watching Young. He looked at her and she nodded. 'It's like it wants to or is trying to stop the fighting.'

An alarm sounded and Martin closed down the feed to the Pentagon. On the main monitor the recordings of the recent combat were replaced with a detailed map of Earth in a flat landscape perspective. 'No! No! No! No! This can't be happening!'

Colonel Young looked at the screen and then at the men and women stood watching the events unfold. *It's all over!*

There was little to say as the unthinkable happened. Russia fired its WMDs towards America, America retaliated against Russia. China fired on Japan and Australia, on Israel and on Germany. Soon everyone was releasing weapons against each other as a hundred lines across the digital map of the world moved in all directions. Submarines posted and hidden under oceans around the world fired their payloads as the inevitable holocaust unfolded. *Only minutes to go!* Young thought. What had all this been over? Hunting terrorists? *Why? Bullshit!* Something else was going on here, and whatever all this had been about, it was now all too late.

'Something's not right here,' Martin said. Young could not concentrate by now and instructed his neural chip to manage the chemical compositions entering his amygdala. Reducing cortisol by inhibiting the hypothalamus and the release of adrenalin, he slowly began to calm down.

'Everyone tone themselves down now!' Young shouted, seeing that Martin kept re-typing and missing keys on the pad he was using.

Natasha followed the early warning system closely on the front screen. 'He's right,' she said of Martin. 'Israel fired on Iran and the weapons should have detonated by now.'

'It's the same for Japan and China, France and Russia, Britain and Russia and Iraq. Our system just made us all shit ourselves for nothing.'

Young sighed with relief. 'Everyone go back to your posts, false alarm *to an extent!*'

The military staff slowly exited as ordered and chatted loudly as they made a move. 'Quiet,' Young ordered. The oddly subdued siren was switched off and the room was now silent.

Young saw that Douglas looked very pale and was mute as he sat on his own, halfway across the room. Violet just watched and made notes on a computer as if writing a report. Edmond shook his head and muttered to himself loudly while remaining fixated on the main monitor.

'I'm getting satellite recordings here that show real missile activity,' Martin said. He appeared to be a little dopey, having toned his mind down.

Young's stomach knotted. 'No, not again, tell me it's a false reading.'

'Relax,' Natasha said to Young. 'Something's gone on all right.

All the missiles were launched. None of them hit their target.'

'That's excellent,' Young said and was relieved for a second time. He reasoned that somehow, as with most countries, their air grid defence systems were much better than had been the general consensus. 'The anti-missile air grids did their job at least, thank God!'

'Oh I wouldn't relax too much just yet,' Martin said, utterly stupefied.

'Why what is it?' Young asked.

Natasha remained anxious as she explained to Young. 'It wasn't the air defence grids, not everyone has them, and somehow over eight hundred and thirty nuclear and anti-matter missiles have disappeared without trace.'

*

On top of a six-storey building Ologun crouched, carefully watching his surroundings. How does an army of two thousand manage to achieve such devastation? As he accessed weapons' tech information gathered by Creed on the initial scan of Earth, Ologun tried to piece together what he might be up against.

In the distance hundreds of blights of smouldering wreckages appeared where downed planes and various aeronautical drones had been shot down. They were either in open fields as plumes of smoke, or out of sight buried deep within the jungle; the old irrigation systems laced throughout the land still worked and doused any further chance of a rampant inferno.

Ologun turned to watch the street below. What he saw made no sense as such, for it appeared no one in this place had any idea of what was coming. Hundreds dead in the streets appeared to have fallen as though caught completely off guard. Police drones, little machines about the size of a man's head, lay destroyed and scattered throughout the streets.

They appeared to have been the first into battle and had been followed by the rest of the police force. Sometime later the army had arrived. All were dead and their machines destroyed which made Ologun nervous. Whoever did this had the organisation and the weapons to pull off one sophisticated hit-and-run operation of the type Ologun found difficult to comprehend. Warfare used to be fought via dropping bombs, firing laser-guided missiles or via insurgency; it appeared the days of bombarding a target and taking out as many as possible had been replaced by something even more exact.

This was a town like any other that smouldered as certain wildlife, vultures and ravens, picked at the dead. Drones of many types lay trashed amongst the carnage. Collapsed buildings and skeletons of vehicles lined the streets, and Ologun realised that the damage had been caused by the Nigerian Army in their desperation against a very advanced enemy.

Ologun dropped from the roof of the building and landed gracefully. He searched the rubble and the cyber network simultaneously. It was almost as though the answer had arrived at once from two sources. As he knelt down next to what he had found, it became apparent that he had misunderstood the identity code numbers given to drones. There were visual representations, three-dimensional images of what he thought were people, perhaps wearing or carrying something. The first thing that entered his mind was that Creed would feel duped, and he wondered how he had missed this.

Ologun was aware of many kinds of tech: air drones and land drones that were based on animals and birds, plus insect drones used for surveillance or spying. What had destroyed this country's own drone army and defence so efficiently? What could cut across a country so quickly in such a devastating way? Ologun stared at the thing lying wrecked on the ground and shook his head. Air drones had gone to war and could be perceived as the most lethal invention, yet the Nigerians had their own and fought back with some measure of success. What they did not have at their disposal was the next and most efficient killing machine: the human drone. It had without doubt been the deciding factor in the outcome of this conflict, for attached to these things were real people that had true ability as soldiers, as killers.

Ologun stood up and felt anxious. There was no more air support left for this army of terrorists, or rather mercenaries, to call on, which made things promising. The fact that nearly two thousand human drones, along with various other types of land drone and vehicle, were still headed east left Ologun feeling fearful. How, he asked himself, was he going to do this?

A sea of dead bodies surrounded him and it felt as though history was repeating itself and that he was always too late; Ologun knew he had to get ahead and stop this slaughter. Once Nigeria's capital was reached and destroyed, this army of mercenaries would head south for Cameroon and eventually the Congo and closer to where this army's true objective would be found.

There was something else, however, as Ologun saw something glisten on one of the dead bodies laid amongst the mass of other corpses. He walked over, knelt down and used a strand of second skin to check the bullet wound on a woman's forehead. The strand dug deep into the hole in her skull and found purchase on what Ologun assumed would be a bullet. He pulled the strand from the wound and with it was something quite surprising if not disturbing. The metal object was dropped into Ologun's hand so that he could begin checking it over. How could a few human drones accurately single tap hundreds of people in the shortest amount of time possible? How does not one single round stray and hit other objects when the opposition tore their own city apart in such utter pandemonium? Ologun searched for the answer on the network and felt even more overwhelmed. He now had in his hand a single unit of another terrible killing machine, the locust drone.

Ologun began pushing and pulling at its parts with fine strands of second skin until eventually he had put its wings together to form a sleek silver rhomboid. Ologun stood up, his head reeling at the sight. Apart from the obvious parallels, he realised that these things were designed to swarm en masse, to find a target and penetrate at a speed equivalent to that of a bullet from a gun.

Controlled by an eighth generation quantum computer, or a head as they were called, these things would never be wasted and would never miss. Ologun searched each wound on the next twenty bodies.

My God! The wounds were empty and it was realised that these things were recyclable and likely on their way to the next set of victims.

Ologun released strands of second skin to act as antennae as he walked the street searching for a digital frequency in the atmosphere. Something powerful, a wide bandwidth would allow information to move back and forth between the machines and their controllers. He saw a pattern and followed it in his mind. Stretched out and across the region a display could be fathomed.

Seven drones eight miles away were lagging behind as defence from any form of flank. Ahead of this to the east there was a small assault convoy, and ahead of this again he found the mass of drones making their way to the capital. Six hundred miles north of this position and held within the master convoy of large wagons moving east, he found the source signal controlling all of these drones.

Ologun cursed in desperation. This would be simple if he ever managed to think ahead. Destroying the trucks and containers that housed the human machine interface units would end this quickly. Instead he was stuck with the much harder option of pursuing and fighting the drones. He made an attempt to contact Creed. Nothing, no response. Maybe it was upset that it had been told to avoid killing anyone when in fact the invasion was comprised mainly if not entirely of machines. Maybe it was busy. Either way Ologun sought options and wanted to intercept the seven human drones that lagged behind the rest of the machine army.

He ran along the street disturbing the birds as they feasted. The smell of burning engulfed his senses as he sought a form of transport, and soon found a car showroom displaying expensive sports cars. Most were damaged but a few were intact and appeared ready to go. Ologun jumped into a particularly fierce-looking car with the engraved make and model Lord SI. It was uncoloured as of yet and shone a pristine metal. He started the engine and its electric drivers spun an impressive roar.

He drove the car erratically out through the shop's front window lens and up the street. It handled well enough as Ologun avoided the destroyed combat vehicles and other wreckage of debris. Driving over a street littered with corpses was disrespectful and disgusting; he could not waste any more time. Eventually Ologun reached an open highway leading east and pushed the vehicle hard. In as little as twenty minutes he reached the last location of the straggling human drones.

He stopped the car on the outskirts of another town with more death and destruction, disembarked and looked directly down the main street and saw that the people here had also been attacked as though out of the blue. *Simultaneous attacks,* Ologun guessed. They had posted teams of three to five human drones across every main town west of the capital. At the very same time each team had unleashed a locust swarm that quickly annihilated whole populations with little effort and extreme accuracy.

At this point Ologun decided that perhaps it was too late; Ray had been right and there would be no justice here. The Chinese had already amassed much of its remaining air force to the northern border of the Congo and were manoeuvring land assault assets into position via air-support ships. Meanwhile the South African Army had already assisted the Special Forces from various African nations to move the version pilots from Luanda all the way to Cape Town. The mercenaries were already finished and yet for some reason they kept heading east and kept on killing.

Ologun had to make a decision here and now. Either carry on and stop the carnage or turn his attention to a much bigger problem: the weapons-grade pandemic. He sat down and started the car's engine then turned it off. He turned it on again and sat there until he turned the engine off once more. He was so full of indecision over this that he repeated this action several times, argued with himself, and head-butted the steering column. At the very last minute Ologun changed his mind a final time. Creed had done the main body of work here and the rest was pointless. Right now the only conclusion that could be made was that this mission was over.

He turned the car around as he searched the network for airfields that might house a plane for him to take, when he noticed that on the ground next to him a vortex of leaves was dancing. It was mesmerising and caused Ologun to look around for a moment as the weather seemed to be changing; perhaps even a storm was brewing. The vortex continued for a bit longer than Ologun expected as it remained a miniature whirlwind of unnatural stability. His mind slowed reality and watched more carefully when the realisation caused Ologun to flinch then jump out of the car. The vortex exploded into activity and attacked.

At the velocity of bullets, each leaf, or what appeared to be disguised as small leaves, ricocheted off Ologun's face and body. First there were maybe fifty locusts then a hundred. Soon the sky darkened as thousands of the things swarmed in unison. They dived en masse and each wave hurt like hell. Ologun staggered around and was soon crawling on all fours for cover; yet again the fear of being attacked by these machine insects seemed odd after a lifetime spent as sustenance for an equally vicious swarm.

A few of the drones latched on and began drilling into his skin with a needle-thin spike. One in the leg, two in the head, and one in the shoulder. They penetrated and then injected something into him.

Ologun got up and created a large flat canvas with his second skin. The flat surface then curved around with perfect timing and scooped up over half the swarm before enveloping them inside as it became a sack. He flexed the skin and began crushing the machines until they were destroyed. Another round of this, then only a handful were zipping around as though redundant. Then something else happened. Ologun felt a pain in his head and another shooting pain in his left arm. *Little shits!* The drones that stung him had injected nano-bots that were now attacking from the inside out. Ologun collapsed as his heart exploded and another minute explosion popped, destroying part of his brain from the inside out.

Over a minute passed, and as his mind reactivated, Ologun saw a human drone running towards him. It opened fire from the long hose it held and blue hot plasma sprayed across the air. The roar of heat splashed Ologun across his right arm as he held it out for cover and watched in horror as the limb vaporised on contact.

He stumbled and fought his way up on to his feet. He then leapt over the car and hid in desperation as his mind became erratic with shock. *Calm down!* Ologun looked at the stump where his arm used to be attached at the shoulder; not even bone had survived that heat. He then checked his left arm and saw that his hand had turned black like charcoal and yet it had not been burned at all. The drone, painted in green camouflage and wearing green combat uniform, had by now moved around the car and took aim with its plasma-thrower once more. The blue substance washed over Ologun and he knew another adaptation had taken place. His skin felt some pain but there was no more damage.

Ologun formed a handless arm out of second skin where his real arm should have been, and he stood up. He smacked the drone hard across the head and sent it flying across the street. Another drone revealed itself, a slightly different design but another metal exo-skeleton with muscles made of tightly woven thin wire. *This might be simple enough.* Ologun ran to the drone with the plasma-thrower and grabbed a long machete-type blade magnetically attached to its leg. He took the blade and sliced at the drone's neck and severed the metal tendons so that it could no longer move its head.

Four other drones took positions above on the roof tops. One fired an RPG directly at him. The explosion threw Ologun though the window of a nearby shop. He lay on his back, checked his right arm and saw that it had grown back to the elbow beneath the fake arm of second skin. Ologun felt that he was being complacent or that he was out of practice for he was sure he used to be better than this. *Get it together!*

Climbing out from the rubble and dust Ologun chose his next target. He ran up the fire escape stairwell of the nearest building and was greeted by one of the machines as he reached the top. It lifted what appeared to be some sort of rifle and aimed it at Ologun's face. What Ologun did not realise was that the weapon released a deep, penetrating microwave burst. Being toasted on the outside by blue hot plasma had not prepared Ologun for the electromagnetic wave. It hit him, went through him and agitated the inside of his brain on a molecular level. Within seconds, Ologun's head exploded and his lifeless body fell back down the stairwell.

'Hostile is down, over.'

'Checking details of combative incident . . . Bring this tech with you, we need to take a look, over.'

'Copy that, retrieving remains, over and out.'

The human drone jumped off the roof and landed heavily next to the entrance of the fire escape metal stairwell. The headless corpse of a body lay quite still upon the street where it was noted by the soldier controlling the drone how the blood or whatever the hydraulic liquid was that had oozed from the dead man's neck was decaying and turning into dust. Two other drones dropped down and took up defensive positions behind burned-out vehicles.

The drone nearest the stairwell knelt down next to Ologun's remains and poked them with a finger. It then looked at the others and shrugged. It appeared that what had first appeared to be an un-stoppable organism remained deactivated or dead.

DEFAULT SETTING

The organism had been on the run for nearly a century. It could only be described as the descendant of what humanity called the Spectra. It was the same and yet different. An ocean of organisms that formed one mind and had been bred for one purpose, except that as with many things made for a purpose, some things become ambiguous.

The organism sat in orbit thirty million miles from a dying white dwarf star within a universe almost spent. The Spectra was still searching while it too avoided its own enemy. It had sent vessels out in order that they search the universe and the multiverse, and still it had yet to find its malfunctioning offspring. A cylinder-shaped shell about the size of Pluto drank from the solar radiation of the dying star while also embracing the experiences of the units it had been created to maintain.

The organism had gone way beyond its original remit. It had been specifically instructed on its launch to keep them in good health only during their natural limited life span, perhaps so that they may be replaced by others if the project was a success. The Spectra had been quite upset with its child for not only had this instruction been ignored, the organism had gone further, much further, in its quest to watch and to experiment. From one reality to another it had given its five units infinite chances when those around them only ever had one. There were unforeseen problems with this unnatural intervention, however, and the organism found it difficult to grasp the internal workings of each of the unexpectedly unique units.

It had stopped using the term unit after a while. Now the organism understood names whether given or self-appointed. Ologun, Hina, Ray, Hershal and Judith, in that order; one to five were still alive and still needing attention. The organism could process the atomic structure of everything within a light year of its position, so replenishing the units and assisting them to adapt and to be better and stronger was effortless aside from the odd impediment. Sometimes it found it hard to comprehend why they did the things they did and had been totally bemused when considering each individual unit's feelings.

It had a direct link to their every thought, their every desire, their pleasures, their pain and their turmoil or satisfaction. Did the organism understand why Ray was presently having sexual intercourse with a female that was not of his species? No. The organism could not understand why Hina had malfunctioned and had sat lifeless for eighty years after its experience on Vanguard, and how when Hershal had placed an organic patch of misinformation on Hina's neck it had brought him back. The organism had tried to re-boot Hina itself and still had not figured out why Hina had begun functioning again and why he had become so different in the process, especially when Ologun and Judith received the same treatment and had suffered no side effects at all. Some information and processes were ultimately impossible for the organism to understand.

Right now Hina and Hershal were quiet, at least in the respect that they were not suffering acute emotional or physical trauma. Judith on the other hand was on the verge of some kind of overload. The organism monitored this and tried to balance the chemical composition in her brain, yet this appeared not to be working as a long-term remedy. Was it that her body had recently been completely vaporised? Probably not. She had been malfunctioning on an emotional basis most of her existence.

At least Ologun was easier to reset, but he remained the greatest consumer of time and energy. This was no real issue as both were in abundance. What the organism found difficult to understand was how stubborn this unit continued to be. When Hina had needed to escape Vanguard the unit grasped the concept of what the organism tried to tell it regarding the nature of reality and that of time and motion. It escaped the planet and was triumphant, regardless of the fact it broke and shut down immediately afterward. Ologun on the other hand was insolent. The unit had not wanted to leave the planet it had been trapped on and had actually found a routine of death and resurrection; stupid thing. Now Ologun came across as slow and without the verve it had once had. It was missing something all of a sudden which was one common factor to all the units. They were tired somehow; they were old without being old as they had all been kept new.

If there was a translation for the organism's next set of thoughts it could only be translated as, 'This just will not do.'

Ologun wanted to eliminate yet another enemy and had failed to figure out that there were very few limits to his abilities. The only thing that seemed to work with this unit was intervention. Such a thing had been done twice before; another thing that displeased the Spectra. Now the organism geared itself up to enter the unit's reality. Right now Ologun had no head and no engine of life: no brain. It was time for the organism to inject itself into the unit's body so that when something had been achieved, this demonstration would live on in the unit's subconscious and hopefully it would remember and learn as though it had done it all itself. It was now time to intervene; it was time to become Ologun Jowett.

*

The truck rolled on down the highway. Two drones sat in the front as three kept watch over the headless carcass now laid flat in the back. The organism that was responsible for replenishing this unit had already injected itself into Ologun's body and was busy building a new head.

Beneath a fabric canvas the body lay still and it listened to the machines that were controlled by their human pilots. Even the organism saw the parallels here. It was actually in another universe transmitting itself into unit one. These machines had their human counterparts projected from another location further east. Soon enough the organism would perhaps feel as they felt, for just as those humans had become the machines, the organism would become Ologun, and soon.

The organism now seeking data, intercepted the avatars' covert comms.

'Fifteen hundred are returning to point, the rest will continue on to the capital, over.'

'Copy that, ETA in two hours, still no activity here, over.'

'Received message, over and out.'

The body was chained tightly and so the organism set to work unlocking and unravelling the restraints with strands of second skin. Its head was now fully re-made and was just about ready. It transferred its consciousness to the brain and it received a new set of senses. The sounds, the smells, the feeling of atmosphere on skin. The organism processed the sensations and quickly learned to accept them.

One of the drones glanced at the sack on the bed of the truck. It thought it saw some movement, stood up and leant over to pull the canvas back. As the fabric was pulled down the drone saw the body had a new head and that its eyes were looking directly at it. There was a synthesized sound of a scream as the machine jumped backwards.

The body jumped up and ripped the drone in half with its bare hands. It then threw another over the side of the truck before turning to the third drone and grabbing it by the head. The machine was used as an object to batter the driver and the passenger drone over and over as it was flung like a rag doll. The truck swerved violently, ran off the road, and hit a crash barrier at full speed. The two machines within the vehicle's cockpit flew out of the truck and into the brush on the side of the road while the organism used its second skin to anchor itself to the ground as the truck flew after them.

If this had been witnessed by someone primitive they might say that it was demonic possession or the devil himself. Eyes glowing an emerald green and thousands of strands of second skin flailing around like snakes, the organism walked directly into the middle of the open road. So Ologun was worried about getting to places on time and defeating so many when it counted most. Save the people, stop the slaughter. If that was one of the unit's last desires then so be it.

The organism had two options at present in order to beat the convoy that was controlling the drones. It stood there and made a choice. The organism cut the stream of information that was unit one, Ologun, and reallocated the projection so that it appeared where it needed to be. Ologun's body in turn fell to the floor where it soon crumpled into dust and ash.

*

'Lou, Lou, we have a problem.'

'Boudrelaux, what is happening?'

Boudrelaux exited the drone control pod and joined the others. 'Captain, the body is now active again, it was not dead.'

More information came from the cockpit of the lead juggernaut of the convoy. A group of men ran to the nearest surveillance screen monitoring the outside of the truck and saw what the fuss was about. 'Another one?'

'No, I think it must be the same one.'

'Impossible. This cannot be!'

The man, the thing, stood half a mile away in the middle of the road as the convoy approached. It did not move and remained eerily still. 'Activate forward aggression.'

The lead truck began to change as mechanisms on the front of the enormous vehicle moved plates to reveal missile silos and heavy artillery guns. 'Ready?'

'In position.'

'Fire!'

The truck fired all its weapons simultaneously at the thing in the road as it approached. The vehicle slowed slightly, allowing the truck behind to gain on it until their bumpers met. As the trucks approached, a colossal fireball engulfed the highway where the being had stood. The smoke cleared and debris rained down just as the convoy reached the location. *'C'est quoi ce bordel?'*

The thing had not moved, had not been damaged or deterred, and just stood there.

'Hit the brakes, stop!'

'No, run it down.'

The truck had now reached a solid hundred kilometres per hour. The organism knelt down on one knee and did what Ologun had yet to master. A compressed field of atoms formed to create a dense, circular plate.

The leading truck accelerated, and hit the barrier, which caused the front of the vehicle to crumple inwards before it flipped up and over, clearing the being kneeling on the highway. The truck landed heavily upside down and slid for sixty metres.

The organism grew agitated as the noise of crashing and weapon fire became deafening. The truck that had been travelling closely behind the first slammed on its brakes and slid into the shield with another loud crash. The next and nearest fifteen trucks stopped, reversed, and began manoeuvring into tactical positions.

The possessed body stood up, eyes glowing, as it drew in more energy for what was about to come. It turned to look at the steaming wreck of a truck next to it and then turned to look at the one lying upside down further down the road. A noise was coming from this direction and the organism checked what rules had been put in place by Ologun, after all this was his body and it did not want to deviate from the unit's original plan. No killing! Unit one obviously liked a challenge.

The noise drew closer as the organism calculated its next set of movements. More artillery fire came from the convoy. They were now parked sideways in a tightly knit barricade twenty vehicles wide and in five rows. This battle formation housed formidable turrets, stampede cannons, mortars, chain guns and missile silos; hell was coming.

A wave of fire erupted directly on top of the organism. Three more waves of bombardment followed. The area lit up as though a miniature nuclear device had been detonated and a mushroom cloud floated into the dusk-lit sky. As the black smoke poured upwards and began to dissipate, it became clear that much of the highway had been destroyed and a huge crater was now in its place. Chatter could be heard above the background of roaring infernos dotted here and there.

Through the smog of the downed truck ahead, the organism saw that a large party of small buggies and other wagons had joined them. It counted and drew a set of grand totals. Ninety eight out of the initial one hundred convoy behemoth vehicles still functioned and were parked ready to fire. Another three hundred vehicles of a smaller type had amassed on this location, and twelve hundred human-shaped machines began to disembark for combat.

The organism never felt fear and processed pain with ease as it had always felt via any of its units. Any sensation the units felt over the many years had been taken and managed as part of the realm of experience. This time it wanted to experience such a thing first hand.

The organism perched on the edge of the crater and watched. It had not yet been spotted amidst the heat and smoke. It took its time and thought about something Ologun had asked himself. Nigeria had the twenty-eighth largest economy in the world. How did it get attacked like this? The organism could not figure out what this question meant; it seemed a complex riddle. It did not understand culture or creed, class or race or hierarchy, or how and why different races found any excuse for conflict. It had no idea why any of this was happening at all in fact, for the thing everyone had been motivated to take, was in its mind worth nothing. Three type-one Version grown by its own parent had so far led to two thousand plus warriors from other lands killing nearly two hundred thousand people of this land. This loss of numbers was ludicrous to the organism and at least it calculated why losing more should be avoided.

It stood up and revealed itself. The convoy fired everything they had, and the drones did the same, so that now the organism was surrounded and being hit from all directions. It moved slowly and deliberately, releasing thick strands of second skin. It walked through the fire, unmoved by the shockwaves of explosions or the force of projectiles. More strands, endless branches, were now snaking and searching. Drone after drone was captured and crushed on one side while thousands more strands reached out to the convoy in front and latched on.

The turrets fired until they were white hot and the thing took it all resolutely. It now looked to be more of an old dead tree with branches growing and pulsating out and over everything. Trucks were crushed, the behemoth vehicles of the convoy were ripped open. The branches of skin reached in, prising open avatar pods and swallowing the people inside whole.

Some of the convoy tried to leave as drone after drone fell lifeless to the ground having had their operators consumed. The organism walked sluggishly under its increasing weight as it grew and mutated. The more it processed the more it threw into the battle. The head on its neck began to distort, jaw elongating and disfiguring, eye sockets expanding and twisting. The top of its skull became overgrown and began to break the skin with long stalagmites of bone.

Hideous and way past being anything human, the organism staggered and felt an odd sensation it had always dismissed in the past. This, however, was first-hand experience and it could not decipher the feeling. It was motivating and all-encompassing, even intoxicating; it was enjoying itself.

Second skin held on to everything and there was no escape. More men and women, the mercenaries, terrorists, were swallowed and held inside long thick strands of it. They were dragged away and held as more were captured. Everything had been laid to waste. Every truck and drone, every turret and every avatar chamber. The last of the mercenaries was rounded up as they abandoned their pods and tried to run; but they could not outrun the tentacles that sought them.

The organism used more skin and whipped at the debris of carnage until the highway was clear and tidy. It moved all of its snake-like strands out and across the highway as if a thousand blackened pythons had been butchered and laid out flat. It admired its work for a moment as it stood amongst the flames checking that all these soldiers were still alive. It turned to the mess of drones and other trash strewn down across the other side of the highway. It smashed everything aside and cleared another path.

It began to walk, its feet breaking the hardened plasma concrete of the highway as though it were walking in soft mud. It dragged half-mile long strands of second skin that were attached to its body. Fifteen hundred bodies alive and subdued were taken as though flies in a spider's web. The organism thought briefly about what it would do now. Five hundred drones were still attacking the capital. All the organism had to do was get itself to the last thirty two trucks that controlled them and its mission was complete.

The organism turned to face its captives then turned the other way to face the emptiness of the highway. It made a dense field of atoms, composed them into a circular shield and held it directly vertical. Then it chose a point directly behind and injected it with energy.

A trick of the quantum world and the power over particles caused the fabric of space to collapse. A whirlpool of light expanded and flowed inward where energised atoms shone en masse and flowed inwards as a sparkling froth. The organism passed through the shield that held Earth's atmosphere from flowing into another dimension and into the portal. Still smouldering from the heat of battle it walked into the aperture slowly and assuredly. Its prisoners were dragged along with it.

SCANNER

The craft probed the solar system and found nothing unusual: two gas giants, one planet mid-range from the sun, and five planets that were baked and bloated as they orbited too closely to the star itself.

Hina sat in the organic cockpit on the back of his craft. Perhaps he considered this thing to be his second younger brother, a sibling that he appreciated more than Hershal. Drifting along in darkness and watching a visible representation of solar winds, Hina wondered about the reconfiguring of code and information. He had gathered much information, yet was aware of how it changed and could be changed. This thing, the warship, contained much of the code that created him and therefore it always seemed so fascinating that it looked the way it did and grew as large as it did. It was apparent that the limits with genetic code were endless.

The craft that had been bred to protect the entity were not much of anything at all, just code that had been adjusted and modified to break certain limitations; all that had ever been needed was energy and understanding without the restriction of ethics and morality. Yet ostensibly, predominantly the craft were human, but hideously mutated via the genome unleashed.

Hina continued to scan the area, then he saw it. One mile in width and one mile in depth, the thing was heading slowly through the system and it, too, scanned the area. Hina thought about the patterns. His mind could see them as though faces in the cloud, a recognition of shapes, and he thought the great ship drifting around out there looked like a hazelnut. Was it some design of strength? Was it some creature that had evolved and had been enslaved by the enemy?

Whatever the answer, this behemoth that was invisible to the naked eye and many other forms of detection, this organic creature, had spotted Hina and his craft. Two organic and animate objects that lived and had their own perception of reality became aware of each other like marine life in the darkness of the deep. One would be predator and the other prey, yet which was which?

Hina linked to the mind of the craft: *time for some practice!* Together their minds were sharper and more reactive. Hina had ideas that differed from the craft's and together they perceived and imagined how this next set of affairs would pan out. The craft folded its wings over its back so that it was now a sleek rhomboid in shape; like a flat, thick dagger. The craft sped on and towards the enemy ship.

Closer and closer Hina watched his second brother approaching as though he were a fruit fly dreading a buffalo; the odds seemed against them. The craft pointed every weapon it had and prepared to fire, then and without warning, the great organic ship vanished.

The craft slowed down and Hina checked to see where it might be. He searched for any information on the network of surveillance buoys. One had activated. Hina instructed the craft to reveal its location and then retracted the order as another buoy activated and another. Hina brought up a visual display of the galaxy and where the buoys were located. He watched as another and another activated yet could not understand what means of propulsion had made this enemy ship cover the distance of light years in such leaps and bounds. Then Hina realised that things had indeed escalated when he spotted the pattern in front of him: the enemy was headed in geometric fashion and at speed, in the direction of Earth.

*

The smell of fire and destruction, broken rubble, blood and sweat filled the air. Dusk approached and the hue between night and day played with Ologun's eyesight. The buildings throughout the city were damaged and peppered with bullet wounds, chinked and charred from many explosions.

The dead were everywhere and only the odd survivor now moved through the streets and the abandoned buildings. Cars, trucks and buses jammed the highway as far as the eye could see heading south and east, a massive obstruction that rose above and beyond Olusegun Obasanjo Way and around the business district of many tall and varying buildings.

Ologun watched as jets belonging to the South African Air Force did flybys, and helicopters landed in the distance at Millennium Park. The carnage was both horrific and mesmerizing.

The Nigerian forces that remained continued to patrol the streets all over the city, their casualties heavy and their numbers thin on the ground. Human machine drones that had belonged to the militia of mercenaries littered the ground, broken and inanimate. Ologun checked a satellite feed covering the region immediately north-west of the city, and it showed that many refugees were making their way towards Kaduna. Infra-red thermal imaging revealed a scattered group, a mass of thousands that had stopped at various points along the way, and others that had already reached the Kaduna city limits. The Nigerian Army was present there, yet in very small numbers that would have fallen if the specialist army of militia had continued past the capital.

Ologun cut the feed and returned to monitoring his surroundings. Those who had left their aircraft had been greeted by the strangest sight. On the Millennium Park grassland were over nineteen hundred captives who had been rendered unconscious and tied up. They sat in neat rows, a sea of bodies belonging to the terrorist army. Ologun felt sick, partly because of the continued attack of the virus and also because he could not remember any of this and how he had got here, which disturbed him deeply.

Ologun turned his attention to the man sitting against the side of a car and at his feet. He was tied up and gagged, yet his eyes remained defiant and full of hatred: General Lou Armistead, or as his last official ranking within the French Army stated, Colonel Armistead. Ologun wanted to perform some terrible acts on this creature. This man had thought it tactically sound to make this ruse look authentic and kill absolutely everyone his mercenaries came across. Ologun knew of such acts; blights on the history of this continent – history of the world in fact. Now, as though a stunt of both sickening evil and an act of some sort of propaganda to fool the world, some sort of fake political, ideological cause had been projected as the reason for the flash raid across this country. Ologun guessed that he had gone to extraordinary lengths to not kill the captured who now lay on the city's parkland himself, although he had no memory of the events.

He did realise, however, that this specialist army of mercenaries may yet still pay the ultimate price when rounded up by the authorities.

Armistead looked up at Ologun with a peculiar expression in his eyes that was pure disdain. Ologun crouched down and, without saying a word, took a knife, put his knee on the man's chest and cut out the man's eyes. He waited as the man screamed beneath the cloth stuffed in his mouth and then injected strands of second skin into the man's neck and Armistead's eyes grew back; the look in his new eyes spoke of fear and horror.

One of the helicopters that had landed in the park lifted and headed towards the highway. It approached with guns pointed at Ologun and his captive. The machine hovered as several soldiers dressed in black combat gear abseiled down to the road a few feet from him.

Six of the soldiers took up positions and sought cover behind vehicles, whilst a woman with very dark skin and a shaven head approached Ologun. 'My name is Commander Amina Gibson,' she said. Ologun smiled as both first name and surname triggered a sense of recognition and irony for him.

'You need to come with us, President Daniel Zuma wishes to talk with you,' she continued.

Ologun said nothing and pondered the surname that had much historical significance.

'He believes that you are here to deliver us all from judgement.' Amina paused, and then said, 'He believes you are Jesus Christ.'

Ologun's left eyebrow lifted in astonishment at this and he chuckled at the absurdity.

'He said he has been waiting for you all his life.'

Ologun walked up to the woman, dragging Armistead by a rope tied around his neck. 'Tell the President that I'm waiting for Jesus too, I'm tired . . . but seriously, I'm not the Messiah and I'm sure I'll answer to him too if he ever arrives. I have a message for every leader of this world,' Ologun continued. 'Daniel needs to log into waqwww/zw.newworldmessage./000.encrypt. It's under the seventh worldwide network with encryption code Alpha 888236. He and anyone in, shall we say, a position of power needs to see what I uploaded there.'

'We need to take you with us,' Gibson said sternly and tightened her grip on her rifle.

'Really!' Ologun said, then lifted his head to his left as though he heard something.

Amina and her soldiers jumped back then cowered when the helicopter pulled back and away as something huge appeared in the sky without warning. The massive black craft hovered and its wings cast a large shadow across the highway. 'I'm going now,' Ologun said. 'I'm sorry I left such a mess.'

Amina Gibson watched with fright as the hovering craft picked up Ologun and placed him inside some sort of cockpit on its back. The craft ascended, stopped to change direction, then disappeared without trace.

*

The land to the south was arid with vast sand dunes of endless desert. The morning sun warmed the air and it blew in through the open hatch of the copter jet as it sped on only thirty feet above the windswept world.

'What are you exactly?' Sergeant James asked. He was sitting opposite Judith, hunkered down in the rear compartment with five other soldiers who were checking their gear.

'They used to teach school kids about me, they used to call me a demi-god, I guess that doesn't happen any more,' Judith replied.

'That's a little narcissistic don't you think?' James said.

'I'm a projection.'

'What the hell does that mean?'

'It's complicated,' Judith reasoned.

'What about that ship of yours?'

Judith looked out over the desert and saw that the craft was still there acting as escort to their mission. It glided along elegantly and silently. The thing was much lower down and sped by the sand dunes, perhaps only ten to fifteen feet above the static waves of sand.

'That too is complicated; you wouldn't want to know.'

'ETA at objective is three minutes,' the pilot informed everyone. 'Hook up and be ready to drop in four.'

Judith put on a headset to speak with the pilot. 'I need you to land the jet on top of that natural structure inside the lip of that cave. Keep the engines hot, and if there's any sign of the Version I want you to bail out, is that understood?'

'Yes, ma'am.'

'The stone tower should give you plenty of warning and the machines would have to climb to your position if they decide to stealth it,' Judith continued. 'On approach you need to fire contour laser pods at and around the tower, and if anything moves on your position you'll know about it before it's too late.'

'Absolutely.' The pilot nodded.

Judith turned to the soldiers and took the headset off. 'I'm going in ahead of you and naturally I'll be taking point. I want you to take up position inside the entrance of the valley and set up perambulation lasers to map the inside of the facility in 3D. I'll take the remaining rods and place them at intervals so that you get full coverage.'

James nodded and Judith began to fill a rucksack with small metal rods which had transparent balls attached to one end. She then took a stampede rifle and a handful of clips of varying round types and placed them inside her second skin on her chest.

'I thought you didn't need that,' Sergeant James said, referring to the rifle, then he nodded to the large blue crystal blades attached to her back.

'I like shooting stuff.' Judith winked. 'You need to hide if anything should happen, do not engage the enemy.'

'There's been no confirmation of any Version left on the planet,' James stated.

'Be prepared,' Judith said and sat down on the ledge, half-hanging from the open side door, ready to jump.

'We have inflate pods with us,' James said.

'Have you brought dead pills?'

'Why?'

'If those things are around you need to play dead. They are able to hear a pin drop in a riot, don't risk it.'

The copter jet slowed and hovered thirty feet above the ground. Judith looked at Damien James and wondered whether it was worth bringing the soldiers. Sam had ordered them to come and to act as

Judith's eyes and ears while she secured the underground facility containing an entire fleet of retired warships.

'Good luck,' James offered.

Judith nodded and jumped from the aircraft. She fell and landed feet first on a sand dune. James watched her progress; it was not long before she had sprinted the whole way to the mountain range ahead. The copter jet moved on and around the side of one of the mountains. The red iron-laced peaks acted as a barrier between the desert and a vast canyon beyond. What could be seen was an illusion, however, for the canyon that looked empty had been turned into a base long ago and the trickery of a sophisticated image shrouded this fact with a past portrait of how it had looked before the modification.

The soldiers abseiled down within the shadow of the main mountain. On landing Sergeant James signalled for the copter jet to take position. The aircraft lifted up and away and towards a tall pillar made of stone, that had at one time been part of the mountain and that had by now and through the erosion of time become secluded. The copter jet fired several small objects from its cannons up and along the trunk of the tower that stood at over a thousand feet in height. It then moved in and landed on a ledge towards the top end of the structure.

The alien craft, meanwhile, had shot up high into the sky and was now hovering in a static position watching the whole area below. James signalled to the men and they tabbed over to the base of the mountain. He checked a map on a small pad and signalled for them to move south and around the side of its base. Within minutes the team had found a large gap, an open set of thick hangar doors that led into a man-made tunnel of fifty feet in height and a hundred feet in width.

Two soldiers were instructed to take positions by the entrance as their colleagues pushed on into the tunnel. As the inside of the underground passage became darker, James and his soldiers instructed their server chips to increase the gain within their eyes so that they could see in the darkness. They jogged along for fifteen minutes and reached another inner entrance where an abandoned gatehouse and several fibre-plate cabins sat outside another large hangar bay door.

The soldiers searched the area for any means of powering up the lights within the facility.

'The control panels are down, I might be able to fix them,' one of the soldiers relayed to James.

'Negative, leave it,' Sergeant James ordered.

James and the others took the small rods with the transparent balls at one end and began pegging them, ball end upwards, into the floor along the entranceway. Sergeant James took his pad and opened an application then turned on the rods. They emitted a long wave pulse of infra-red lasers in unison that acted as a form of sonar. The void beyond was mapped as the light hit objects and collected data. Within moments the inside of the underground base and as far as three thousand metres in depth, had been mapped in a visual three-dimensional image. James checked the scale of what he was seeing and used a selection key in order to decipher it. Then another screen showed that it was available for access as Judith had obviously managed to place the rods that she had taken. James opened the tab so that now two representations covering both the entrance and much further into the underground facility merged to present one schematic. James noted what he saw. By now the whole base was covered, or at least the expanse of the main floor where the ships were sitting. Among them and to the rear of this enormous cave, Judith was running around, an ant next to the retired ships.

'This is going to take time,' Judith's voice came over the comms. 'I'm going to open the roof, although I think it will take twenty minutes or so. Make yourselves comfortable.'

*

Judith made her way up to the flight control office. The place was on complete shutdown – the ships had been left here to hibernate perhaps decades ago. Dusty retroactive computer consoles filled the exterior of the room. Judith swept aside an empty mug, an old computer pad, and a picture of someone's family from one of the desks she needed to access. She searched her server chip for local access points and switched on the computer terminal directly in front of her.

Quickly, she located the control panel for each of the ships' AI;

there were no Version pilots present. One at a time the ships' systems were brought online and their reverse mass engines fired up. Judith then accessed the controls for the hatchway that acted as roof to the underground facility. The sound of creaking metal and groaning machinery echoed throughout the entire place. Dust and sand fell from above in the darkness, yet Judith could see everything. A long beam of light shot down, hit the concrete floor, and widened until the underground complex was revealed to be an expansive yard filled with thirty five ships in waiting. Judith sat down for a moment and was awestruck by the magnitude of what she saw. *Excellent!*

*

The craft watched and listened. The wind moved sand and whistled as it passed the mountain range. It knew that what it saw was not the entirety. It became aware that as the usual movement of everything down to the last atom within its perceptive range was as it should be, something was about to disrupt the fabric. It moved slowly towards a disturbance.

The craft the colour of bone glided silently, like skeletal remains of some great creature that had died in the barren wastes and been resurrected. It felt the shift and stopped moving in order to watch a particular point in front of it.

A torpedo shot through the curtain of reality, a great ship suddenly appeared in front of the craft, causing it to close its wings over itself and fire its weapons. The human vessel, a long, rectangular construct, banked starboard as it took the punishment of thousands of energy bolts ripping at its hull. The ship's hull hissed and boiled as the metal evaporated and its inner decks were exposed. The ship opened fire from its port side and stampede rounds pummelled the tiny speck that had attacked it. The craft took this onslaught in its stride and continued its relentless attack as it hovered, panning from left to right like a turret had been embedded in the sky.

The human ship listed badly as it continued its journey towards the red mountains beyond the dunes. Its starboard side was dragging low, and it passed over the sea of sand, dropping what appeared to be droplets of blood. The craft scanned this activity and saw that many humanoid figures had been peppered along the ship's route and that the crimson figures were running at an impressive pace towards the base of the mountain.

The great ship took a thousand more shots of energy and was now a skinless structure of framework akin to a burned Zeppelin. The ship crashed and slid through the dunes creating a neat path of flatness behind it, and as it did so it littered the area with debris until the colossus ground to a halt. This great feat of human engineering now seemed more like the remains of a great whale that had been picked clean by scavengers.

The white craft continued to fire its cannons, picking off many of the red-skinned creatures that had been deposited along the way. Over two thousand of the things scurried across the dunes showing tremendous stamina in such terrain. The craft released more and more firepower and yet too many broke through the net and escaped. It broke off from its pursuit as it hit the mountain range and it wondered if Judith could handle the swarm of over a thousand drones by herself; it was about to find out.

*

'This is Atlas One. Come in, over.'

'This is Sergeant James, go ahead, over.'

'We have multiple contacts on approach, ETA five minutes. Go dark. We are taking the copter, punching out, over.'

'How many contacts?' James asked. 'Over.'

'Nine hundred and counting. Get the hell out of there. Over and out!'

James signalled to the men and they ran into the facility. The whole place was now exposed under the midday sun and they sprinted to the nearest ship. They stopped and took defensive positions underneath. One of the soldiers took off his satchel and opened it, pulling out a reel of thread. The rest of them took out small hand grips and the thread was attached to a harpoon gun. It was fired up and on to the ship's hull where a flat, adhesive tip stuck to its metal.

'Go!' James instructed. The first soldier attached his hand grip to the thread and was quickly dragged up and to a hatch on the side of the hull sixty feet off the floor. The others followed. James pressed into his ear to activate the comms. 'Judith you got the message? Over.'

'Affirmative, go dark now,' the response came.

James hooked on to the thread and was pulled up via the handgrip to the open hatchway. He climbed inside the ship and on to the junction way of a corridor. 'Split up and find a place to hunker down. Activate your packets and take the pill. Let's hope this doesn't go on for more than an hour.'

The soldiers nodded and headed off in opposite directions down the four passageways. James ran to a ladder and climbed on to the next level. He ran until he had passed the leisure deck and through what used to be a bar with fixed tables and chairs next to a dance floor. He jumped the bar, knocking into an empty glass fridge behind, smashing several glasses off a shelf. He then opened a hatchway on the floor and jumped down into a storage cellar.

James activated a small, round pack of fabric so that it inflated within the confines of the enclosed space. It was shaped like a coffin and made of a stiff board-like substance that would mask his thermal output once inside. He climbed in, lay down, then strapped the lid down over himself from the inside. He lay there for a moment listening in the dark until he took out a small capsule from the same chain as his dog tags, placed it in his mouth and swallowed. His heart slowed and his mind went blank. The chemical compound would stop everything and place his body in stasis, keeping the cells in his body from degrading until his heart began to beat again. He took one last breath and faked death for a few hours.

*

Judith ran to the entrance and saw to her right and above that the soldiers had entered one of the ships. A hatch had been left open and a thread hung down to the floor. *Idiots!* Judith climbed the thread and closed the hatch. She then dropped to the floor and yanked the thread to pull it off at its adhesive pad stuck to the hull's metal.

The sound of many feet approached; an unusual sound that defied the Version's weight and power as an agile light-footed machine of grace. Judith walked over to the hangar entranceway and watched them flood down the large passage, wall to wall and all the way back as far as she could see.

The machines exploded on to her position as she fired magma-tip rounds at them from her rifle. Many fell as they melted from the inside out. Judith walked backwards as they swarmed towards her, reloading clip after clip. Explosive rounds, vampire rounds, liquid-tip nitrogen rounds. She emptied all her ammunition into them and still they came.

The machines split up and darted around the ships to her left and right and would soon be flanking her, surrounding her. She unleashed her blades and prepared herself. The after-effect of her former annihilation meant that she had become indestructible for longer, which meant that these things should not win. Yet Judith felt that the sheer number sent was a tactical choice to consume her time as only a few needed to be able to climb on board each ship to steal them from right in front of her.

The craft appeared overhead and above the open top of the hangar. The Version poured in and attacked Judith. She hacked at them and destroyed them while the craft above fired down on them. If they climbed on to a ship and tried to gain access, the hovering craft picked them off first. The room was soon filled with fallen Version, and Judith found it difficult to keep fighting as she lost her footing on the floor of crimson corpses.

Higher and higher the wall of Version bodies climbed and Judith became hemmed in. The ivory craft supporting Judith shot off suddenly as something else seemed more important. Without its help things became almost impossible.

She heard stampede fire, the calibre only a mighty warship could use. It sounded as though it were coming from above and was very close. The craft must have been in combat with yet another ship that had been commandeered only a week earlier. The shadow of a ship passed over the opening of the valley and above the yard of ships. It was on fire and half-destroyed as the ivory craft followed in close pursuit, relentlessly firing its weapons. Judith was grabbed by a Version drone and then another until many of them had formed a vice-like grip around her.

More and more piled on, linking hands to form a larger ball of bodies lying atop a mountain of their own fallen. Judith could not move and was being crushed.

More Version came over the top of the walls surrounding the shipyard. They dropped down and poured in, filling the valley as more and more latched on to each other, imprisoning Judith in layer after layer of hundreds of machines. Judith could still hear the craft firing its weapons, but whatever it was up to, it had failed to help her. Judith panicked and felt claustrophobic. Her mind became a whirl of fear and anger, for losing the last of the Prospect fleet to the Version was unthinkable.

Judith felt hot, felt as though she were burning like the fire coursing through her body. The pain and agony caused her to scream, yet she saw that the Version closest to her, hugging her, had burned to a crisp. More heat built up and Judith felt weightless as if floating through oblivion, dizzy and impaired. A great flash of light ensued and thousands of Version were vaporized in an instant. Judith landed on her feet; her body smouldered and smoke poured from her shoulders and head. She watched the ash and debris drop from the air and saw that even the mountain of dead Version had become a charred, blackened mound. The craft hovered above the valley, watching her carefully.

'What would I do without you?' Judith said.

The craft grumbled and whispered to her. It said that it had done nothing. It said that Judith had just released a burst of energy and it wanted to know from where. Judith continued to smoulder all over her body and went to touch her head. Her hair had been burned away to the scalp once again and she rubbed the smooth skin back and forth. She had no answers for the craft and for a moment was slightly upset that she would have to grow her hair yet again, until realising that such things were completely unimportant.

Judith looked over at the ships. They were red hot in parts where a heat of high intensity had hit their hulls. Judith sighed and crouched down as though out of breath. The only thing she was absolutely glad of was that none of the ships had been damaged or stolen.

FALLOUT

The avatar had almost finished giving President Kawle's speech to the country. For all intents and purposes it looked and sounded exactly like her. The key reasons for using a machine that represented the President could be stated as safety and security, yet in reality most people knew that the machine mimicking the woman had to be used for other reasons. People were prone to involuntary body language: give away, tell-tale signs in their facial expressions and so any secrets and lies were secure via the translation of a device that gave nothing away. Members of the press were now asking the machine questions as it stood on the podium behind a lectern.

'Could you explain to the country once again, to confirm to the American people, on what true basis this invasion took place?'

'Can you tell us what happened over there, is it true that the South African government released a new kind of weapon on our forces?'

'We are still waiting to see real proof that no nuclear weapons were launched; there is a lot of conflicting evidence that suggests that contrary to what every country involved is saying, in fact weapons of mass destruction were launched.'

'There are reports coming in that American and European forces entered Africa with two agendas, will you comment on what the second agenda was?'

'In fact, Madam President, was the terrorist organisation Eyes of Truth a fabricated American allied ploy in order to justify the invasion, as President Zuma is now claiming?'

President Kawle watched from behind a one-way mirror offstage. She spoke her responses to each question and in turn her replica uttered the words without any emotional indicators. 'We are now, due to the recent events that have occurred, about to make history. In two days there will be a meeting of all prior members of the United Nations, the first in over thirty years.'

The room erupted with all members of the press shouting

questions. 'That is all, thank you,' the avatar said.

The machine walked offstage and was met by several technical personnel who stripped it of its synthetic skin to expose its metallic exoskeleton. Once the thing was naked it was placed in a mechanical coffin of sorts and wheeled away.

'How many presidents can say that they are responsible for a nuclear holocaust?' President Kawle asked. She walked into a corridor and towards a lift that would take her to the top floor of the building. The President seemed very tired now and was quite drained of colour.

'There was no holocaust,' General Dean replied as she joined her in the lift.

'Alien intervention,' Kawle said, and Dean saw that Kawle was in complete turmoil. The lift moved quickly and stopped six hundred floors up.

'We are working out the particulars,' Dean said.

The President moved into a large apartment, followed by the general. Kawle stood by the reinforced window lens and gazed out across the city of Washington DC. General Dean sat down on a sofa and watched the President play with the window lens setting in order to adjust the zoom function on the city.

'I think about past presidents and how some of them were caught in lies. I think about all the reasons I started out and how if I became president that I would be better than that, that all the death and destruction and the callousness of how the value of human life . . .'

'You will survive this,' General Dean said.

'The world is on hold. The world is holding its breath. A part of me is terrified and the other part of me is . . . relieved,' Kawle said as though talking to herself.

'What do you want to do?'

Kawle moved from the window and sat down. 'I can't get away with this, if there is to be a UN congregation. There are talks regarding criminal charges, war criminal charges. I may have to step down in order to appease many of the other nations.'

'I read the minutes from this morning, whatever happens can't happen yet. Not with there being a state of emergency,' General Dean said then tilted her head, having been interrupted via a message on her neural chip.

President Kawle also received a flagged message on her own server and was reminded to contact the Secretary of Defence, Gregory Chapman. She replied to confirm a National Security Council meeting in the next three hours, and he in return confirmed that he could only be present at this particular engagement and nothing prior. Kawle scrolled through several menus, her left eye twitching slightly with pupil fully dilated. She found and read a message that included all other appropriate bodies that confirmed the congregation. There was another meeting to be held before this, however, and Kawle turned her attention to General Dean to see that she was busy organising something using her neural implant.

'Have they arrived?' Kawle asked.

'Colonel Young and Natasha Forbes are waiting with Dominic now. The biologist and historian are there also.'

'Have they seen the file?' the President asked.

'No, not yet,' General Dean said, stood up and moved to the lift, and waited by the open door for President Kawle to enter. 'Colonel Young and his team have compiled a full report and from what I just scanned, they may have just shed some light on this matter.'

*

The meeting convened in the main dead room within the underground complex to the White House. Dominic Brooks, head of homeland security, took position at the head of the table in order to address the room. Colonel Young was next to Natasha Forbes amongst members of the presidential cabinet and some high ranking military personnel. Young nodded at a woman he knew from the CIA: a director of special operations, Joanna Rogers, who was sitting next to Vice President Eric Blane. Young could tell by their eyes that they were away upon the digital highway giving and receiving messages via their neural chips. Perhaps they were messaging to each other or to the outside world. Whichever it was, the room would soon be cut off from outside signals as the fire walls of the dead room were erected.

Colonel Young then watched Douglas and Edmond as they sat

quietly for a change, in contrast to Rogers and Blane, seeming utterly absorbed by the proceedings.

Dominic Brooks began. 'For those who have privileged clearance to be here, please be aware everything that is about to be discussed is classified. Any attempt to leak or disclose this information outside of this dead room will be classed as treason and punishable by any means deemed appropriate. We have a lot to discuss here so let us begin with Colonel Young's findings. He and his team have some important information. Colonel Young, please proceed.'

The colonel cleared his throat and remained seated. He looked to Brooks at the end of the table and then to the President sitting at the opposite end. 'We searched through archives using a facial recognition programme, we set no parameters in order to access any materials available. We believe the person as such to be an Ologun Jowett. On the data file provided for you is a historical account of the man.'

Screens embedded on the desks were accessed by all except Young's team who were already familiar with the information. 'This can't be right,' General Tong said after some time.

'The recognition software used by the quantum head devices is a hundred per cent match,' Young replied.

'Then he is over two hundred years old.'

'Let us discuss these things in a while,' President Kawle insisted.

'The individual was once part of IMC's asset protection division.'

'Asset protection?' Kawle asked, reading a key index within the file. 'Excuse me, Colonel Young, please continue.' The President listened yet all the while felt even more anxious at realising that IMC, or rather the Prospect Empire, was involved; that one of their assassins had returned to Earth. She then looked to Joanna and Blane and wondered how this small team assembled by General Dean had come up with this intelligence, when literally thousands of central analysts with access to more resources had yet to get this far.

'We have little information on his career there as such, but we do know that he was sentenced for crimes committed in North Africa and sent to the planet Deceiver to work on the mining installations. Note, this was before the ice age,' Young professed.

'From what we have seen of this man so far, if indeed that is what we call this thing, there seems to be every chance it's the same individual, or a clone. Definitely some extensive, extraordinary genetic modifications have gone on here,' Brooks added.

'For what crimes did he receive such a sentence?' Kawle asked.

'Turn to page six of the compiled visual aids, Madam President,' Young insisted.

Everyone skipped to page six and saw an unthinkable scene of horror.

'Jesus,' Kawle blasphemed. 'What the hell is this?'

The old and faded Flickr files revealed twelve heads on poles and many body parts scattered around a blood-soaked scene. Entrails had also been hung in some sort of twisted decoration on the neat line of poles. More pictures from different angles showed that other bodies lay slumped on the ground, people who had been executed at close range by gun shots to the back of the head.

'We shouldn't take any of this out of context,' Edmond said.

'What context could justify this?' Kawle said, raising her voice. 'Is this what this Ologun Jowett is capable of?'

'This is distracting us from the main topic here,' General Dean intervened. 'This man was sent to Deceiver around the same time God's Blade arrived. Colonel Young, you may continue in a short while, but first I think everyone needs to see this.' Dean turned to the President to confirm she was authorised to show everyone in the room something. President Kawle nodded and the file was accessed ready to be shown.

'This file that is about to be shown was uploaded on to a primary secured international administrative global web page I.A.G. Seven. We believe the file to have been uploaded by Ologun Jowett. The site has been shut down and protected for security reasons. However, I'd like some feedback on what you are about to see.'

'This thing left us something?' Young asked.

'He left us what we think to be a warning,' General Tong said. 'All authorised personnel have seen this, what we believe to be an event of some kind.'

'It came with the word "Unite" as a header to the file.'

'Unite?' Young said.

'Just watch and see,' Dean ordered.

The main holographic display at the front of the room was switched on and some strange images were played, a live event through a first-person perspective. The footage moved around at speed revealing decaying grey concrete buildings overgrown with vegetation that lined the wide streets of what appeared to be an abandoned derelict town or city. Whoever it was that had taken this footage was moving forward until they knelt down next to another man with bright blond hair. Something was said and the viewpoint changed to look towards a pillar of green light leading up towards a bright orange sky way above. At the base of the green blanket shield was a barricade with soldiers waiting and watching among tanks and other turret fortifications that were clearly archaic in design. Then, this point of view was interrupted as it jerked upwards, focused on and followed something dropping from the ceiling of light, what everyone in the room had by now recognised as an enormous digital lens.

'Is that the star lens from Black Ball? I think that's Black Ball!' Edmond said.

'Please be quiet,' General Dean ordered him.

The event continued to unfold in front of them as something great and hulking lumbered across towards the person that had taken this footage. The person then ran and was pursued by something humanoid with a white flesh-like armour and a mirrored face. The room's occupants gazed in astonishment as the hulking beast reversed on knees that pivoted backwards, then fired.

'Pause,' General Dean ordered. The footage stopped. 'Close up of the creature's mirror mask times eight.'

The holographic image zoomed in and was adjusted.

'That's Ologun Jowett,' Tong offered.

'What is going on here, what is this?' Colonel Young asked.

'It's within the basin of the Black Ball complex,' Edmond said.

'The shard,' Natasha added as something had begun to make sense to her.

'What exactly is the point to this?' Colonel Young asked.

'There is much more of this up to the point where Ologun Jowett gets up on to the star lens, has a conversation with another man and then proceeds to climb aboard a ship of what can be described as . . . what we think to be alien as such,' General Dean said. 'What we have gathered so far is mostly through assumption, although it is believed that whatever is going on here may not involve Prospect.'

'That is your opinion, General Dean,' General Tong argued. 'We have no way to authenticate any of this information or what it means.'

'We have experts that believe this to be a memory that has somehow been adapted in order to be placed in the public domain,' Dean continued.

'Impossible!' Douglas scoffed. 'Are you saying that someone took a memory and translated it into digital reality? I assure you that such a thing cannot be done at all.'

'This man,' Dean said, 'this thing, proceeded to kill every living creature on that ship and was completely unscathed. There are now recent yet verified reports that this thing attacked and captured the terrorists in Nigeria. After destroying their combat drones it, or he, detained and secured we think up to two thousand in under three hours. Besides this, it is also involved with a craft that can only be described as being alien. I think we are beyond impossible in this instance.'

'What is clear to me,' the President said, 'is that this thing took out the very target, the very terrorist group we intended to eliminate. Why would it do that *and* attack our forces?'

Admiral Wass had remained silent throughout the proceedings and looked uncomfortable at this question. Young also noted that Joanna Rogers and Vice President Blane had remained quiet and he wondered what they were thinking. No one in the room responded until President Kawle spoke again.

'Natasha, why don't you explain to us what you think about all this?'

All eyes were now on the woman who began to feel nervous and flustered. 'Well, I ran tests to look for inter-dimensional spatial anomalies, after all the alien ship used a very accurate ability to nullify its mass, and reduced mass um . . . on its approach. I used our satellite to monitor for energy cascades to scan the planet and found that there were millions of cascades. I think the virus is being projected here, I think this man, Ologun, is being projected here in the same way.'

'From where?' General Tong wanted to know.

'That is beyond our abilities for the moment,' Natasha responded. 'All I can imagine is that a construct of some kind can analyse, adjust and adapt to whatever stress is applied. Basically any element required, any information can be sent through a deliberate and accurate stream to replenish this thing or this man, the same reason we are unable to beat the virus.'

'Like a clone,' Brooks said.

'Possibly, but I mean if he is hungry or thirsty then whatever it is that he is attached to just sends it on through. If he is shot or burned or whatever then he is re-made and becomes stronger, a perfect adjustment, a measured adaptation.'

'Perfect soldier,' Tong said.

'I think we are missing the point to all of this,' President Kawle said. 'We went to war for an objective that seems insignificant now that we are faced with . . . whatever this is.'

'I don't follow,' General Tong interrupted.

'We are running out of hope, we may have inadequate defences, and we are almost out of time!' Kawle shot back at the man. 'We need to master this cascade portal technology, and not just to build ships. Some of us have known that the virus was being sent through these cascades, we know that it keeps adapting to every measure we take to destroy it, and so here we have a being that is from the same technology, the same means. I am hoping this is our chance. We need to find this man before anyone else. If this message is authentic and we are facing a, dare I say it, alien threat, it needs to be discussed within the UN convention.'

'The UN is not just convening because they believe an alien species or some other threat is on us,' General Tong argued.

'Well,' President Kawle said, nodding, 'I'm going to make sure this is brought to everyone's attention.'

'We are moving away from our main objective here,' Vice President Blane said. 'As far as I can see, Colonel Young's team have come up with little in the way of useful information.'

'I disagree,' Young fired back at the man. 'We may find a reason for him being here, perhaps this is less simple than or more complicated than we expect. We need to figure out why he is here, if we get to know him.'

'Prospect sent the thing and it is testing our capabilities,' General Tong warned. 'It doesn't want anything, it is under orders like any soldier, worse still it probably isn't a person at all.'

'Really?' Young said. 'Then why did he travel all the way to Morocco? The only connection we have regarding this is that he used to live in that country, spent much of his youth there. Strange behaviour don't you think?'

'Enough!' President Kawle ordered and stood up to address the room. 'I can see that in reality very few of us know enough facts and conjecture is getting us nowhere, we are wasting time. I want all information to be transferred between relevant agencies and for key personnel including yourself, General Tong, to read and assess all findings by all teams. I will not have assumptions distorting the choices we make regarding this matter. Be very aware that this has just turned into a global manhunt of a magnitude never seen before. And in all honesty I'm not sure yet whether or not it would be better for another nation to find this man first.'

The vice president coughed as though trying to interrupt the President. 'Obviously we will need to continue in our initial aims. General Dean, if you will.'

'We need to find Ologun Jowett. That is our main objective,' General Dean said. 'We find him and find out why he's here and what his real intentions are. Colonel Young, you and your team continue in your work.'

General Dean then nodded to the President.

'That will be all, you are all dismissed,' President Kawle said and turned to vacate the room.

Everyone else then stood up to leave but General Dean called over to Colonel Young. 'I need to speak with you in private please.'

The colonel remained until the room emptied and Dean sat next to him. 'What are your thoughts?' she asked him.

'On what exactly?'

'There is a being out there that may be able to save us all and yet we find he is a butcher and a murderer.'

'I think that under certain circumstances we all make compromising decisions under duress.'

'You're referring to Rashad,' Dean said.

'I think that everyone is afraid, everyone is scared of Prospect and worried that everything is about to be lost. I think that unless we find some hope and soon . . . Look, we went into Africa for reasons beyond fighting terrorists. I don't wish to speak beyond my authority, except that something is very wrong here. No one, and I mean no one with any sense, believed we were invading Nigeria for the reasons stated.'

'I cannot discuss that with you,' Dean said.

'Then may I ask what it is you wanted to talk about?' Young said, 'I need to know what the hell is going on here, I need to know in order to do my job. There is talk over the legality of the Rashad mission. The militia, the terrorist drone army that we went in to stop. The South African government and Chinese government have accused the United States of paying the army of mercenaries that attacked Nigeria. The world is divided in two over the idea that the allied force response for military aid was a ruse in order to invade Cameroon and go even further, as far as South Africa. What for? What did we want in Nigeria or South Africa?'

Dean sat and listened and thought about what Young was saying. 'Young, you are not authorised to know certain aspects of the mission . . . We need to discuss how you deal with your mission, Colonel.'

'There was nearly a nuclear holocaust over this,' the colonel said, still venting his agitations, 'so I think we both know, everyone knows that such an obvious lie, such a blatant act of war . . . there's only so much we can get away with. Don't get me wrong, I'm a patriot and I love my country but intervention from this thing, Ologun, and that animal, ship . . . I think for once someone wants us to be saved and for the world to unite and just stop fighting.'

Admiral Dean stood up. 'Listen to me, Colonel, I'm trying to speak with you here off the record so stop talking and listen! I want you to promise me that you will find Ologun on peaceful terms.'

'Peaceful terms?' Young said.

'There are many departments looking for him now: CIA, NSA and many other small teams such as your own. Not to mention the rest of the world who might believe they can seek and perhaps capture him for their own intent. Perhaps they will want to unlock this technology. But I suspect that if they antagonise this individual, if whoever gets to him first does so in the wrong way then disaster will follow. I think that no nation is capable or equipped enough to deal with this thing.'

'I don't think that Field General Tong agrees with you on this, does he?' Colonel Young said.

'If that ship that attacked our task forces had made its way back here . . . Let's just say that I think no one on Earth can stop such a thing.'

Young nodded. He had his own ideas about it all and had so many questions. Deceiver, the shard and the possibility that there had really been an alien battle within that basin outpost. Part of him was glad that it probably had nothing to do with the Prospect Empire. Another part of his judgement told him that whatever was happening here might be far worse.

'What I am specifically saying here is that I want you and your team to get to him before anyone else and only report to me,' Dean added.

'What you are asking is that I betray my country,' Young protested.

'What the hell do you think is going to happen when we instigate our usual policies in these circumstances? The fact is that you and I are under orders to treat this thing as a terrorist.'

'What for? The damage and destruction of billions of dollars' worth of assets?' Young intervened. 'A terrorist that fights and detains terrorists?'

'Whoever finds him will try to destroy or capture him. There may well be a way to stop him, kill him, and I have no doubt that others as qualified as Miss Natasha Forbes are working on such a thing, but what if we get it wrong? What if we succeed and that ship that was with him retaliates?'

'How do you propose I find him before anyone else?'

The general reached into her shirt pocket and plucked out a small tablet device and keyed in something upon its screen. 'Here,' Dean offered to Young, 'I believe this may help.'

Colonel Young looked at the device and read what was on the screen and felt some apprehension. 'I can only hope that you know what you're doing,' he said.

*

Judith had returned from her mission and was now on board one of the retired flag ships, *Perpetual Productivity*. She sat on the bridge, swinging on her chair and rubbing the stubble on her head through her fingers. Half of the fleet of ships were now in orbit while the remainder of the retired fleet had landed close to the crisis management zone to provide shelter and a better means of operational capacity.

'Judith.'

Judith turned to see that Sergeant James had risen from his temporary demise. 'What?'

'Admiral Langmead wants to see you immediately.'

'Is that so?' Judith said. She stood up and walked past James. 'You did well out there.'

'Thanks,' he said.

Judith made her way to the operations room and found it empty. 'Ship, locate Samantha Langmead.'

'Medical quarter deck six,' came the reply.

Judith thought nothing of this and continued on her way. Eventually, and after a twenty minute walk, Judith found a guard outside one of the recuperation rooms.

'She in there?' Judith asked the guard. The woman nodded and Judith entered.

Judith was shocked when she saw the Admiral. The woman was lying in bed with the covers up to her chin, and her small, shrunken head rested on a pillow.

'What's going on?' Judith asked.

'I ran out of Span treatments, Judith,' Sam's voice croaked quietly.

Judith sat down on a chair next to the bed. The room was tiny and completely metallic, which helped to amplify the weakened voice of Samantha Langmead.

'You look awful,' Judith said.

'Thank you, Judith, I knew I could count on your bedside manner. I have no time left so listen to me carefully.'

Judith stood up and went to a medical unit within the room and found a scalpel ready to cut into her own arm.

'What are you doing?' Sam asked.

'I might be able to help, to reverse this.'

'You know that is the one thing you cannot do. You know that, Judith, please sit with me a while.'

'I can try, maybe it's time I learned,' Judith offered and sat next to Sam once again. Judith felt desperate all of a sudden, knowing that there were no answers and that with all her capabilities, stopping death from all kinds of physical trauma was very different from stopping the natural process of time that was the constant decay of life. 'My God, I need to get Glynn out of stasis, I'll have someone go planet side to get . . .'

'No, Judith.'

'No what?'

'Leave my son be, I don't wish to see him now.'

'You're dying,' Judith argued.

'I know, but I want to go peacefully. My son only serves to remind me.'

Judith sat in silence in thought at this then said, 'Remind you of what?'

'Our failures . . . his mistake that cost so many lives.'

'You blame Glynn for this?' Judith said, both angry and bewildered. Her voice raised and echoed back at her from the solid metal walls.

'Yes,' Sam said in a cold, yet frank response.

'You always wondered why I disliked you.'

'Judith, there isn't time for this, and who exactly have you ever liked? You're a child with Asperger's, a dyspraxic fool, a sociopathic . . .'

'Be careful I don't kill you before your time's up,' Judith said. 'You will break his heart if he can't say goodbye. Especially in these circumstances.'

'Then you tell him something else. Tell him anything, there are too many things for me to tell you, Judith, please.'

Judith calmed herself seeing that the life within this woman was quickly dissipating. 'What is it?'

'There's always been a protocol for every eventuality. Further south along the same route to the retired ship facility there is a back-up city. Everything is automated and under a vast digital lens, the same lens taken from the basin after that alien entity, Spectra, made its own liquid sky.' Sam chuckled at what she had just said and continued, 'There's food, water and shelter, more than enough to accommodate those who are left.'

'Why didn't you say anything before? There are people down there who need help.'

'It's an evacuation site in case we were invaded by . . . There is no military left, Judith, I don't want to hand this installation over to just anyone. You need to find the right set of people to take over.'

'Fine,' Judith said. She watched as the once powerful and dignified admiral struggled to breathe as pain ravaged her frail body.

'This is retribution isn't it?' Sam said after some time.

'What was done to Earth is unforgiveable,' Judith replied.

'So you think this all happened for a reason then.'

'I think that a few had it coming, but everyone paid in the end. Maybe there is something watching, maybe it has just all been a terrible mistake. I don't know, I'm still too numb to even face any of this yet,' Judith said, shaking her head.

'Why did you always hate me, Judith?'

'I never hated you,' Judith said and sat thinking about this woman and what she meant. 'All right,' she continued. 'When Frank and I arrived on Prospect, when we walked and talked and saw the six cities and the vast lake from a distance, it was the last time we were close, I think. He saw you and you ran to him . . . the moment he held you in his arms I felt . . .'

'I know,' Sam whispered. 'He missed you too. You got busy, everyone became so busy. Then the strain of it all got too much. Knowing that Rita nearly killed Glynn, knowing she had made the Coda Virus and I— I think he needed both of us and we just weren't there.'

Judith felt herself welling up and took a deep breath. 'I can't deal with the shame of it all, if you won't see your son then I will.'

'Don't leave me, Judith. I haven't long now.'

Judith sat with Sam for a while in silence and remained there watching and waiting. Sam's breathing slowed further and further until it finally stopped.

'Goodbye, Admiral,' Judith said and leaned over to kiss her on the cheek. 'I never hated you.'

Judith left the small room and spoke to the guard. 'The Admiral's gone, make preparations please.' She wandered off down the corridors of the ship. Her mind was in a state of disarray as she thought about everything. Passively, by subconscious interaction Judith soon found herself at the ship's mess area searching for something to drink behind the bar.

'You looking for this?'

Judith looked up to see James had found her and brought a few bottles.

'We have some old Merlot wine, vodka and rum.'

'You're a saint, I'll have a vodka,' Judith said and sat on one of the barstools.

James sat next to her and pulled some glasses from over the counter. He wiped the dust from them with his shirt, put the glasses down, and poured the drinks.

'Are Glynn and May on board yet?' Judith asked.

'Not yet. The team's down in the triangle now.'

'Triangle?'

'That's our shorthand term for the three main ships and everything that's sitting amongst them at ground operations. People should feel . . . I mean they have shelter now, or at least feel a touch safer with them there.'

Judith said nothing and poured another drink straight after downing her first.

'Are you okay, Judith?'

'The world just ended,' Judith said and looked at the man. He had green eyes and copper hair which perhaps was not exactly to her taste, although she could not deny her own mood.

'Nothing's wrong,' Judith said.

'Okay, well, look I have a few things to do so . . .'

'You ever been in the captain's quarters of an Empire flag ship?' Judith said, cutting him off.

'No.'

'You know where it is?'

'Yes, of course,' James said.

'Bring the wine, you're due an inspection, Sergeant!'

'Are you acting as medical officer on board now?'

'I'm the best there is, be there in ten minutes, that's an order.'

Judith grabbed the bottle of vodka and walked away from James. As she exited the room, he watched her body as it moved within the second-skin suit. The skin did not leave much to the imagination, but James felt that he still wanted to see what was underneath. He drank his drink and grabbed the wine. He did not want to disobey a direct order.

LIMITISM

'I'll take the distance chopper, the Russian fireproof army coat and the Jackal walking boots.'

'Very good, sir, would you like to add damage and loss insurance to the bike?'

'No, I'll take the bike as is.'

'Oh I'm sorry, I already added them on.'

'Just take it off, I won't need it.'

'I'm afraid you'll need to contact the bank to cancel the ten monthly instalments there, so sorry.'

Ologun looked the shopkeeper up and down and then began browsing through all the junk within the cluttered shop. 'Whatever,' he said.

The craft had dropped him off on the southern border of Ethiopia, and Ologun was now thinking of ways to leave the continent. His objective was to reach Italy as soon as possible and to journey across Europe. Eventually he wanted to get to North America; he had an agenda that required him to be there. Ologun startled the man by inserting a strand of second skin into the payment machine. 'It's the new thing,' Ologun said.

'Oh I see. It seems to have worked. I'll bring the bike around to the front of the shop.'

Ologun nodded in agreement. He took his by now very broken boots off and put the new ones on. He then put on some trousers and a T-shirt over his second skin, then finally the coat, which was of a thick, dark green material yet remarkably light and flexible. Ologun exited the shop and stood on the pavement outside.

The town was virtually empty as with most places. It had begun to dawn on Ologun that he had returned to a post-apocalyptic world. It was not like he had imagined nor indeed how many forms of media had led him to believe it might be. A nuclear holocaust or a swift and natural pandemic, or perhaps a meteor hitting the earth, or a supervolcano blackening the skies; the list went on. The reality was something different. This was the painfully slow demise of the world's remaining human inhabitants as nature took hold and buried the rubbish left behind by a once over-successful species. The world had limped on quietly until nations finally went to war out of frustration through desperation. They all wanted the Version pilots, everyone wanted to unlock the secret to time and space. They feared the Prospect Empire and were terrified they would one day return, and it was with some irony that the meaning of the word 'prospect' had now become a dirty, horrible, twisted version of its original semantic value.

'Here you are, my friend.'

Ologun looked over the bike as the shopkeeper parked it next to him. The IMC logo had been rubbed off and other, newer components had been added to a very old military bike; built to last as they always were. Ologun thanked the shopkeeper, mounted the bike and held on to the elongated handlebars that were at shoulder height. He revved the electronic drivers that purred a healthy spin. He thought about the Version pilots held by the African United Council and how they had failed to capitalize on the technology. Ologun could not help but think that it was a shame the Americans and allied forces had been forced to try to take the technology. He could not truly blame them in a sense and considered that if the African alliance had simply offered to share the Version pilots with the other nations then collectively, they might have successfully reverse-engineered the Version and created what the world really needed. He also figured that it was the same old chaos going around over and over again. He recalled how the GSA invaded the basin and how he had tried to stop them, that he had attacked the side that was only making desperate moves against those who had in turn killed billions on Earth. Such madness; and now he had stepped in and done a similar, perhaps equally detrimental, thing once more and Ologun found that he could not do right now, no matter which choices he made.

Ologun nodded to the shopkeeper as the man went back inside his shop. He realised that there were only a couple of things left for him to do now and so he thought of a new objective and set off down the empty street and towards the rest of the emptying world.

*

Colonel Young took the lift heading down to an old weapons cache located beneath a bank that had been built during the last redevelopment drive to renew the city of Los Angeles. As with almost every city in America, *especially* America, it had been pounded to rubble during the Prospect War.

He read the data file projected into the vision of his left eye. Asset protection, and all the history that had led to the near-destruction of everyone on Earth. Young felt apprehensive and disgust at this new set of orders. If it were not for the asset protection agents, things might be different. Maybe someone, a physicist or some other scientist, could have figured out the secrets of energy cascades and perhaps the war with Prospect would not have been so one-sided. The construct that was releasing the apocalyptic virus could be found or may never have been made or released. So many ifs and maybes filled the colonel's mind.

The lift stopped and he exited into a warehouse filled with metal crates, various technologies, and tall rows of shelves that led off in rows into the distance. The place smelled of sawdust and the air was dry, causing him to cough. Young turned to his left to see the stock-keeper in a small shack waiting behind the open window hatchway.

'Colonel Young?'

'That's right.'

'The canister needs to be signed for, place your eye in front of the scanner please.'

Colonel Young did as he was told and put his face up to the scanner. Once the machine had finished, he placed his hand on a DNA scanner.

'There must be some mistake,' Young said.

'In what way?' the stock-keeper asked.

'I came to find a man, someone in stasis, asset protection. A very old stasis chamber perhaps.'

'Oh, I see. Well, our friend is in the canister. You'll see what I mean when you read his file.'

'What's in the canister?'

'Sonny Camden.'

'I'm not sure I follow,' Young said, baffled.

'You were asked to take him to R&D at Nevada complex fifty three?'

'Yes,' Young confirmed. 'I presumed it was for equipment, specialist stuff maybe.'

'Oh,' the stock-keeper laughed. 'Your man here is nothing but his base component.'

'Meaning what?'

'In that canister is his brain. Lost everything during the war. That's the price you pay for being a long-term stasis assassin. My bet is they're going to fit his brain with an adapted avatar machine. Hope he doesn't mind not being a real boy.'

'I see,' Young said. 'Thank you for your assistance.'

The colonel picked up the canister and went to the lift. He turned to look at the stock-holder, a small balding man that appeared much older than his mid-twenties. The man gave Young a strange look that he could not quite place. The lift doors opened and Young got on board. He had been ordered by General Dean to pick this man up, this Sonny Camden. Some argued that he was too dangerous regardless of being the best hunter they had available. Colonel Young had his doubts, for this brain held the life of someone who had killed innocent people for a living, a man who should be tried and convicted for deleting many brilliant minds from existence in order for his employer to excel without competition. Now Young had been told that they were to put this man into the body of a machine. He would be faster, stronger and tougher than a man.

The doors to the lift opened at ground floor level and Colonel Young stepped out, canister in hand. He felt that he could destroy the canister and the brain within, he felt that this was all a bad idea. Then he thought through what Dean had told him. Sonny Camden was from another time and another set of rules just like Ologun Jowett, yet most importantly of all, Sonny knew Ologun.

*

Judith disembarked from the shuttle craft and saw that the great white alien craft also hovered way above and beyond everyone else's eyesight. 'Stay here,' she ordered James and two other soldiers.

Three bombardment-class ships had been docked in a large triangle surrounding the initial crisis zone. The ships dwarfed everything, casting a shadow over the people that had gathered. The control centre sloth block tank now seemed terribly insignificant at the centre of events, a tiny speck made redundant now the ships had arrived. Crowds of people remained within this contained area and Judith struggled to get to the vehicle. She pushed her way through the hordes and emerged on to the ramp of the tank.

Judith scanned the vehicle's interior and made her way to the room where Glynn and May had been left. Judith opened the door, saw the room was empty and began to panic. No soldiers, the tank's ramp was open and the stasis pod missing. Judith moved rapidly outside the tank and grabbed the nearest person she saw. 'Where are the soldiers? Where's the stasis unit?'

'I don't know,' a young man said.

'I need to find out who took them now!'

'You need to speak to the new government leaders.'

'What do you mean?' Judith said, releasing the man.

'The representatives of each frontier zone declared martial law this morning.'

Judith saw a few men brandishing rifles at the far side of the crowd. She moved quickly and emerged next to them moments later. She grabbed one man by the neck, kicked another in the head and punched the third person, a woman, fully in the face. Judith dragged the man she was choking along with her as she climbed a long flight of stairs to a hatch on the side of one of the ships. She typed in a code on the hatch, the door slid open, and she threw the man into the dark quiet of one of the ship's corridors.

'That weapon is Prospect combat urban issue, where did you get it?'

'I, I was issued it this morning, listen I'm just a regional reserve commando . . .'

'Commando,' Judith scoffed. 'Where are the people who now claim to be in charge?'

'They're aboard the *Punishing Cadence*.'

Judith left the man there, moved through the crowd once more and up another set of stairs leading to a hatchway. She typed in the code. It failed. Judith tried another code and another until the tenth time her access codes failed.

She took off one of her blades and smashed it into a seam on the hatch door. Judith yanked left and right using the blade to prise the door ajar. Eventually the locking mechanism gave way and the door popped open, yet with remarkably little damage to the hatch door at all. Someone ran up the steps towards Judith just as she was about to enter. She quickly knocked him back down the stairs and Judith entered the ship.

Once at the end of the first corridor she gained access to one of the ship's computer portals. Judith searched using the ship's internal thermal scanners for any clue to the whereabouts of the people she sought on this enormous vessel.

The odd person walked the decks here and there, as security perhaps. More scanning revealed that on one of the middle decks there were two people standing outside a conference room and that inside the room six people were sitting around an elongated table.

Judith sprinted to the nearest lift. Once there, a man close by shouted at her and lifted his rifle. She moved at him and knocked him unconscious with a brutal palm to the nose. The lift arrived and Judith boarded. Several decks later and Judith was nearly at the conference room. Two more soldiers were beaten up out of sheer spite and Judith burst into the room.

Startled, the six people – four women and two men – stood up.

'Who the hell do you think you are? Get out!' a woman shrieked.

'My God,' another man gasped, 'it's the abomination!'

Judith nearly said something but instead realised that she was going about things clumsily. She ordered the white craft to find out whether Glynn was inside the stasis chamber or not. It could find an ant on the ground from the stratosphere if needed. All Judith had to do was think of Glynn's face and the craft would work it out. She did so and sent the message via her second skin.

'Who are you?' Judith asked.

'My name is Anna Staines, to the left of me . . .'

'I don't need a full introduction,' Judith vented impatiently. 'I mean how have you all come to be in charge?'

'We were all once the council lead representatives for our districts,' one of the men said. 'My name is Wai, by the way. Please excuse my colleague's rudeness earlier.'

Judith received a message from the craft that it had retrieved Glynn and May and they were still in stasis. It then relayed the fact that a convoy of trucks was headed somewhere and that during the attack sixty humans had escaped incarceration.

Anna became distracted as she turned her head to one side. Then she stood up. 'Outrageous!' she shouted. 'You have no right, we're trying to reassert order here.'

'How?' Judith asked. 'You just arrested the remaining Prospect military personnel, so you are doing so under no authority.'

Judith then learned from the craft that the trucks were headed for execution squads and that many had already been killed.

'We are the authority!' Anna screamed.

'Perhaps,' Judith answered. 'But if you had killed my boy, all of you would be . . .' Judith could not finish the sentence, realised that she was just about to kill them all and decided she had to leave quickly.

'This is not the end of this matter,' Anna said. 'Glynn Sharplin caused the death of billions, he will pay.'

Judith moved without being seen, grabbed Anna by the neck, and held her up in the air. 'You don't get it, do you?' Judith screamed, then threw the woman to the floor as the others ran for cover.

'There's a base down south that could house everyone,' Judith said as she tried to calm herself down. 'I'm headed there now if any of you wish to follow. And, by the way, there are fifteen more craft inbound sent by the Spectra. They will remain in orbit and try to protect those who are left from any further attacks.'

'The who?' one of the council asked.

'You couldn't protect us when we needed it most,' Anna said, brushing herself off and adjusting the collar on her shirt. 'We don't need you or the alien ships.'

'The alien ships as you call them have just been ordered to target and kill anyone who even attempts any more bloodshed. Work that one out for yourselves and spread the news.'

'Who do you think you are?' one of the council fumed.

'The one with the biggest stick!' Judith shouted back.

She said nothing more, but headed out on to the corridor where a number of armed people were waiting. 'Excuse me,' Judith said and walked at them; they moved quickly to get out of the way.

Half an hour later Judith was aboard the white craft within a small compartment. James sat next to her and appeared uncomfortable.

'It smells in here,' he said.

Judith said nothing and James continued to touch the flesh-coloured bone interior of the compartment and then sniffed his fingers. 'Judith.'

'What?' she said, staring blankly ahead.

'When are you going to revive Glynn and May?'

'They're better off where they are.'

The stasis chamber was presently in another compartment aboard the white craft and James wondered whether Judith would ever let Glynn and May out.

'We need to find out what happened and if Glynn did anything to instigate all of this.'

'No, we don't,' Judith said, flatly.

'There's talk.'

'So what?'

'They say he needs to answer for what happened with the machines.'

'They say you need to answer for being a soldier,' Judith said. 'Nothing is going to happen to anybody.'

'You can't just order those alien ships to kill anyone who steps out of line, Judith, you're losing it here.'

The craft slowed and lowered to the ground. Then the bottom of the compartment opened and dropped the pair of them the two-foot distance to the dusty floor beneath. James swore at this as he landed awkwardly and then covered his eyes as the craft shot up and away at great speed.

'That thing scares the shit out of me,' he said, dusting himself off.

Judith said very little as they headed around the side of a mountain. 'Wait here,' Judith instructed as she saw a tall, thick pillar made of black granite in the medium distance. It was early and the day was beginning to heat up within this desert region.

Judith approached the great pillar and searched it for a small keyhole. When it was found she used the pendant Sam had given her and inserted it in the socket. A click and a hum ensued, and a wide passageway into the mountain opened up. Judith waved James over and he double-timed it to her position. 'Right then,' Judith said, 'the passage leads six miles under the mountain, and the outpost's at the centre of the mountain range.'

'Six miles,' James grumbled.

'I thought you were fit,' Judith criticised.

'Why didn't the craft just drop us on the other side?'

'There's a vast defensive battlement embedded everywhere around here, like an iron shield of continuous bombardment should anything invade the air space.'

'You could have told me this earlier and I'd have taken a jet and had it carry a buggy,' James said as he walked towards the opening in the mountain's side.

Judith followed him, keeping very quiet.

They walked in through the entrance and Judith's eyes adjusted. 'Wait here,' she instructed James. Moments later she switched lights on to reveal a gatehouse and a large car park full of various vehicles.

'Holy shit!' James said, as he made his way into the compound.

Judith scanned the tunnel, but lost sight of it as it curved off to the left.

'You know my uncle had one of these,' James said as he used his elbow to wipe dust from a truck's hood. 'You'd think they would have upgraded stuff once in a while, this stuff is what, seventy years old?'

'Fifty,' Judith answered and pulled the power plug and cable from the socket on the side of the truck. She then sat in the driver's seat.

'Still, they could have put some new stuff here.'

'The whole point of a secret base is that you don't have every

Tom, Dick and James turn up every time there's a new vehicle on the market. Are you getting in or what?' Judith asked.

'I was thinking of taking one of those quad bikes over there.'

'Get in the truck,' Judith said impatiently.

James was glad the tunnel was relatively straight and had no sharp corners as Judith drove the truck as though she had stolen the thing. He buckled himself up just in case and watched the chemical lights overhead whizz by.

Soon enough there was a light at the end of the tunnel and the truck shot through and exited into daylight. Judith braked hard and James lurched forward violently. He shook his head and sat back. 'Shit in hell's inferno,' he said, taking in the scene.

They were now on a road that led around the circumference of a vast lake that led into a distant horizon. Near the shore where they sat within the armoured truck, the lake was in the shadow of the mountain while the rest shone a rippling mirror. The area was filled with activity as millions of birds took full advantage of the oasis deep within this desert region. They both disembarked from the truck and walked towards the lake's edge. 'We could do with a stampede turret about now,' Judith said.

'Why, what's going on?'

'I was thinking of the flying vermin and that bloody racket,' Judith quipped dryly.

It was indeed deafening as the close-knit quarried cliffs of the mountain range only amplified the ruckus of the many variety of birds living here.

'I don't get it,' James said, looking out over the lake. 'Where's the base?'

'Come on,' Judith gestured and stepped into the water. It was only up to her chest and she waded in towards the centre.

James stepped in and froze as the cold water hit his body. 'You'd think it would be warmer being in a desert, right?'

'It gets cooled at night, like just about everyone knows who is taught about exposure, especially you soldiers,' Judith said. 'Stop pissing around and get a move on. Those council members will be here in the next few hours.'

James waded through and was surprised to see large fish swimming around him, perhaps curious or oblivious; he hoped they were not vicious. Then he saw some sort of motorised underwater vehicle moving slowly across the floor, and noticed through the purity and clarity of the water that the floor was glass or a mirror. 'Judith what the hell are we walking on?' he asked.

By now Judith had found something and ducked under the water. Five minutes passed until she broke the water's surface again and stood back. Something then shot up: a fifteen-foot tall cylinder that was ten feet in diameter. The cylinder released steps that led up to another level a quarter of the way up its side. This was closely followed by a loud hiss as the side wall of the tube opened up.

'Come on,' Judith said and ran up the steps out of the water and into the interior where she sat down on a wall-hugging sofa, soaking its fabric.

James waded heavily from the lake and walked up the steps. He sat down and said, 'You'd think the seat would be waterproof, eh?'

'Don't be stupid. There are concrete containers with boats in them on shore.'

James sat there cold and wet and was further stupefied at this remark. Judith pressed a few buttons on a touch screen and the cylinder hatch closed before it began to descend.

'What kind of base is this?' James asked.

Judith said nothing until the lift stopped and the door swivelled open. The two of them disembarked on to a wire-mesh platform and walked into a fibre-mesh cabin. They continued through an old room that was filled with archaic hardware, computers and desks covered in dust, and where rather thick cobwebs covered every nook and cranny.

James could smell that it was derelict or maybe damp, perhaps from being an underwater facility, but there was something else. There was nevertheless a freshness to the air as it blew through, which was filled with the fragrance of flowers or pine; there was too much of an aroma to distinguish each element.

'After you,' Judith said and stepped aside for James to proceed out on to another walkway.

James stopped just outside the cabin doorway and was now outside, but inside. 'What the . . .'

He stared for a while and looked into the distance, at the crescent-shaped city below and then further still towards the endless green of forests. 'Judith, this isn't a military base, this is a country.'

Judith strode out on to the walkway and stood next to him. For her, it was just as mesmerising as it brought on the feelings of nostalgia and some form of comfort. 'Welcome to Black Ball Two.' She smiled.

HORIZON

'We can't get there on time!' Hershal exclaimed.

'No,' Hina agreed.

'Ray tried to go back to the Spectra vessel,' Hershal said.

'I know, he was sent back to Earth, the disobedient tool.'

'Then it's up to Ologun and Creed,' Hershal added in a slightly nervous tone.

'You know,' Hina said, 'why I hated Ologun so much?'

The two sat on the bridge of the *Ryu Yo*, both staring into the aether. Hina thought he saw something amongst the mass build-up of trapped photons, amidst the blinding light. He thought it was one of the other ships within the fleet of sixty but could not be sure.

'It wasn't that he was stupid, which he is, it wasn't that I envied his life. It was that he always tried to distinguish between people in a sort of way where he was only ever drawn to people he thought were vile and couldn't find a way of relating to the rest as if they were above him, better than him.'

'Are you meant to be making any sense?' Hershal asked, with a hint of sarcasm.

'What have we all achieved exactly and why? I realised recently that no matter what we think, we are in the end but slaves.'

'I don't know what you mean,' Hershal offered, becoming disturbed at the patterns within the aether. 'We should close the link to the probe before either of us goes mad.'

'You think that being in charge of people and helping to build ships to defend Prospect is your own agenda? You think Judith staying on Prospect all this time is what she wanted, and that her having that nervous breakdown has nothing to do with programming of some kind? Or that Ologun's indefatigable need to run around doing what he does is for his own gain? Do you think . . . well, I'm not sure about Ray . . . But I can tell you that I hate people, humans and their pathetic merry-go-round of selfishness and lies. I hate, and yet I am anxious that they are in trouble. I hate them and by hurting them I inadvertently did the Spectra's bidding. We are without ambition except the salvation of humanity and their numbers as intended.'

'What the hell are you talking about?' Hershal asked.

'I gathered information.'

'You killed people for the Spectra? I don't follow.'

'The Spectra knew the enemy was heading for Earth way before we did,' Hina said, moving on. 'They put Ologun on Earth because they think he is the ideal candidate to greet them.'

'How do you figure?' Hershal asked.

'Playtime is over,' Hina said. 'We tried to make our fleet and failed to get it ready on time. Now it's time for Mr Death-Incarnate to have a go.'

'That's rich, coming from you,' Hershal scoffed.

'I think you'll find that when Ologun gets going I pale in comparison. I always found it odd that the fool believes himself to be different from what he actually is.'

'And what would that be?' Hershal asked.

'A masochistic, schizoid killing machine.'

Hershal could not really gather what Hina was trying to say. Maybe Hina was paying Ologun a compliment. Then again, discussing Ologun's personality faults seemed redundant due to the fact that all of them, including Hershal himself, had issues with the perception of being real or even valid.

Hina stood up and headed to exit the bridge.

'Where are you going?' Hershal asked.

'I'm going into stasis, I need to close down until we get to Earth. I'm feeling rampant. I can only suggest you do the same, you look . . . spent.'

*

Judith watched the same surveillance feed over and over. She sat within the fortress's main control room and had managed to hook up to the research and development facility's computer which she had already set up for dominion over everything else that had survived nearly a week ago. The systems at the fortress might be considered old but in truth there had not been that many advances in recent years and only a simple interface modifier had been required. The security footage of Glynn's last few hours in the Version production complex made no sense. He could be seen getting on with anything other than work on the machines. Feng came and then went. Then May showed up. Judith switched security feeds around the time Glynn and May appeared to leave the office, then typed in a sequence command to follow the two as they left the complex. Camera after camera followed and switched from one to the other as the computer edited together the full timeline.

Judith sat up with more interest when she saw that the pair of them had taken a left and headed into the warehouses. It was a tour, Judith understood, and she watched with the growing realisation that Glynn had not uploaded Feng's mind to the Version mainframe at all.

Judith then watched two screens simultaneously. One was the repeat of Feng talking to Glynn where it appeared they were having a heated discussion, and Feng, after some finger-pointing, then left. She watched the general as he exited the compound with his ensemble of goons and became confused as to what exactly had happened. Everyone thought Glynn was responsible. Sam, his own mother, had assumed, and everyone else had gossiped, even those who only knew him from the news stories regarding his accomplishments. No one seemed to have any reason not to assume the Version were his responsibility.

Judith rubbed her head. Her thick black hair had grown back very quickly and was now three inches long. The footage of Glynn and May continued so that now they were in the cryogenic stasis pod store room. They both seemed to be getting along well and Judith watched with fascination. May kissed Glynn, and they were petting heavily. Then Judith spotted a security guard heading in their direction from further across the warehouse. Returning her attention to the pair in the store room, Judith's eyes lit up on seeing that May had dropped to her knees and was unbuckling Glynn's trousers. *Kids!* Judith thought, with a wide smile.

'You found anything yet?' James said, as he entered the room.

'No,' Judith said and stood up quickly to block the screen.

'Right, okay, you seem shocked or something, everything all right?'

'You just broke my concentration by barging in, that's all.'

'Sorry, I'll leave you to it.'

Judith waited until he was gone, then sat down. She leaned in, ready to watch a car crash about to happen as the guard approached the storeroom door. The guard must have made a noise as Glynn and May were spooked and decided to climb inside one of the stasis units. The guard entered the room, shone a torch, and began to walk down the aisle of pods either side of him.

Judith watched with anticipation and yet she knew the outcome. The guard received a call on his server chip and ran out of the room in a hurry. A few moments later all surveillance stopped.

*

Judith walked out on to the roof of the fortress to see James watching through a pair of binoculars he had found. He turned to look at Judith briefly and then raised the binoculars once more. 'Did you know there are chimpanzees here?'

'There's everything here, you should see the marine preservation pool, its one hundred times larger with an underwater facility, it's off the coast of Jovani.'

James put the binoculars down and walked to the roof's inner concrete stairwell. 'They knew how to build stuff, I'll give the fascist bastards that much.'

'I didn't find anything on the security recordings,' Judith said.

'Then what now? If you want Glynn to be innocent . . .'

'We need to see the keeper of this place.'

'Right, what's that then?'

Judith looked around and seemed hesitant to answer. 'It's one of the original Version pilots.'

'Dear God, we need to destroy it right now!' James said. 'Where is it?'

'No,' Judith argued, 'we find out what happened and then decide.'

'This is too dangerous,' James protested.

'It's on an isolated domain and may not know anything. We detach it from everything and then interrogate it.'

Judith took James deep beneath the fortress and through several long corridors to reach the room where the Version was held. 'Leave this to me and don't say anything,' Judith instructed James.

James followed Judith and all he could see was a square pool of brightly lit water. He waited as the chemical lights were switched on and warmed up. There at the centre of a large square room hung the Version. It was odd to say the least as it hung on cables that extended from its sides and over the small, square pool.

'This is creepy.'

Judith put her index finger over her mouth and gestured for James to be quiet. She then began working on one of the computer consoles in order to isolate it from any weapon systems. When finished, Judith approached the machine as it hung lifeless and waited. Then it moved: a twitch, then another before it finally moved its head.

'Error detected, functional capacity of base defence system link error.'

James sat down next to the console desk on a chair and was perplexed as all he heard was whining and hissing. 'What's wrong with it, Judith?'

Judith turned to glare at the man and shushed him. 'I have taken you offline, Version Six Thirty, I need to ask you some questions.'

'Please reactivate link to defence systems . . .'

'I need you to pay attention,' Judith said, interrupting the thing. 'I need to know what happened with the Version. Why did they attack, why did they malfunction?'

The Version pilot hung in silence, perhaps in thought as its head kept flicking every few seconds. 'Authorisation of project value required. Please state . . .'

'Judith Magda Gibson. Access code: three nine seven three six one dash four six three eight chew.'

'Judith do you know what this thing is saying? It sounds like screeching.'

Judith was by now livid as she turned to James and screamed at him. 'Get out, get out now!'

'All right, take it easy. For heaven's sake, Judith.'

'Prospect clearance level invalid. Unit five of Version type two override accepted.' Judith was distracted from her annoyance at James and listened as the Version kept talking to her. 'Organism one instructions gives priority over value one, value one supersedes priority over value two.'

'I don't understand, what is organism one, value one and two?'

The Version, with an empty face, appeared to be looking directly at Judith. On the walls either side of them, eight small, round glass beads embedded in the concrete lit up and emitted a hologram that formed directly between Judith and the Version. Even James at this point regained some interest at this.

'Organism one, Version developer one through fifteen class type . . . human reference Spectra.' The hologram showed a small representation of the shard and then changed to that of both Earth and Prospect. 'Value one, value two. Value one to be protected from hostile species. Accurate status, species to intercept value one in three thousand six hundred and twelve hours. Version type one to intercept hostile intersection in three thousand six hundred and eight hours. Command accepted. Command viable.'

Judith stepped back in horror as she began to piece together what the machine had told her. She then darted from the room and sprinted down the corridor.

'Judith!' James shouted after her and followed. Down each passageway James ran, but was unable to keep up. He reached the fortress's main courtyard and saw that one of five cylinder lifts had gone and was heading towards the star lens. James climbed into the nearest lift and pressed for the lake's surface. He was anxious and was wondering about the hologram and what it had shown. The last image was of sixty blips and then a representation of what he knew to be Earth.

The lift approached an opening in the star lens and slowed down as it passed through. The door slid open and he saw the great white craft hovering above the water, sending it into a violent flurry. James exited the lift carefully and saw that Judith was screaming at the craft. He could not quite hear what she was shouting as the birds protested at the craft's intrusion and were presently flying around en masse, screeching and squawking to create a deafening roar. James stepped down into the water, which felt warmer now the sun had been up a while. He waded chest-deep towards Judith, who had her back to him.

'Why?' Judith was screaming, over and over. She was hysterical and threw one of her blades at the craft. Then something else happened as the craft flinched back and upwards. The white of its wings began to burn up red hot as though re-entering a planet's atmosphere. The thing did not like what had just happened and released what looked like multiple cannons across its wings and from beneath its body then pointed them directly at Judith.

James waded through the water as fast as he could. 'Judith, Judith!'

The craft did not fire its weapons and simply watched as Judith slumped face first into the water. James reached Judith and turned her over. 'Judith, what the hell, Judith?' He then saw that her eyes were open and that she was staring and he was now terrified that she might be dead. He checked her breathing and placed his ear to her chest to check her pulse, unsure what was wrong.

The craft released a tentacle from underneath its body and snatched Judith from James' arms. He was flung forward and dived into the water. He shot back up and watched as Judith was tucked away inside the beast's underbelly. 'Judith!' he screamed after her.

The craft then used the tentacle and brought something else down and plonked it into the lake. James held his head tightly with both hands as the craft pointed directly at him and told him something. He cowered in terror until he realised that silence had returned. James looked around, to the sky and across every direction of the lake where a boat was approaching. He looked to the sky again and then back towards the boat. The object the craft had dropped sat upright in the water and James realised that it was the stasis chamber in which Glynn and May were hibernating.

'What's going on here, Sergeant?' a voice called out from the boat.

James saw that it was one of the new leaders of Prospect; Anna had arrived with other people. Twelve more boats were also on their way, containing groups of men and women dressed in civilian clothing, who were all armed and keen to reach James' position.

'James, what is going on, where is Judith Gibson?' Anna asked again, trying to grab the man's attention.

James looked at her and then to the sky again. 'I don't know.'

*

The white craft folded its wings to make a perfect sleek rhomboid. It then fired a laser that spun round and round directly ahead until it expanded into one large circle. The fabric of space began to collapse in on itself, a waterfall of energy dropping into emptiness. As the portal was complete, the craft shot through and into the aether. Unit five, Judith, had a problem and the craft struggled to grasp the reasons why. Did this unit not stand idly by when the human race broke in two? Did Judith not accept that the sacrifice or depletion of numbers appeared to be compulsory?

Whatever Judith agreed or disagreed with was beside the point. The original Version, the creatures grown for humanity to create portals in order for faster travel, had been given a new set of orders. Prospect was of no value to the Spectra and the organism had given the order to protect Earth, for the Version to leave Prospect and intercept the enemy.

Perhaps, the craft reasoned, Judith was unaware that the organism, the Spectra, had priority control over all the original Version pilots. The answer to this did not matter to the craft for between the two organisms, the Spectra and its child at odds and humanity's insatiable appetite for destroying one another, there appeared to be no sense found anywhere.

There were problems with this continued interference. The Spectra did not want to get involved with humanity after the great time of division and yet could not leave them be. Then there was the issue of the second organism, the Spectra's true offspring, to which the five medical units belonged.

Unit five had seemingly shut down and only organism two could provide the answer to this malfunction, indeed should have corrected the problem already. The craft set course for the Spectra and for further instructions. It did not expect Judith to overload in this way, and it was not that she was mistaken in what she said, for the white craft had sent the programme signal for the Version uprising and had indeed been responsible for billions of deaths.

The craft mulled over the facts and considered the results of each decision that had been executed. It most definitely wanted to send more specific instructions next time for things had got out of control. The Version had been ordered twice not to attack Judith, and twice they had failed to comply, even causing the craft into taking action against the drones at one stage.

Regardless of this glitch, the craft was still satisfied with the outcome of the plan; this plan of numbers and all that had happened was still acceptable. In the end there were still more than enough human beings remaining.

*

Lies. Her mother had told her when she was young, "You have to be smart to lie, very smart, so don't lie." President Kawle swept her dark hair back and caught her reflection on a nearby surface. Her very dark skin could not hide the blackness under her eyes and she felt very tired. Arti Kawle stood in the vast emptiness of a hangar bay where the Secretary of Defence, Gregory Chapman, General Dean and Vice President Eric Blane had joined her. Many scaled-down holographic projections filled the space, a reconstruction of the last incident recorded by a US military satellite: imagery of Ologun Jowett's attack upon the terrorist's avatar control convoy in Nigeria.

'I assure you we can stop this thing,' Gregory said.

'Just as I was assured the outcome of Operation Rashad,' the President replied.

'I think caution and understanding would still be advised,' Dean offered.

'Without a doubt some humility should be afforded at this juncture. At least until we can ascertain how the technology works,' Eric Blane added.

President Kawle examined one of the avatar control tanks. The hologram projection was quite detailed and as she walked the length of the machine she could not help but ask herself exactly what limitations this creature, this Ologun had. There was a representation of a complete undamaged tank to Kawle's left and she looked over at it before returning her scrutiny to the one closest to her. The tank she stood next to had been ripped open, smashed and damaged almost beyond recognition.

'General, what would it take to destroy a tank such as this?' Kawle asked.

'These machines were top of the range seven years ago. Russian engineering, exceptionally tough. Titanium asaronite tri-weave hexagonal casting, advanced metal weave muscle flex coating. Nothing a bunker buster would not take care of. It's a beast. It has – had – state of the art anti-aircraft capabilities . . . it's a formidable asset. Facing a hundred plus of these without the tools to stop them would usually be problematic for any nation,' Dean said, tailing off in further thought.

'Thirty six minutes. That's all it took for this man-creature to destroy these machines along with . . . God help us,' Kawle stated.

The President walked over to the exact holographic representations of Ologun Jowett. She inspected the one that was more of a man. Six feet five, slender and athletic in build, the man could be like any other. She then walked slowly over to the next representation. A monstrous and hideous mutation that walked on thick tentacles of blackness. A monster that had grown to nearly fifteen feet in height towered over the President and amongst the density and chaos of hundreds of tendrils that reached out and over everything, a face could be seen and was almost devoured by the rest of the creature. With twisted features, its skull had been crushed so that its hideous face sent the President into a state of panic. 'Turn this image off now!' she ordered.

President Kawle walked quickly towards a set of steps leading up to another level in order to leave the hangar bay. The others in her company followed until they were at the next level looking out over the full expanse of the room. Kawle took one last look out and over the reconstruction site as many hologram emitters gave a full representation of all one hundred and thirty three avatar control tanks including the undamaged illustration used as a reference. Even though none of it was real or really there, the President could not help but feel the magnitude of destruction and the power it had taken one creature to achieve it.

'Once we find a way to disrupt whatever is feeding this thing, we will defeat it,' Greg Chapman said with a bravado that neither the

President nor General Dean appreciated.

God help us, Kawle thought to herself once again. She exited the hangar bay through a small doorway and out into another more massive interior void.

'I need to take a flight back to Washington. I will see you tomorrow, Madam President.'

Eric Blane nodded and said goodbye to Arti Kawle; all the while the two made eye contact and she knew what he was thinking: that deep down the man was extremely nervous about what might yet happen. The two men walked to a buggy parked against a nearby office, got on board the machine and drove back the way they had come in.

'We have further demonstrations here, do you wish to observe?' Dean asked President Kawle.

'I'm going to see my husband,' the President said. 'Can you take care of this?'

The two women walked through the underground hangar bay beneath the arid lands of the Nevada desert in one of the most classified locations in America. Around them and beyond a scale that was comprehensible, one hundred great space ships, war ships that had been assembled over the past fifty years, were ready and complete.

'What does he think?' Dean asked.

'What? Of me remaining in power? He understands.'

General Dean nodded and was pleased with how the UN meeting had gone. Thirty six hours of fraught discussion had led to some sound decisions. The President had been endorsed to remain in power by the Chinese, including Israeli and European votes. Russia vetoed, along with the African states as expected. The Middle Eastern countries, however, had surprised everyone and sealed the deal. The President would remain in her position until this crisis was over and then she would have to explain her actions, perhaps even step down if necessary.

'I'm having problems with the team you assembled,' Kawle said. 'Glochman has taken this as far as he possibly can, he thinks it compromises his authority.'

General Dean kept walking. None of this concerned her. In fact she was expecting the director of the CIA to try to intervene at some point. 'The problem with the organisation has always been that they ignore good intelligence to suit their own agendas,' Dean said of the CIA. 'They could have identified Ologun using the same techniques as Colonel Young's team and yet chose not to. Young is thorough and naturally very inquisitive, so much so that I took him away from the collective and posted him on star duty with Forbes,' she continued, with reference to the collective counter intelligence unit that encompassed all, and had access to all US agencies regarding terrorist threats.

'An irony then,' the President said of Young's present command.

'Young's had a lot on his mind lately, but I'm telling you now, I know why Bill Glochman wants to shut him down. Colonel Young will likely figure out why we went into Africa and he will find Ologun Jowett, hopefully before any other country or agency.'

'No unauthorised personnel can know about Africa,' Kawle ordered.

'You'll have to excuse me for saying this, Madam President, but all it takes is for one African state to reveal the truth about the Version and it's over in any case. You could do with Young as an ally.'

'You sound overly confident in such a small team,' Kawle said in a critical tone.

'It's surprising what a small system a specialist group can achieve for better or worse. I'll admit that politics isn't my favourite subject, yet I have to ask you what has this Ologun cost us so far? South Africa is reported to have given the Chinese one of the Version machines for their part in aiding them, which if we'd won . . .'

'It doesn't matter now,' Kawle said. 'I have my own battles to fight in Washington, I need to make sure that this is all handled in the best possible way. Of all the times to be dealing with those vying for control. If only I were a dictator.' The President smiled and the general's eyes narrowed at this, with some internal agreement and sympathy for Kawle.

'So, we either emerge from this as heroes or we face total destruction. No pressure then!' Dean said, and smiled back.

*

They left the vicinity of the hangar installation and walked down a long corridor and towards a room where voices could be overheard.

'I shall leave you to it,' President Kawle said to the general and carried on walking. Dean opened the door to the room of a small office and entered.

'Are you kidding me? Something hacked every military installation on the planet and set off over eight hundred nuclear warheads? Fifty of them were anti-matter! Do you know what *one* of these weapons is capable of?'

'He's an admiral,' General Dean said to the man screaming at Admiral Wass. 'He knows more about such things than you.'

Donald Holland, the head of the United States largest military contracting firm, Ethica Systems, had graced the installations with his presence and he was not happy. 'This thing didn't crack a quantum code, which by the way is still almost impossible, it confused the network into doing exactly what it wanted. How does that even work? What the hell is next? Power stations, utilities, banks!'

'There have been reports of several companies being compromised, including two banks,' Admiral Wass offered.

'Excuse me? I'm sorry did you just say that there have been occurrences pertaining to this discussion that have not been imparted to me and my company? Do I look like an idiot to you, you dumb shit?'

General Dean sat down and noticed that the room was a mess in testament to Holland's fit of rage. She understood the implications of what was being said, yet even though it remained frightening it also remained a mystery. The big picture, when disregarding threats of alien invasions as seen on the file sent by Ologun, was that there were two of his kind here on Earth and two organic craft, both making moves and causing havoc. One of these things had infiltrated the AI of every nuclear launch site, including submarines, and launched WMDs using pre-programmed software that automatically chose targets.

The warheads had then been plucked from existence which meant that they presumably had an arsenal that could destroy the world.

What no one could make sense of was why? If there was no immediate intention to use the weapons, what was the point? One outcome had been that every capable country, every remaining superpower on Earth, had formed a closer relationship. There were alliances now being made where the international community was preparing for a hostile invasive encounter, albeit for a change it was not against each other. Dean thought it could have been perceived as ironic if it were not so tragic that the world's nations could not agree on much except this rare union in order to protect the world.

General Dean continued to listen to Mr Holland, all the while considering, hoping that these things that had come here were not looking to attack Earth at all and that they had been particularly smart. How do you unite the countries of Earth? They had done it and, even as Dean sat in contemplation, the international community had held a number of meetings regarding any assets they could bring to the table. The general was herself now preparing to partake in further discussions. Dean had already seen what each country had proposed, given specific details of hardware, ships and planetary defence capabilities in case Earth was in fact in danger and an invasive force attacked, whether from Prospect or aliens. All Dean could think was that contrary to what most heads of state from around the world had once feigned regarding their military assets, that all its countries combined to make Planet Earth an astonishingly hostile target for potential enemies.

Holland continued shouting this and that, which did not interest Dean. None of what had happened was the man's fault and she waited for him to calm down for she needed two things from Ethica Industries. Thus everyone revealed they had ships and everyone wanted to launch before something showed up. Prospect, aliens, whatever, the world was getting ready, although the portal technology was desperately required. There were, however, other things to consider.

'If they can pluck weapons from the sky then they can just put them anywhere,' Donald vented.

'You have bigger problems,' Dean said to Holland.

'What? Bigger finding a way to secure our systems from some

alien thing stealing our most powerful weapons? The world just got its ass kicked and everyone is blaming my company for this. Ethica's stock dropped forty points in the past five days.'

'Listen to me!' the general ordered, losing patience with this tirade. 'There were two points of intrusion. The missing warheads is one issue. Setting them off in the first place is obviously a major concern. The other hack, however, the reason you were brought here, is because of the drones.'

Admiral Wass breathed deeply and exhaled for he knew what was coming.

'Shit' Holland shouted and wiped his face hard with his hand.

'Mr Holland, I need to know that there is no way that this man or that creature can trace the two thousand drones and their control combat vehicles back to us here,' Dean said, slowly and concisely.

'I think we're tight on that front. Those machines, all apparatus were purchased from secure remote market sources or bought from carefully chosen international companies. Most of the drones were ex-Swedish and the vehicles were Russian stealth tanks. No, there is no tracing going on here. Hey, listen to me, the deal was for the artificial pilots, those Version drones, I need assurances . . . I need . . .'

'We have something else for you,' Dean said, interrupting Holland. 'You need to come this way.'

General Dean left the office and Holland and Wass followed. Through numerous corridors of the underground base they walked while they talked; for the most part, Donald Holland talked and fretted.

'Whatever this thing is and if Forbes is right in her assumptions – after all they are only assumptions and we have no controlled experiments, no data to back anything up, what I'm saying is how exactly can information be transmitted instantaneously? Especially when you consider that there are meant to be variables that slow down matter even when in the aether. Is the construct here or in our solar system? Is it further away and if so, none of the time factors make any sense at all. Nothing can transmit without some sort of delay.'

They arrived at a large, unused room where several soldiers and more men in white coats were busy prepping for something.

'I hope you know what you were doing with Colonel Young,' Admiral Wass said to General Dean.

'If this plan fails we have nothing.'

Wass nodded in agreement. 'If we should fail then this is our main backup. Mr Holland, I would like you to see this.'

Soldiers began emptying something out of a container at the centre of the room while the technicians stayed close by in case they were needed. What was poured out on to the smooth concrete surface looked to be a powder of sorts. Then on top of this a small metal cylinder was placed.

'What is this?' Holland asked.

'Watch,' Dean replied and handed him a pair of ear defenders. Everyone followed and placed the protection over their ears. A fifty-calibre round cannon was wheeled into the room by three soldiers and pointed directly towards the centre and directly at the mound of dust. General Dean gave a thumbs up to one of the technicians who used a digital pad to perform tasks on the screen.

Silently and quickly the cylinder rose into the air and, following this, the dust moved and began to surround the device. The dust compressed until eventually it formed into the shape of a man. Donald Holland watched with deep interest as the fifty-calibre cannon was unleashed. Even with ear protection the noise was tremendous. The rounds hit the figure over and over, dust exploding in all directions and into plumes.

A few moments later the figure was destroyed and reduced to dust once again. The cylinder then rose from the floor a second time and the figure was formed anew.

'Interesting,' Holland said. 'Nice to show off tech that I haven't thought of. Are you trying to tell me something?'

General Dean continued to watch the figure of amassed dust particles and then made a cutting action across her neck for the instruction to discontinue so that the figure collapsed once again. She took off her ear defenders. 'This technology got lost in our stores over eighty years ago. You see, during the war this tech was being developed by GEA scientists as a super soldier.'

Dean walked over to the centre of the room, picked up the cylinder from on top of the dust and walked towards Holland. She handed it to him and he examined it closely.

'Do you know how it works?' he asked.

'It uses precision magnetic fields to move metallic filings around,' Admiral Wass said. 'The dust on the floor is a toughened alloy that has been microscopically shaped in order to link together and form any shape. For the purposes of this demonstration we made the shape of a man.'

'Well, what are its limitations?'

'It's not complete yet,' Dean said.

'Oh?' Holland said.

'We only found this technology when we began investigating all historical aspects of the shard, along with any classified operation regarding the Black Ball facility. These were weapons to be utilised by an Admiral Novex of GSA for some classified mission,' Wass continued.

'What happened?' Holland asked.

'We don't know, but it was sheer dumb luck that we found this technology, and only due to this thing's arrival here on Earth,' Dean offered.

'So what do you want from me in regards to this?' Holland asked.

'Well,' General Dean said to the man, 'we want you to complete the weapon. Make it combat-ready as a drone. If things go wrong, if and when we make contact with Ologun Jowett we need something that can contain him, it. We want you to complete the technology, and then make as many of these as your company can manage.'

'By when?' Holland asked.

'Yesterday,' Admiral Wass said.

*

'I'm here to talk, that's all.'

'I have nothing to say.'

'Ologun, why don't you tell me about what you think about . . . yourself?'

Ologun sat opposite the woman sent to assess his psychological state of mind. Eight months at Mirage Six and he had crossed the line way too many times. The room was dim with a ceiling fan spinning lazily above. Doctor Page had instructed him to lie down for the chat on a sofa at the rear of the room. Instead, Ologun sat on a chair directly opposite her. The woman portrayed a false confidence and Ologun could tell that she was slightly nervous in his presence.

'I don't think anything.'

'You perform a dangerous job here at the camp. You seem to place yourself in more danger than the others you work with quite regularly. Why is that?'

Ologun worried her for he had no facial expressions and she could not gauge his responses.

'Dangerous for whom?'

'You used to be a sales person up until fifteen years ago, then became a territorial soldier, weekends at first. Why is that?'

'I was fired.'

'Is it because of your wife leaving you? How did you feel about that?'

'She left me for someone else. It happens, we married young.'

'Where is she now, may I ask?'

Ologun sat back and exhaled. He could feel the heat at the window in a constant battle with the air conditioning. He let his head fall back slightly and saw the fan, and wondered why it was there at all.

'She runs a health shop with her new husband and does charity work on the side.'

'May I ask what happened between the two of you?'

'No.'

Doctor Page kept writing notes with every answer Ologun gave.

'Your father passed away the same year. Tell me how that affected you.'

Ologun felt differently about this question, and Doctor Page could tell as Ologun's eyes glazed over that he was distant in thought.

'I'm not sure,' Ologun said. 'I felt numb, I felt good, I felt as if, like . . . I had died and was set free at the same time.'

'Do you feel numb now?'

Ologun failed to reply.

There are a number of incidents that have occurred here in recent times. Three weeks ago a girl was found raped and killed. No suspect has yet been found. How does that make you feel?'

'It doesn't matter what I feel.'

'I'm sorry?' Doctor Page said, intrigued.

'The girl you are referring to was eight years old. And your assumption that anyone would or could be caught for the crime is naïve. Investigating crimes is beyond the limitations of IMC policy here. We break up disorder and violence as it occurs, we do not investigate.'

'Do you think that perhaps for some reason you are not allowed to feel? Surely without the freedom to feel you become lifeless and without normal values. I would say that is a contradiction to your behaviour. I think that you are saying that your feelings do not matter and yet you act on your feelings all the time.'

'You ever see a father holding his deceased daughter, Doctor Page? There's something about mothers and sons, and fathers and daughters. The father of the girl who was murdered . . .' Ologun sighed with recollection. 'He cried so hard I thought he would, wanted to . . . I don't feel like that, I never felt like that.'

'Perhaps if you had children, or maybe you are very good, too good at supressing the way you feel.'

'Compared to other people, at times, I think I'm artificial,' Ologun said.

'You feel anger. I'm here to ascertain why and to help you . . .'

'You don't get it, do you? I don't feel real, I have no desires and no ambitions, I have no interests or passions, I have nothing. I own nothing. I have nothing to portray to other people . . .'

'Wise up,' Doctor Page said, interrupting him. 'You need to keep going, do you understand? You're not just a projection, you are real. You will make a difference, now get up!'

*

Ologun opened his eyes to see a vast field of digital lenses rotate towards the last ebb of sunlight over the horizon. The lenses flashed a crimson burst and then darkness came immediately as nature flicked a switch. His eyes adjusted to the darkness and Ologun

245

wondered if he had actually been asleep; he never slept.

A woman curled up in a foetal position, not far from where he sat, shivered as the air cooled down rapidly. Ologun placed a hand on the bike next to him and stood up. He walked over to the woman, who in turn screamed at him and scurried away. Ologun grabbed hold of her, picked her up, and sat down cross-legged bringing her into his arms. 'It's okay, I know,' he said to her.

The woman screamed once more, 'Iblis, Azazel!' and began to cry uncontrollably as Ologun held on to her, and wondered if he had done the right thing by her.

There were things, many things Ologun failed to understand about the world. His journey north had led him to a town that he would have passed without a second thought. Having such accurate sight over great distances, however, made sure that he caught a glimpse of something on barren wasteland just outside the main street.

An investigation had led Ologun to find the woman stripped naked and buried up to her waist. Unconscious and badly injured, the woman was close to death, having had various-sized rocks thrown at her with some force. Ologun had dug her out, healed her and dressed her in a burka that had been left behind and that he presumed was hers.

Ologun took a moment and tried to contact Creed via his second skin, via that laser dish in South America. By all accounts the craft had attacked a Chinese rapid tank force as it headed towards Israel. The thing had then disappeared, after wiping out the entire complement of three thousand tanks and various other vehicles. Ologun considered that the craft might be upset due to having instructed it not to kill anyone when there had been no one to kill.

Ologun shook his head. Some things were difficult to know or consider in such a short space of time and all he could do was mull over the same things in his mind, over and over. There was an outcome to all that had happened and Ologun could not decipher whether it had simply been the message he had sent or whether it was because of what he and Creed had done.

Either way it appeared that through various meetings of the United Nations, the first meeting of its kind in decades, and despite some potentially harmful skirmishes like the one between China and Israel, the state of Europe and the kingdom of Saudi Arabia – the list had become extensive; the world had begun a fraught process to unite as one.

Ologun lowered the woman to the ground gently and stood up. He waited and watched as the Hercules plane landed in the distance on the empty highway and until it drew near to his location before coming to a standstill.

The engines to the plane were switched off and a few moments later the doorway hatch at the front of the plane opened and automated steps were released and lowered to the ground.

'This is the last favour I'm doing for you, unless of course you fancy making more generous donations.'

'I need to go to Italy,' Ologun said.

'No way, the whole of southern Europe is out of bounds. I can take you to Turkey, that's as close as I can get with the help of my contacts,' Nova insisted.

'Fair enough,' Ologun agreed.

'Who's this?' Nova said, referring to the woman rocking back and forth on the ground.

'I need to get her somewhere safe, a shelter of some kind. She was stoned.'

'Sharia law stoned?' Nova asked, shaking her head.

'Well, I didn't catch her with a reefer did I?!' Ologun spat, seemingly annoyed. He walked over to the woman and scooped her up in his arms. He then carried her to the steps leading up to the cockpit of the plane. 'You have anything to sedate her?' Ologun asked Nova. The virus had infected him to the point whereby he dare not make intimate, penetrating contact with anyone.

'Yes.'

Ologun climbed the steps and Nova followed. He walked down the interior of the plane and found a bed that he presumed Nova used for sleeping.

'Make yourself at home,' Nova said with sarcasm and moved to check on the woman. 'She have a name?'

'We're not on speaking terms.'

'Hi there, what's your name?' Nova said softly in Arabic. The woman shivered with exhaustion and whimpered.

Nova stood, opened an overhead compartment and took out a small box, opened it and found a set of patches in a transparent sheath. She took a patch out of its wrapper and placed it on the woman's left arm. 'She'll be out cold in a minute, we need to go now.'

Nova made her way to the pilot's seat and buckled up. Ologun followed and sat in the co-pilot's seat. Nova started the engines and prepared for take-off.

'The whole continent, scratch that, the whole world has gone nuts in the last twenty four hours. Religious crack pots think it's the second coming or something – just when I thought this planet couldn't get any worse!'

The plane shot forward and accelerated. A few moments later they took off and headed towards the stratosphere.

'Take us to a medium altitude, I'm in no rush,' Ologun said.

'So,' Nova said.

Ologun switched on the media device located above the cockpit controls. Music blared out and he kept pressing buttons until he heard an Arabic voice talking. He listened and felt he was a little rusty but understood enough to maintain his interest.

'What have you been up to exactly?' Nova asked.

'Wait a minute,' Ologun said.

'Listen to me when I tell you,' the voice on the broadcast said, 'how can the likes of America and Europe be held accountable for this, what can we call it, chicanery?'

'There is no solid evidence to prove that the Americans paid this military force, or forces to attack Nigeria.'

'America has never offered military assistance to any country unless there was something in it for them, and the South African Government state quite clearly that their interrogation of those captured . . .'

'Captured and tortured! There has never been any reliable information gained through the torture of terrorists.'

'The captured mercenaries admitted that they were funded and ordered by someone American to invade Nigeria under the pretence of being a religious or politically radicalised group that would carry out a coup d'état.'

'Why? What does Nigeria have of any value? The Western allied forces put together Operation Rashad in order to seek out and destroy this military faction.'

Ologun turned the media device off and sat back deeper into the chair. He felt sick and ached from head to toe. The virus had been fought to the point of destruction many times over and he wondered how often it would keep coming back.

'It was you, wasn't it?' Nova said.

'It was me what?' Ologun asked.

'You went into Nigeria and destroyed the drone army.'

'You don't think that sounds ridiculous?'

'Not if you're Jesus Christ,' Nova said in a peculiar tone.

Ologun chuckled and shook his head. He peered out of the cockpit window into the night sky and then into the jungle canopy miles below. 'I'm not the Messiah, he would have more to say than me . . . they say he was a carpenter, I never built or made anything in my life.'

'But you are something. No one walks into a war zone and comes back out . . . where are your friends?'

'They went somewhere else.'

'Who are you?'

Ologun nearly told her that she would rather not know and then thought about the question some more. 'I could tell you that I'm no one, but I have to ask, do you really want to know?'

'Yes,' Nova said.

'First I want to know about you,' Ologun said.

'Like what?'

'You're French and you fly aid in and out of war zones and other areas that have suffered natural disasters. You're a qualified nurse and what else?'

'There is nothing else.'

'Why do you do this . . . work?'

'I would have thought that was obvious.'

'You don't have a boyfriend or girlfriend or someone back home?'

'I have a genetic pick waiting for me when my tour is up if that's what you mean,' Nova said.

'I don't understand?'

'You know, by law I have to breed with three different partners before the age of twenty three, although this line of work has allowed me to get away with only having to have one child so I suppose I've had a full life.'

Ologun sat, deep in thought at this for a while and then said, 'When do you have to go meet your pick?'

'In the next six months. Once I'm pregnant I'm free to pick my own partner. You know, natural selection rather than genetic matchmaking.'

Ologun understood and yet was appalled. He had a lot to catch up with on this world. It made sense that breeding programmes meant stronger children that might resist the virus. If a person was poor or of average wealth, the breeding programme was instigated for them. The wealthy, on the other hand, had modified offspring that were even better in many respects; the laws of the past had indeed been changed. It did not matter though, everyone died more or less at the same time, around their mid-thirties or perhaps a little later if lucky.

Ologun's stomach cramps became worse and he accidentally let out some rather loud flatulence. Nova pressed a button so that a jet of air shot up between them as a dividing wall. 'Excuse you,' she said.

Ologun felt miserable and said nothing as the pain in his body intensified.

'You said you would tell me your story,' Nova said after a while in silence.

'Sure,' Ologun said and began telling her about Deceiver, the shard, what he was, and what he was made for. He told her about everything except the Spectra and the alien enemy and simply made out that the Prospect Empire had produced him. Whilst he spoke, he thought about the aliens that had attacked the basin and wondered if the whole reason he was on Earth was because something had happened.

'My God! Is Prospect coming back, is that why you are here? I don't understand.'

Ologun shook his head. 'I don't know, I haven't seen anyone from Prospect in a very long time.'

'Why, what happened?'

'I'm tired and this conversation could go on and on, sorry,' Ologun said, shrinking into his seat.

The world was doomed enough as it was, Ologun thought, and one or two alien invasions just added insult to injury, he decided. Still, there was no greater danger than the one humanity posed to itself, it appeared. Ologun knew that his efforts were needed and that he should start doing what he was designed for in the first place. With all that had happened and with all the dread that seemed inevitable, Ologun just hoped Prospect was doing better.

MANO-A-MANO

Practice made no difference to what was coming. The mission Ologun had sent it on was too easy and could not even be added to the resolve of experience. It had now come down to this. The enemy was directly ahead and moving at great speed. The human terms for locations were noted in its mind: Kuiper belt, dead binary, Jupiter, Neptune.

The enemy ship moved so quickly it appeared to teleport the distance between Neptune and Mars. The great animal that was this ship moved more slowly at this juncture, stopped and began scanning the red planet; this would not do. Humanity once lived all over the place in various colonies. What would the enemy make of abandoned cities and other now derelict deep space constructs? Would it piece together that the species it was headed for had destroyed each other? That much of its progress had come to a halt simply because humanity could not rein in its aggression towards each other for the most peculiar and unnecessary of wants or needs? Surely it was in every species' nature to be successful, and what had happened appeared to be against all common sense. Back to the rock from where they once came and retreating as a wounded parasite; humanity was not ready for what was coming.

The craft folded its wings, a jet-black shell that became a minute replica of the Spectra vessel. Its sleek, rhomboid shape sped on towards something that was vastly superior in size, in mass and in fire power. This would have to be an accurate attack, a one-off attack that might lead to the craft's own demise. It thought about death and it thought about the first real fight that it had ever had as an infant. That had been a good time; this would be even better.

The enemy craft approached and it saw Creed at the last moment before it attacked, before it had the chance to retaliate.

*

It sat in what might be described as a seashell of sorts. Hooked up to its custodian, the ship, it watched as the scan of this solar system took place. *What a near perfect set-up for life,* it decided. Gas giants as defence against random debris. One sun and a planet at perfect distance with its own singular moon. The creature felt that this place was so mild and, most likely, very consistent. Information of more interest was accessed to reveal a fourth, very red planet where some unnatural structures of old had been abandoned with no signs of activity.

It then returned its attention to the third planet and its moon. The moon told a similar story of many structures, what the alien could perceive as a mass of oddly fashioned constructs. It tried to imagine the moon or Mars as once having thriving city landscapes filled with habitats in order to house millions of people, also long abandoned.

The creature finally gave its full attention to Earth. It smelled the information, read it in fact as an intricate map of scents was released where the alien began to learn very quickly about the constructs and the technology and of the dominant species that resided on this small blue planet. This would be an issue, the alien decided. How to get in and out in order to retrieve that which it had come for.

It seemed unbelievable that this planet had so much activity and that some of the occupants had . . . the alien continued thinking and reading the scents. These bipedal creatures . . . It scanned further. Human beings, as identified in this species' humanities own library of information, had already conquered and unleashed the power of the atom, had already grasped the concepts of the inter-dimensional fuzz of reality, the cosmos at its most basic level. *Impressive,* the alien decided.

It then wondered if this species was aware of her kind. She searched and found one incident that had happened over a century earlier. It was an unfortunate incident. Many years later in a quadrant nearby, a custodian had also gone missing.

Something did not quite make sense to the female alien. The planet this incident took place on was too great a distance away for this species to traverse in reasonable time. She searched further and became fascinated. This species was not one; humanity had split in two. It made sense and it appeared that the second half of this human kind had indeed worked out the fundamentals of a type of travel that not even her own kind used any more; the very kind of technology that her species had forgotten how to access and the very useful technology that this vessel had been sent to retrieve by any means necessary.

A thorough scan revealed the constructs they had come for. She locked in on the items that needed to be retrieved and told the custodian where to orbit the planet humans called Earth. During this process something else happened. A projectile of solid mass hit the custodian at tremendous speed. Before the alien's next thought entered her head the ship had been killed, all oxygen had been sucked into the vacuum and the Unison of her kind were about to die.

A cocoon, her safety pod, latched on and dragged her inside and slammed itself shut. She immediately began accessing this real-time incident and key strategic information. Eight hundred pods had launched out of three thousand. Seconds later, seven hundred pods were destroyed as the custodian exploded. Now there were a hundred heading for the planet Earth, three million miles distant from the schools of the escaped pods' present location.

The alien female sent an inter-dimensional laser pulse; a distress call from her command pod. The message said: 'The human species were hiding weapons that defeated the greatness of a custodian, the mission will fail, assistance needed.' That was all she could do. The pods would travel at good speed and use all their energy and try to get to Earth before the oxygen ran out. Some pods might make it, yet it seemed most likely that many if not all would burn out before reaching safety, if Earth could be considered safe.

The Unison, her kind, the remaining survivors, signalled her. They were all equal and all capable, except that it was this female alien's turn and her time to lead, and this leadership would continue for some time to come, although death had already begun to intervene.

*

Creed continued to sprint and, for the first time in its existence, panicked. The enemy ship had released sentinel craft that had been hugging it like Remora. Dispersing of these would be a simple affair; the great ship that Creed had killed was a much tougher adversary, except that now Creed began to lose consciousness as its injuries took hold.

Orange gas seeped from its body along a deep wound and one of its wings had been shattered. It carried on towards Jupiter via reverse mass, and pushed hard to gain a speed several times the speed of light. It chose what to do next for it needed sustenance in order to repair and to survive. The gas giant could be a good hiding place, but it was too violent and there was too much pressure inside. It needed heat and saw Europa, even though coated in deep ice, would be a good choice.

The sentinels fired their weapons of thin energy beams and just missed Creed as it flew closer to the ice plains of the planet. The craft dropped an energy bolt that hit the ice and began to sink as a bright blue flare.

The craft sped on and did a full circle of Europa, managing to avoid the pursuit of the other creatures. It fled until it returned to the point of incision into the ice, sped down the tunnel and through the fifteen-mile depths until it hit Europa's subterranean oceans. The sentinels tried to follow and found that the tunnel was too narrow for their bulbous size. They flew back and forth in a figure-of-eight formation, looping around and waiting; they had realised that they had the wrong fire power to traverse through this deep, frozen shield.

Creed floated down, barely conscious as it scanned for thermal vents. Eventually it found a split in the ground that spewed out core magma. It watched passively through thermal vision as various marine life swam around and picked at the creatures living off the thermal vents in the floor. Creed headed for the rolling magma as it crawled across the ocean floor. It found an opening and delved down into the flowing inferno that looked almost like its own master.

The magma washed over Creed's injured torso and wings, engulfing them completely. As the craft lost consciousness it had one final thought about the failure to stop the enemy and that they were about invade Earth. *It's up to Ologun now, he should know what to do!*

Reviews

If you enjoyed *Prospect>Earth* please consider leaving a rating and review on Amazon – all genuine comments and feedback are welcome.

Reviews and feedback are extremely important to Craig Jenkins, as well as other potential readers, and would be very much appreciated. Thank you.

More Books by Craig Jenkins

Version

Coming Soon

The Almagest Principle

Printed in Great Britain
by Amazon

25575534R00145